The shaman looked up [barcode: D1462727] a spirit summoned?'' Sh

"Then I suggest you stand near *him* and don't do anything unless he tells you to. Spirits know what might happen."

Cara nodded and moved alongside Chase. She grabbed his arm again. "What's he going to do?" she whispered.

"I don't know," said Chase. "Every shaman summons spirits differently. It's very personal. Hermetic mages have tried- and true- procedures, almost formulas. Shamans have specific rituals too, but I understand they make some of it up as they go along based on what feels right."

She nodded and grabbed him tighter. Without thinking, he reached his arm around her. She moved closer.

"Now," said Farraday. "I'm going to do this the long way. I could be done in pretty much an instant, but why give myself a headache?" He dropped from the squat and sat Indian-style in front of the pile of toys.

He separated them so that none touched, and then reached into his pocket and pulled out a greasy bag.

"What's that?" asked Cara.

"French fries," said Farraday. "Cat just loves Nuke-It Burger fries."

SHADOWRUN

NIGHT'S PAWN

TOM DOWD

A ROC BOOK

ROC
Published by the Penguin Group
Penguin Books USA Inc., 375 Hudson Street,
New York, New York 10014, U.S.A.
Penguin Books Ltd, 27 Wrights Lane, London W8 5TZ, England
Penguin Books Australia Ltd, Ringwood, Victoria, Australia
Penguin Books Canada Ltd, 10 Alcorn Avenue,
Toronto, Ontario, Canada M4V 3B2
Penguin Books (N. Z.) Ltd, 182–190 Wairau Road,
Auckland 10, New Zealand

Penguin Books Ltd, Registered Offices:
Harmondsworth, Middlesex, England

First published by Roc, an imprint of New American Library,
a division of Penguin Books USA Inc.

First Printing, April, 1993
10 9 8 7 6 5 4 3 2 1

Copyright © FASA, 1993
All rights reserved
Series Editor: Donna Ippolito
Cover: Richard Hescox
Interior Illustrations: Larry MacDougall

 REGISTERED TRADEMARK—MARCA REGISTRADA

SHADOWRUN, FASA, and the distinctive SHADOWRUN and FASA lo-
gos are trademarks of the FASA Corporation, 1026 W. Van Buren, Chi-
cago, Ill. 60607

Printed in the United States of America

PROLOGUE

SEATTLE, 2048

Awakening *n*. Refers to the return of overt magical activity to the modern world and the reemergence of races and creatures previously believed mythical, such as elves, dwarfs, orks, trolls, dragons, and other beings. This return is marked as occurring on December 24, 2011, though some evidence of the incipient return of magic exists prior to that date.
—*WorldWide WordWatch, 2053 edition*

The line outside Dante's Inferno was long, mean, and as alien to him as the people who stood in it. He'd been to Seattle before, even to this very club, but the sights never failed to astonish. Certainly, he understood dressing for style, for effect, but physical extremism repelled him. Home, they ran the shadows as hard as any, and their colors showed it. There they wore the clothes that suited them, that made their work and their lives easier and simpler. Every policlub had its own look, its special expression, but none of them would ever have considered overt physical mutilation as a symbol of superiority. Customize and internalize, yes. Flaunt it, however, and you were asking for trouble.

In America, especially in this town, it seemed to him

that you weren't anybody unless people noticed you walking down the street. For him, though, a man whose life *was* the streets, to be noticed was almost certain death. A friend once joked that the American affinity for chrome came from some racial memory of century-old automobiles. Here, now, in Seattle, he believed it.

How little subtlety they have, he thought, passing a line of impatient people all wanting to get in to the same place at the same time. A place where they were obviously not wanted. To them, the attempt to penetrate the inner sanctum of Dante's Inferno was as valuable as actually dancing on its glass floors. In Berlin, he thought, people wouldn't play the fool standing in line just to be rejected. They'd simply find another club .

Reaching the door, he stifled a laugh. Dwarfed by the size of the huge troll working the door was a gander-girl looking slick in black and red trying to talk her way inside. A waste of breath. They didn't know her and she wouldn't get in.

With a nod to the troll, he brushed past, earning a curse from the gander-girl. But her City Speak was so mangled and uttered with such guttural inexperience that he stopped and turned to look at her. She was shorter than he, but jacked up to nearly his height by a pair of gleaming black razor-spike boots. Her hair, its color shifting from iridescent blue to white and back again, made a perfect frame for her face. She was beautiful by the standards of either side of the Atlantic if one ignored the cold look in her eyes. She glared at him, waiting for an equally venomous response, but he resisted. Far too much was at stake tonight to humor her.

He gave her a deadpan look and was about to turn and be gone when she surprised him by cursing again, this time in perfect City Speak. He smiled in amusement. Her first curse had been sudden, impulsive, and fractured. The second time was perfect, even down to the crosstalk inflection. She was chip-trained, no question, but trained only. If she'd actually been wearing and accessing a language chip, her first curse would have come out like a veteran's.

He couldn't help but smile even more broadly as he gave her a closer inspection. The clothes were right: all the proper straps and chains tight or loose as fashion demanded. Quad-colored earrings dangled from her ears, glittering and dancing in the lights of the street and the neon of the club's facade. Her iris tint was near-phosphorescent, designed to pull another's eyes to them even in the darkest club. She was absolutely perfect, the ultimate gander-girl. And therein lay the failure in her appearance. But it was that which so intrigued him.

He weighed the options, her paradox versus his own purpose, and decided to take the risk. He nodded again at the troll and spoke just loud enough for him to hear, "Say, chummer, she's with me."

The girl apparently overheard, starting slightly at the words. When he motioned for her to take the lead, she glanced once at the troll, then turned away quickly from his sudden, feral grin. As she stepped forward, he guided her with a gentle pressure of his fingertips at the small of her back. Once again she gave herself away. Her jacket was real denim, not the cheaper synthetic look-alike that a "real" gander-girl would wear.

They continued down and into the uppermost level of the Inferno. Though he hated the place, he'd gradually become a semi-regular out of sheer habit whenever he was in town. There were certain things that always brought him back. He'd first met Dante in London, where he'd performed the club owner some services that had ensured him first-class service in the club thereafter. Information could be a priceless commodity.

The band had apparently just taken the upper stage. A staccato riff from the lead ten-string triggered the sync-systems, bathing every level of the club in pulsing light and liquid noise. Shag metal was apparently the latest rage in Seattle, making his desire to go transcontinental all the stronger. It was enough that he might die tonight, but the idea that his death might be to the accompaniment of a pitiful rendition of "Bangin' the Duke" was too much.

He wanted to believe that his people were not like these nighttrippers thrashing around him. He wanted to believe that back home things were different, that his people had some memory of, and some honor for, the glory of their cultural past. He wanted to believe that he was superior to these Americans with their all-consuming lust for the new. But he knew that Europe's magnificent past had all but vanished from mind, as though it had never been. Technology had blurred the differences between nations, chipped languages had weakened the borders, and the Euro-Wars had utterly destroyed them.

The Restoration might be physically reviving Europe's lands and people, he thought, but it's destroying us culturally. The driving force behind it were the Euro-corps pursuing the grail of unrestricted growth. If the corps could erase national boundaries, it would mean no more import-export tariffs. It would mean the availability of vast pools of cheap labor. It would also mean death to three thousand years of dynamic social expression. Radical politics and a return to nationalism were the only hope for rescuing individualism, the uniqueness of the continent's many peoples. The Neo-Europe District of the global village must not come to pass.

The policlubs had been born out of the urgency many felt for another kind of restoration. They, too, wanted to rebuild Europe, even if it meant a return to more contentious times. Theirs would not be a Europe homogenized for mass consumption. For better or worse, it would be Europa Dividuus. These groups alone kept alive the flame of political activism and individual expression. Without the policlub movement, Europe would soon become a corporate Disneyverse.

The various policlubs did not, of course, agree on the means or even the ends, but was that not as it should be? On the surface, the Restoration might appear to be proceeding apace. Behind the scenes, however, Europe was at war—in the streets, in the datafaxes, in the hearts and minds of those alive enough to listen. Europe would not become another Manhattan, not even another Seattle. He'd come to make sure of that.

He blinked, realizing suddenly that he'd been lost in thought, staring at the pulsing, thrashing crowd for longer than he'd have liked. The girl was still there, a few steps away. He tugged gently on her arm, and she turned to eye him quizzically. "Watch the dancers," he said, leaning against a light-filled pole. Relaxing his body and mind, he focused his attention on the pulsing lights of the lasers, letting their silent rhythm take him.

A moment passed.

Then a longer one.

His vision shifted beyond the confines of his body and he was free, viewing the worlds as few others could. He saw the ghostly auras of men and women dancing madly, locked in the mundane world and oblivious to him. He ran his gaze quickly over this level. There was some minor magical activity in the faint auras of cheap trinkets hawked on street corners, but no bright blossoming or dazzling oscillations to warrant further interest.

The iridescent bodies of the dancers on the glass floors at each of the levels below him blocked much of his immediate view, so he released his astral form. Dropping quickly down all the levels, he came to where he could contemplate his destination. He saw the cool green power of the mystical shield-wall enclosing it, but no sign of the person he was supposed to meet. The shield prevented him from knowing whether she was already within its protection. The only way to penetrate its mystery was to walk through, physically, unhindered. The shield was nearly impenetrable to the pure astral body, but to break through it was something neither he, nor most other humans, could do unassisted.

His body jerked once as his wandering spirit returned. He'd discovered his mystical ability very late in life, just a little more than ten years ago, and was still not totally used to it. The girl was looking at him, as though to ask what was next. Taking her hand, he led her away.

They moved down-ramp a few levels. Halfway to the bottom, he paused at the sight of a posturing corporate cowboy. Boldly emblazoned across the back of the man's jacket was the Saeder-Krupp corporate logo showing the dragon and the German flag. The coincidence gave him pause, but he shook off the thought that the woman he was to meet had already completed her mission. It wasn't, after all, so unusual to see people wearing the dragon-logo design. Besides, he was counting on the fact that the woman would know very little of his motives, or his knowledge, at this point. She was both crafty and powerful, but he'd been careful to keep her guessing. "Know your enemy and then use that knowledge against him," was a motto of her following. Well, he hoped that all she knew about him was what he wanted her to know. Regrettably, he knew even less about her.

Reaching the sixth level, he and the girl went to the nearest bar and signaled for the barkeep. Feeling the girl move gently against him, he turned and looked into her eyes. Her gaze dipped and then rose. Behind the slightly glowing tint, her eyes were bright blue. "My name's Karyn," she said, "with a 'y.'"

He smiled. "No it's not."

She blinked twice as the bartender appeared, wiping the counter in front of them. Leaning across with a touch of hesitancy, the elf barman pitched his voice so that no one else could hear. "Greetings, my friend," he said in clear, unaccented Russian. "How are things?"

"Harried, as usual," he replied in the same tongue, though definitely rusty.

"A man named Shavan is waiting for you in Hell."

"A man?"

The dark-haired elf shrugged. "Figure of speech. I was only given a name."

The man nodded. "*So ka.* The usual for me and a Firedrake for my friend." He pulled a credstick from its wrist-sheath, but the elf waved it away.

Now the elf spoke in English as he moved down the bar. "All taken care of, chummer," he said. "The In-

ferno still owes you. And if we don't, then it's on me for
old times." The man returned the credstick to its sheath.
Old times, indeed. He chuckled and wondered just how
much the elf hated him, or feared him.

Just then the crowd roared as a glare of hard, colorless
light cut across the level. He'd seen the act before and
figured the lead singer must have just triggered a small
bit of nightlight and was gleefully trying to shove it down
someone's throat. Ah, art.

The girl pressed against him again, her hand lying casually on his arm. "Nice line," she said, dropping the
timbre of her voice. "I almost believed you did know.
Just for a second."

This time he didn't smile. "You still aren't sure."
Their drinks arrived as he spoke, making her gape in
surprise at the Firedrake. He took his Blind Reaper in
one gulp and touched her arm.

"That's your favorite drink." She looked up at him,
eyes still wide. "And your name isn't Karyn, either with
or without a 'y'. And you're not from anywhere near
here." Fear swam in her eyes now. "But no matter," he
told her. "Tonight you're with me."

He brought her hand up to his face, gently kissed the
palm, then closed the fingers one by one. "I have business. It may take some time, but I want you to hold
something for me." Power danced quietly behind his eyes
and she gasped. She'd felt the change.

As she slowly opened her hand, a jumble of brilliant
red silk unfolded, first forming a flower, and then falling
open in a drape that covered her hand. He gathered it up
and tied the flare of color around her throat. She touched
it and stared at him, an odd glistening in her eyes. The
corner of her mouth twitched slightly.

"You can give it back to me later." His voice was low,
barely audible, and she strained forward to hear it.

She'd felt the silk appear in her hand, but still wasn't
sure if he'd used bar-stool sorcery or the real thing to put
it there. She'd think about it, and then think about it
some more, and then want to know. Later, he'd let her.

He brushed her cheek and then her hair with the fingers of one hand, then moved away without looking back. If his business went well, he'd be alive enough afterward to need to disappear somewhere, *pronto*. And if he'd read the girl right, she was the bored daughter of some equally bored ultrasilk-suit type. Weary of the macro-glass scene, she'd become enraptured by the rhythm and color of the streets, but remained blind to its workings. Afraid of being rejected for her real identity, she'd gandered herself up the way they did it in the trids. By following the templates to the letter, she'd given herself away.

The quadruple ramps spiraled downward around the outer edge of the club, mimicking the curve of a DNA spiral. Deeper and deeper into corruption he walked as each level echoed the names and places of Dante's nightmare: the author's and the owner's. He ignored the screams and the other sounds, preparing himself as he descended.

Below the lowest dance floor, down a short, winding ramp, was Hell. No sign marked its location. One had to know it was there. Flanking its entrance were a pair of scantily clad, androgynous figures who watched every step of his approach with a near-feverish interest. He stuck his hands into his pockets, and the twins twitched. He flashed them a grin. "Shavan is waiting for me?"

The one on the left nodded, and the one on the right spoke. "Indeed," it said in a tone of menace. "You are expected." The bodies of the twins were perfect, scarless, some say the best ever made. He doubted that, but they were the ideal guards for Hell.

Flash the fat credstick and you could rent Hell and be assured of complete privacy. It was swept magically and electronically before and after every meeting. Once the participants were inside, no one else got in. No magical eavesdropping was possible: the astral shield prevented that. No way in through the higher planes, either, which was what Shavan would be counting on.

Hell's designers had been kind enough to include a sizable foyer just within the outer doors to allow one a

moment of preparation. Unfortunately, there were few
spells he could raise and sustain that she wouldn't detect.
Keeping her calm until just the right moment would be
the key to walking out of this meet alive. He checked his
gear once, then dropped down into a lotus position on
the floor. The rhythm of his pulse released him, and he
gave the shield-lattice and his surroundings a quick astral
once-over. Everything was quiet, but it was still early.
His senses returned to his body and he prepared himself.

Shavan was an enigma. The leader of a policlub known
as The Revenants, she wielded great power. Little was
known about her, and less than a handful had ever actually met her. The only description he'd ever heard was
that she was of Nordic descent, but in this day and age
only a DNA test could tell for sure. She was a powerful
sorceress, an adept perhaps, and had relied on that to
conceal her trip to Seattle. She needed to speak to someone, and that individual was not about to come to her.
What she hadn't counted on was that someone else knew
how to look better than she knew how to hide.

Shavan had been surprised that he'd known she was in
Seattle, let alone that he knew where to find her. She'd
believed that her business was deeply buried in the shadows. That was her first mistake. Her second was believing that what he offered her was sincere.

He'd chosen the meeting place, one known for its
security, and she'd chosen the time. His only guarantee
was her word that she'd be there, and that was enough.
They both had reputations to live up to.

He stepped through the inner doors to find her waiting,
exactly according to the plan. He was late.

"Alexander," she said, a slightly wicked smile crossing her face. "Fancy meeting you here."

The sight of her was so different from what he'd expected that he scanned the room to hide his surprise. In
startling contrast to the woman, the room and its accessories were pure white. Everything about Shavan was
dark. Her clothes, her skin, her eyes, even her voice.

She laughed. "I believe this is yours." Reaching into

her pocket, she pulled out a wad of bright red silk and let it drift gently onto a sofa.

The odds against him walking out of here in one piece suddenly fell radically. His mind raced through the possibilities of how she could have gotten the silk, and he rejected every one just as quickly. There was no way she could have gotten it and still beaten him here. Regardless, she'd used the ploy to good purpose: his momentum was broken. With his options already halved, he was still at least five minutes away from playing his real cards. Until then, a bluff would have to do.

He picked up the silk and tied it around his throat. "Like it?" he asked, keeping his voice as level as he could manage.

She seemed amused. "Like what?"

"The silk."

Her amusement grew. "Ah, yes, it's lovely, I must admit. And real no doubt." Keeping him in view, she turned slightly to mix a drink.

"One hundred percent."

"Only the best for Alexander."

He let several long moments pass as he wandered over to the audio-visual console and casually scanned the selection menu. "Only the best for Gunther Steadman," he said, pressing on the touch-sensitive screen. He cued the first selection to fade up midway through and the second to follow it after a short pause.

The mention of the name Steadman gave Shavan such a start that he caught her surprise even as she mastered it. She already knew that Steadman was dead. He sensed the fear and anger that washed over her before she regained her calm. For someone of her power, Shavan was proving far too easy to read.

Nonchalantly, she finished mixing her drink and turned to face him directly. "Red was never Steadman's color," she said coolly.

The music he'd selected had begun to play, giving her another pause and him another opening. Choosing the piece had been a gamble. Hearing it now, he wondered briefly if he'd overplayed his hand.

"It is now." He said, letting the music almost drown his words. She heard him, though, for he sensed another wave of tension wash over her.

"This wouldn't be some kind of threat, would it?" Only her eyes followed him as he moved to sit on a nearby float sofa. "I think Mozart's *Requiem* is hardly suitable background for a business meeting." Her voice was flat, expressionless.

He shrugged. "I like it. It relaxes me. Just think of it as being in honor of Steadman."

She relaxed fractionally and said, "So, he's *dead.*"

He nodded, stretched his arms out across the back of the sofa, and told her what he was fragging sure she already knew. "Three days ago in Hamburg. Bullet to the skull. Nasty, very nasty."

"So who's running Der Nachtmachen now? Who do you represent?" She was studying him intently.

"It's not really important," he lied casually. "The offer's still the same."

"On the contrary. It's very important." She crossed the short distance between them, and gracefully lowered herself onto the sofa opposite him. "I want to know."

As the first part of the *Requiem* was coming to an end, he knew his five minutes were slowly ticking away. Standing up, he placed his left boot on the low glass table and adjusted the straps. He moved slowly and carefully so as not to alarm her, wanting mainly to annoy her with the delay in his response. When he'd finished, he sat back down exactly as before.

He smiled before speaking. "Technically, I'm the one who's running things now."

Her eyebrows shot up. "You!" She was incredulous. "You're lying. The Nightmakers would never accept you. You're a runner and too fragging close to what they hate most."

He shrugged slightly. "Think of it as a kind of military coup," he said, staring her straight in the eyes. "Besides, I said 'technically.' I issue the orders, but they come from Steadman's mouth. Rather, what's left of it.''

False understanding glinted in her eyes. "You're playing on that fanatic edge the inner circle always had, aren't you?"

He nodded, aware that the "Introitus" had ceased. The next selection was about to begin after the pause he'd programmed. It was time to play his cards. He stood up.

"Enough talk." His movement, pitch, and inflection snapped her onto the defensive. "We've made a decision. Der Nachtmachen no longer finds it acceptable for you to be the shadow-liege of The Revenants. Our unification offer is withdrawn."

Shavan stood up to face him, her eyes taking on a Medusan quality. "No longer finds it acceptable?" she hissed. "You think you can bully me? Bully us?" He didn't need his astral sight to see the power building. "Saeder-Krupp has already agreed to the funding, my stupid friend. With their nuyen, The Revenants will yank the reigns of the Restoration out of the hands of the bureaucrats and put them back in the hands of the people!"

He shook his head, turned, and step-vaulted over the float coach, putting it between them. Landing with a turn, he said, "Didn't I read that in your last propafax?" He pushed back his leather coat and jammed his thumbs into his pants pockets.

Her voice and anger rose together. "You of all people know I'm right!" Her left hand shot out to point at him. "How many trillions have already been spent so that the contractors and analysts can build their villas?"

He shrugged again. "I don't know, but I was always fond of The Revenants' little hideaway on the Riviera. Great view."

Shavan's anger solidified as her arm slowly came down. "Why now? Der Nachtmachen has always supported our view. Steadman did, his people did, even you did—when you cared to comment. Why have you changed your minds *now*?" Her tone was clipped and hard, and without realizing it she'd shifted into German.

"Why? We haven't changed, and you haven't been listening." Alexander slowly spread his hands wide. He walked clear of the furniture and dropped into lotus position again, in doing so declaring a duel. "Der Nachtmachen firmly believes in Europa Dividuus," he went on. "No question. You, however, made the wrong move."

Standing about ten steps away from him, she dropped down too, mimicking his position. He nodded, they breathed, and the world changed. The furniture, devoid of life, became dark, hollow shadows and the boundaries of the room vanished to become walls of scintillating green energy. The shield that kept out prying eyes would become the limits of the astral battle, Alexander thought. Nothing could get out and nothing could get in. Nothing expected, that is.

"You went to Saeder-Krupp," he said. "You wanted the nuyen, but you could have gotten that from just about anyone. You kept it quiet because you didn't want anyone to know you were getting backing from a corp." The glare in her eyes was blinding, and her aura left no question that she was prepared for battle. Alexander knew he had to keep talking, keep her interested just long enough. The music of Mozart's death mass surged, still audible, but now coming to their astral hearing as the anguish and the tears of its composer rather than the musical notes the physical world heard.

"More than money, you wanted the dragon, and you wanted him enough to come to Seattle to see him." Alexander paused and her eyes narrowed. "You wanted Lofwyr behind you," he said.

"So?" she snapped. "With the dragon backing us, we could rally the apathetic Awakened."

"Saeder-Krupp is one of the controlling corporations of the Restoration. Why would Lofwyr betray it for a bunch of street hustlers?"

Her eyes glinted as she saw an opening. "I've spoken with him. You forget how *old* he is. A Restored Europe would quickly become a concrete and steel Europe. He wants to return it to the way he remembers it.''

"Damn it, Shavan! Haven't you ever looked at Saeder-Krupp's profile? They're Saeder-Krupp *Heavy Industries,* for god's sake. Who the frag do you think is going to be pouring all that concrete and casting all that steel? Who do you think pumps more toxins into the air? Who do you think pollutes more rivers?''

"Those are all companies he's bought. It takes time to bring them into line environ—''

"Don't you know that wonderful American saying?'' Alexander said, cutting her off. " 'Never deal with a dragon'? Don't you know why that's true, Shavan? It's because the likes of you and I could never hope to understand them. They have more secret motives, more plans, than we could ever suspect, and to them we're just along for the ride. Trust me on this.''

She snorted. "What would you know? I've spoken with Lofwyr; he is very direct, very aware and concerned. . . .'' A dark shape moved somewhere beyond the shield. She let her words trail off and watched it circle the room. The time had come.

"I don't run Der Nachtmachen, Shavan. A friend of mine does. A friend who's also very concerned about who has influence where. And he doesn't want his brother fragging around in Europe any more than he already is!''

They both moved. Alexander's hands slammed together and he pumped every drop of his will into a shatter-shield spell. Raw astral force ripped around them, and power streamed upward out of him, tearing into the lattice of the shield. He felt tendrils of ice whip into him as she struck with her own energy. He reeled, trying to control the power arcing around him. As his mystic bolt impacted, the shield was hit hard from the outside. Unable to withstand the dual concussion, it shattered, raining prismatic energy. A giant dark form poured through the opening and past the falling shards.

Alexander felt his power slipping from him as he saw her for the last time. The dragon's astral form slammed into her, its unearthly claws tearing great, jagged rips into her spirit body. Magical energies flowed from her to dissipate harmlessly around the dragon. Alexander shuddered as her screams merged with the dragon's roar.

"Shavan, meet Alamais!" he cried out, unheard.

The world spun into red-tinged darkness, the music stopped, and he became utterly calm. Floating in darkness, he smiled. He would survive, the dragon would see to it. A new road was opened before him.

Dosvidanya, my past, he thought. You are behind me now.

PART 1

MANHATTAN, 2053

Shadowrun *n*. Any movement action, or series of such made to carry out illegal or quasi-legal operations.

—*WorldWide WordWatch, 2053 edition*

1

It took a careful, knowing eye to perceive the subtle changes in the shades of the black plasticrete rushing below the aircraft's landing gear. Except for Jason Chase, who forced himself to watch, the pilot was the only other person who noticed. Feeling her craft pass safely over the spot, she offered a silent prayer of thanks. Though the scars had long been covered over, Chase could see them as as he had in the days after the accident. There was one long, jagged fault, one hundred meters or so in length, and a second one running parallel. That one started a short distance after the first, but ended almost immediately at the point where the metal that carved it out had bent and shattered.

The orbital bounced twice, finally touching the black. Chase leaned back in his seat, eyes closed, as the braking jets fired and struggled to bring the sleek craft to a safe stop. Feeling the pressure ease, he unplugged his data cable from the seat's system jack and then from the datajack set behind and below his right ear. The cable, remembering its unpowered shape, wrapped itself into a neat coil that Chase dropped into his pocket.

Calling up the time display on his retina, he adjusted it for Manhattan time, and sighed. Twenty minutes late. Chase, personally, didn't mind being late, but Eric Sieboldt did. And he was still Eric Sieboldt, for at least another hour or so.

The jetway was already in place by the time he'd gotten his carryon bag together. He was one of the last off, winning a smile from a flight attendant as he passed. She was attractive in the old natural way. He spotted no sign of alteration, neither in her slim but shapely body, nor in the color of her shoulder-length, ash-blond hair, nor in the gentle shape of her face and the unforgettable blue of the eyes. And she was young, enough so that he was aware of it. Because she'd been so attentive during the flight, he decided not to inflict Eric Sieboldt on her. He smiled back.

Once in the terminal, he detoured from the surge of people moving toward the baggage claim, in search of the nearest information desk. It took but a moment to locate one of the token, manned desks most airlines had somewhere in the terminal. This woman also smiled as he approached, but he saw the battle-hardened steel behind the veneer and prepared for it. Eric Sieboldt complained loudly, and often. The records said so.

She nodded vacantly, all wide smile and rehearsed charm as he raved and she typed. The woman apologized, pointing out that the flight's delay was due to local conditions at their origin point, Damascus. That put the delay under the "Act of God" clause of his arrival insurance and precluded compensation, but the airline would happily provide him with a free drink upgrade on his next flight. Chase almost laughed, but Sieboldt didn't see the humor and managed to thank the woman curtly as he turned on his heel.

The maglev ride to the baggage concourse was short, but surrounded by the flicker of myriad holographic color advertisements and filled with the scents of a hundred different perfumes and colognes. No one spoke. Few looked at anything other than some reading screen, one of the ads, or some undefined spot on the car wall. All wore custom, corporate-cut suits of one style or another, except for one leather-clad joker-boy who stood with his back against the doors, arms folded, grinning at anyone who would meet his gaze. The joker was out of place, knew it, and wanted to have fun. Chase looked down and held back his grin: twenty-five years ago he might have behaved the same way.

Resealed and sporting a bright white clearance tag, Chase's bag was waiting at Carousel Twenty, as the announcement had predicted. The joker-boy watched the line of fashionable bags nervously, apparently not finding what he was looking for. Picking up his case, Chase turned toward the nearby ramp to customs. As he hit the moving walkway, two bulky customs agents emerged from an unmarked doorway. Gazing idly at an ad for this year's Toyota Elite hanging in the air above him, he let the walkway carry him on while thinking about the kid. Twenty-five years ago he just might have made the same mistake.

The wait at customs was short and, remembering to be Sieboldt, he engaged in almost-polite, idle conversation with an elderly ork woman traveling with her normal-enough looking grandson. For some reason she wanted to talk about how safe transorbital air travel was. He decided not to argue the point: she hadn't seen the runway scars.

She had the manner of the naturally aged, which marked her as one of those who'd changed with the first wave of returning magic. The newer of her kind, the second and more recent generation, were all cursed with rapid aging; they reached physical maturity far ahead of their emotions and then died only barely having experienced life. That was true for the goblin races anyway; the fae races, on the other hand, the dwarfs and the elves, seemed blessed with retarded aging, even unnatural youth. Chase hoped this boy would remain human and not change at puberty. Here in the secure confines of the airport, he and his grandmother were protected from any overt racism, but the rest of the world was very different.

The customs agent didn't smile as he took the transit pass from Chase and slipped the encoded end into the reader. While it scanned, the agent reopened Chase's carryon and checked the garment bag and removed the tags. There wasn't much more than a few changes of clothing and some data chips for the datadeck in the carryon. The agent scanned the list the airline had printed on the white tags. "Do you certify that these chips contain no contraband data, Mister Sieboldt?" The agent's voice was raspy from too much city life.

"I do."

The agent nodded. "You realize that transport of contraband data across state and national lines is in violation of—"

"I said I don't have any." Chase let an edge slip into his voice. The agent glanced up at him and then over at the display of the transit pass data. He noted the residency code.

"Of course, Mister Sieboldt," he said, smiling now. "Regulations require us to mention it."

"I understand."

The agent closed the cases and attached green tags showing the state seal. "Welcome back to New York, sir. If you need any special arrangements, a transport assistant in the main concourse can help you."

"Thank you, but that won't be necessary. I assume the city express is still running?"

"Yes, sir, it is. Now, if you'd just stare at the sign on the wall behind me a moment while we update your transit-pass image," the agent said, cueing the system. Chase complied. It was normal. The sign welcomed him again to the city. He thought about the woman and her grandson.

The machine beeped and the agent handed him the pass. "Thank you, sir. If you'll just pass though the sensor gates again, you'll be on your way."

Chase took the bags, the pass, and a deep breath, then moved through the nearest gate. No alarms sounded, no lights flashed. At every airport or border crossing he always wondered, just for a moment, if the sensor gates had been upgraded without his knowledge, just waiting to reveal his secrets. So far he'd been safe. Twenty years was a long time to be safe. The day of reckoning couldn't be far off.

He moved toward the main concourse, but once clear of the customs area, veered off into an adjoining corridor. An airport page mispronounced his mother's maiden name and he laughed. He wondered how much like her this other person was. Out in front of the terminal, he hailed a cab, which he took to one of the remote parking lots. An untraceable credstick paid for a drab car he'd left parked there months ago.

Chase drove the car east on the Belt to the Cross Island Parkway, then took the Throgs Neck Bridge up into the Bronx. From there he traveled north and then west to the second span of the George Washington Bridge. On the far side he paid the twelve-dollar toll with the credstick that showed the ID to which the car was registered. Hitting the Jersey Turnpike, he went south, stopping only briefly to change into some clothes from the black nylon bag in the car's trunk. Newark Airport was only a couple of exits down the road.

Arriving there, he again parked in one of the remote lots, but this time took a shuttle bus to the airport. He'd left his good bags in the trunk and had mixed some of those clothes with the ones in the black bag. The datadeck fit neatly into an outer pocket.

Once in the airport he took the tram to the transit terminal and paid cash for the PATH ticket into Manhattan. The subway car was cold and grimy and reeked of urine, sweat, and smoke. No one wore suits. The ads were two-dimensional. He stood with his back to the car doors and grinned. The only one who met his gaze was a punker—a rat shaman wannabe from the look—festooned with far too many talismans for them to be practical. Chase nodded, but the boy looked like he wanted to spit.

Eight minutes later the subway slid into Terminal. As the passengers filed through the check station, Chase handed over a different pass and the clerk almost smiled through her Plexiglas face shield. One armed guard in black and blue Port Authority security armor rifled Chase's nylon bag, while another ran a portable scanner over him. Those Chase wasn't worried about.

"Welcome to Manhattan, Mister Carpenter," the clerk said, the microphone system clipping her words. "Good to have you back," she joked amiably.

Chase nodded. It was good to be back.

2

Security won out over society, and Chase decided to set out across Terminal toward what passed for civilization, and eventually his apartment. As he left the Port Authority building for the hustle of the city, the street drek and the humidity rushed at him together. A pair of trickers wearing half-concealed Sister's Sinister colors bounced up as he stepped out into the harsh, late-summer sun. He kept moving, but eyed them skeptically over his sunglasses.

The first, a tousled blonde with an iridescent purple undertint and a red synthleather dress that would have stopped any traffic that could have run Terminal's blockades, took his arm. "Bigs," she said, rubbing her fingertips against the palm of his hand, "odds we got the feel you want."

The other, a tall brunette with hair cropped short and eyes hidden by sunglasses, took up a position on his other side. He caught a glimpse of almost-invisible cosmetic scars just beyond the black of her glasses. The datajack nearly hidden in the shadow of her left ear gleamed of fresh chrome. He was tempted: it had been awhile.

He smiled at her, then turned back to the blonde. I'm sure you do, *kirei*, but I'm still mostly meat. I don't think I'd live."

The blonde's face formed into a silicon-perfect pout,

but before she could say anything, he leaned in quickly
and kissed her lightly on the lips.

"Chip truth," he said as she jumped back, eyes wid-
ening slightly. Then he reached out to grab the dark-
haired girl's hand and pulled her toward him, attempting
to repeat history. To his surprise she deflected and count-
ered him, the look on her face passing from something
cold and violent to what could no longer be mistaken for
mindless amusement. As her left arm snapped up, he
extended his own arms to block, nearly as fast. She
stopped with her arm half-extended, the palm flat toward
him. It was then his thoughts turned suddenly to the
blonde, who was now somewhere behind him. Careless.

Chase pivoted slightly, balancing himself between the
two, but clearly favoring the brunette. On the blonde's
face he caught the last hints of amusement dissolving
back into that perfect pout. He was alert now, and noticed that her posture, though seemingly relaxed and
careless, was perfect for a hard move against him if he
made any further maneuvers toward her partner.

"Ladies." He finished his pivot and ended up between
them, arms lowered. "It's been wiz, but I think today's
not my day for magic." He took a step back as the brunette glanced at the blonde. Obviously the more polished
of the two, the blonde continued her pout, made a small
tsking sound, then turned to walk away, her heels snap-
ping smartly against the plasticrete. The brunette looked
back at him once, attempted a shrug, and hurried to follow her friend.

Chase watched the pair until they hung south on Tenth
Avenue. The brunette gave him another half-glance as
they turned. He waited a few moments for his pulse to
come down enough to catch his breath. Stupid. Stupid.
Stupid.

Sighing, he turned and crossed the street, hoping to
put distance between him and them. The last thing he
needed was involvement in some incident in Terminal.
He was carrying the wrong IDs for such troubles.

Not that he didn't deserve them, he thought. He'd spent

too long wearing dark suits in the middle of the desert. The corporate liaison life had fogged his brain. Maybe there was still some nerve gas left in Tel Aviv and he'd gotten a lungful. His mental flagellation complete, he decided to frag security and get a drink.

At this late hour of the afternoon, the check zone between Terminal and the Lower Westside was calm and quiet, letting him breeze through easily on his resident pass. He moved angrily, making the street-sellers bypass him for more hospitable-looking marks. He crossed Eighth and went underground, grabbing an "A" Express toward downtown. The evening work cycle was just beginning and the rush-hour migration begun. He hopped out at East Fourteenth and hiked the rest of the way.

It had been nearly six months, but he was sure his destination would be exactly where he'd last seen it. All kinds of troubles had failed to move it for all these years, and he couldn't think of much that could. The alley looked about as he remembered, except for a couple of newcomer cats rousting some rats near a pile of fiber cases. They watched him scornfully as he passed. Brave souls.

A fresh piece of scrawl gleamed at him from the loading dock, something in German about causes, effects, and sexual organs. Policlub stuff, no doubt; it was tough to avoid the drek.

The stairs next to the dock were as trash-strewn as ever, but there seemed to be no new stains. He stood at the bottom, for the thousandth time reading the No Entrance sign on the steel door. After a moment a cheap, weather-beaten speaker tacked onto the door frame squawked, "What?" Chase knew the voice to be much deeper than the speaker allowed.

"Open the door. I gotta take a piss."

The speaker gave a distorted chuckle that sounded more like a bark, then Chase heard the electronic locks slip aside. The door had only just begun to swing open before he'd slipped inside. His low-light optical system kicked in as he entered the darkness and patted the arm of the man who'd let him in. "William, *mi amigo,* you look like hell."

The ork smiled, a sharp, gap-toothed monstrosity that forty years ago would only have been possible in fairy tales. "It's what I get paid for."

Chase tapped the ork hard on the shoulder, and knocked him back a half step. William chuckled. "You're a nasty critter for an old man, Church."

Chase shrugged expressively and continued on. Drek, he thought. He'd forgotten that around here they knew him as Church. Too many places, too many names.

The ork called after him. "Teek already knows you're here, so don't try sneaking up on him."

The short corridor led him to the slightly raised area that bordered half the place. There was really only one room, but it had been divided up with partitions and sound-dampening wall sections. If customers wished, they could sit in the main area near a stage that occasionally presented live acts, but more often displayed cheap, sixty-four color holograms of some exotic dancer. The more select could pick the raised area or else a sectioned-off area where they might pass the time. Without fail, midnight or midday, there were always people there. It was a biz club, which meant that anyone present was quite obviously in the biz. Chase wasn't in that line of work anymore, but came anyway.

In the last few years, Manhattan had become the place around which Jason Chase revolved, the site of his brightest as well as darkest days. Those who knew him, and who he really was, tried to get him to be anywhere else but Manhattan, but the memories didn't care where he was standing.

Teek's was neutral ground, a place that didn't connect with anything on either end of the scale. Chase came there for the atmosphere, the sixty-four color women, and Teek.

"Well, jack me into a light socket, his holiness is among the blasphemous," came Teek's voice suddenly.

Chase had been heading toward the bar, and turned as

the owner of the voice approached, hands thrust into the pockets of his Indian-weave cardigan, a wide smile on his face. Teek was moving away from a group of sharp-suited Japacorp types who seemed somewhat displeased at the interruption. Chase felt no pity for them.

"Damn right, and I've got a pocket full of absolutions hot off the presses. Figured you might be needing a couple by now."

Chase let Teek pass, then followed him to the bar. He seemed shorter, maybe more stooped, maybe a little more shuffling. Things had happened. Chase suddenly thought that maybe he should have made some calls first.

"So," said Teek as he stepped up behind the polished, genuine mahogany bar and began to pull out glasses and bottles. The usual bartender, a moderately cute girl named Shawna, gave Chase a quick wave from the other end of the bar. He returned it with a smile. Teek rarely worked the bar anymore, but when he did the staff knew to give him wide berth. "That's quite a tan you've got there."

"Been doing some business under the sun," said Chase. "Putting my language talents to good use."

Teek swept the room with his gaze, let it light briefly on a couple of patrons, then glanced back at Chase. "Just talking? That seems so unlike you."

Chase laughed. "Hey, *amigo*, I was slow and old ten years ago. I've got tech in me older than the geniuses who are designing the latest stuff." He grinned. "I'll tell ya, it's certainly a pleasure to know that I can spend my golden years working off the bennies of my reputation."

"Golden years, huh? You're barely middle-aged."

Chase laughed ruefully. "If I were still working they'd be referring to me as 'venerable' or some other drek." He shook his head. "Not for me. I walked while I could."

Teek smiled. "How long you in town this time?"

Chase gave a careless shrug in reply, watching Teek mix up a couple of drinks, their usuals. He was surprised to see the older man's Special Forces ring back in its old place on his right hand. Sometimes he wore it, but more often he did not. Chase knew the feeling, but his own ring had been sitting at the bottom of the Black Sea for twenty years. "There's nothing in the works right now, plus I seem in dire need of a rest."

Teek's eyebrow raised. "Oh?" Half a lemon liquefied in his hands and splashed into one of the glasses.

"I'm not in Terminal cinco minutos when I almost get thrashed by a pair of thrill gals. The blonde was a pro, but I think the brunette was new."

Teek's eyebrow dropped and a grin began. "A pair, eh? Blonde and brunette? Blonde's got a light purple undertint and favors short skirts, usually black, Aztlan style? Brunette's close-cropped, Euro-style, likes red, sometimes black too?"

"You know them?"

Teek shrugged. "Semi-professionally only. A few months back they used to come in here and work some of the rear booths. When I came back I asked them to stop. Didn't want the wire." He finished mixing Chase's drink and slid it over.

"I'm sorry," Chase said after a moment.

Teek looked full at him, maybe for the first time since the other man had arrived. "You hadn't heard? I just assumed you had."

"No, I hadn't. When was it?"

"Four months ago. I took a month off, wandered around a bit to work out the cold. It wasn't unexpected. The drugs finally stopped helping, and he was dead within days. Just like the doctors said."

"If I'd known, I'd have come back for the services. Marko was a good man. I'll miss him."

Teek nodded. "I know, but there was no service, really. I was afraid of who'd come. Too many old ghosts."

"I understand."

Teek almost smiled. "Yeah, I'll bet you do." He finished making up his own drink and took a long sip. Chase let him savor it before changing the subject.

"So why'd you throw the girls out? I don't remember you being that morally discerning before. Though I guess with that pair. . ."

"No, those two aren't dangerous that way. They're loopers."

"Loopers?"

"Sim looping." Teek read the blank stare in Chase's face and laughed. "You have been away." He finished his drink and started another. "They've got a three-way hookup or some such rig. The two of them and their client rig up and sense-tap each other doing whatever they feel like doing at the time."

"You've got to be kidding. What the hell does that kind of hardware cost?"

"Not anywhere near as much as a few months ago. From what I understand they've got a basic portable sensory recording deck that's been rigged to route the sense signal to another unit instead of recording it. Instant feedback. Since the link is two-way I imagine it can lead to an escalating loop that builds until the circuit breakers trip. Aficionados call it 'shooting the hoop' or something."

"Is it illegal?"

Teek shrugged. "Not yet, too fresh. The signal the portable equipment handles is pretty crude, well within legal levels. There've been no direct psychological effects that I know of, but. . ."

"You suspect otherwise."

He shrugged again and looked off toward the back of the bar. "I've had enough of twisted realities myself, thank you very much. I know what that stuff can do the gear's hot enough. There's a new batch of psycho-traumatic sense chips hitting the market every week. I understand Knight Errant recently grabbed up a bunch that have a behavior-modifying secondary signal. Anarchist Euro-policlub drek, but strong enough to make an impact on some."

"Great."

"Figures we'd start importing the crazy stuff. Couldn't

bring over the British sewing circles or beer-chuggers. No, this is America. Gotta have the radicals.''

Chase shook his head. Teek was treading on dangerous memories. "Bomb the lot, I say. See how *they* like it.''

Teek looked at him for a moment, then smiled lightly. "So speaks the voice of experience.''

Chase shrugged and looked at his friend. "You play the game, you live by the rules.''

3

A week passed easily.

His apartment was as he'd left it, the little he had still intact. The Home Secretary expert-system had done its job of answering electronic mail and paying bills, but sometime over the last few months the ventilation system had decided to back up, throwing a pall of dust over nearly everything. He surprised the building management company with a quick call and got a promise that they'd clean the place up the next day.

They did, and he spent that day and the next, and the one after that, just knocking around. He fired up the brewkaf machine and sampled the diverse selection of coffees he'd forgotten the cupboards contained. He laughed often at the easy banality of his life.

Three days back, and his Vienna contact forwarded a couple of job offers through a blind route. Each offer came tagged for the name they knew him by, and got routed by the private, secure systems of the Vienna data haven to similar systems in Denver. From Denver it bounced to Manhattan via a protected mail-forwarding system in Boston. It was safe, but not foolproof. If someone wanted Chase bad enough they could track it all, but there were enough safeties along the route that he'd probably know they were coming. He planned to live his life very pleasantly and with the only risk of surprise visitors being the roaches that occasionally made the trek up from downstairs.

On the fourth day, Teek called.

"I thought you'd want to know that someone's been looking for you," he said, his face looming six times its normal size on the telecom screen.

Chase sat up. "Oh?"

"I wasn't here. Nick was working the door—you haven't met him—but he told me when I came in."

"Nick, whom I do not know, knew my name well enough to tell you someone had been looking for me?"

Teek laughed. "One of my employment criteria is the ability to memorize lists of names. People I keep track of."

"Great."

"Nick thinks she was a streeter, or close to it. She asked if he'd seen you lately, and he said no, never having had."

"Good," Chase said.

"I'll feed you the security camera recording. You can take it from there," Teek said. "Just tell me when."

Chase picked up the remote and told the telecom to accept the data signal when Teek sent. "Go ahead."

Teek leaned forward, pressed a button, and the red words "Receiving Data" began to flash across the bottom of Chase's screen.

"That's it," Teek said.

"Thanks." The words turned green and disappeared.

Teek nodded. "Anytime. Call me if you need anything."

"I will do that, my friend. Thanks again." Chase flicked the remote at Teek's image, turning his face back into the flat black of the screen. By the time he'd hung up, the telecom had automatically decompressed the trideo data into usable form. He told the unit to play it.

The camera angle was high and to the right of the bar's outer door. Chase hadn't noticed it before. Next time he would look. The image was clean and sharp, even in the low evening light. High-quality. Thank you, Teek.

Even with the good image, it was hard to see the girl. Her body language, which was contradictory, placed her somewhere between eighteen and thirty. His guess was closer to the former. In her green minidress, black sheer stockings, and half-calf boots, she was dressed for success, if turning tricks was the career path of choice. Her auburn hair was cut short and she wore a shoulder bag that could have been holding anything. The way the front wave of her hair fell it was tough to see her face.

"Can I help you?" came a voice through the cheap speaker. It must have been Nick; William was never that polite.

"Yes, I'm scanning for Simon Church," she said, her voice a little deeper than what he'd expected and with the trace of a British accent.

"I'm sorry I don't know the man." *Gracias,* Nick.

"I'd heard he was hereabouts some."

"Told you I don't know 'im."

"Older, I guess by now, big shoulders, dark hair."

"You just described my mother."

"He's an old term—chummer—of mine. Lots ago."

"Look, chica, I told you I don't know the man."

She looked down and away from the camera, and Chase still hadn't gotten a good view of her face. There was, however, a gnawing familiarity. When she looked back at the door, the movement of her head tossed her hair away from her face for just a moment. It was still too brief for him to make her out, but he knew he could reverse the recording and still-frame it, so he let it run.

"Sure, sure. If he shows, tell him Cara was looking for him. I need some help. I've got a room at the Caina, Eighth and Fiftieth. Okay?"

"Whatever."

"Great. Thanks." She stepped away and the recording ended.

Chase didn't need to check, but wanted to. Older by now, she said. Older by twelve years. The recording ran back to the turn of her head and he froze the picture. The image was clear enough that he could zoom in until only her face was visible.

When Chase looked at pictures of himself from twelve years ago, he saw very little difference. Most of the changes from ages twenty-seven to forty-one happened under the skin, normally invisible but painfully present at inopportune moments. It was different with Cara. The only similarities were a certain posture, the movement of a hand, her mother's eyes, her father's tone. She'd been only eight years old the last time Chase had seen her. Twelve years from being an eight-year-old was a lot longer.

He remembered, the memories coming back sharp and fresh.

She runs at him, clothes dirty and torn from her slide down the hill. She's smiling, though, ignoring the scrapes and the trickle of blood running down her arm. "That way?" she asks, giggling for punctuation.

He shakes his head and glances at the familiar Land Rover coming up alongside, kicking dirt and gravel. "No. Not unless you like eating dirt," he says.

The Rover door opens roughly. "—*fragging* Christ, Cara, are you insane?" Her mother swings herself from the seat, careful not to catch any part of her evening dress on the door's accessories. "Have you any idea what your father was doing tonight?"

Cara turns toward her mother and never changes her expression. "He's still there, right?" she asks.

"Of course he's there! Did you really think he'd come chasing after you just because of this stupid stunt?"

"No. No, I guess I didn't."

"Tonight was important, Cara. Tonight was crucial. The Japanese don't look kindly on executives with unmanageable children."

"But Daddy didn't come, right?"

"No he didn't."

Cara doesn't say any more, only looks back at Chase

for a moment before beginning to walk around to the far side of the truck. She brushes some dirt from her arm and then climbs into the passenger side of the Rover. She sits there, waiting.

"She was where we thought, Mrs. Villiers," he begins, careful about how he addresses her.

"But how in god's name did she get out of the compound?"

"She's very good. She must have listened hard at the family security briefings and learned our schedule and procedures. We'll start varying the patterns. That should slow her down some."

"You'd better. This can't happen again while we're here. She has no idea what she's risking."

"No," he says, "I think she knows exactly what she's doing."

He'd spoken to her one last time before the family left.

She's standing on one of the sundecks watching a pair of falcons dance in flight. She glances over her shoulder as he walks up. "Are you coming to Seattle with us?" She's gotten taller.

"No, Cara, I'm not. My contract with your family is up. Your mother has decided not to renew it."

"I got away from you too many times, huh?"

He nods. That was as good a reason as any.

"How about you catch me? I could run away again, and you catch me and I tell my mother you were really good, the best." She's watching the falcons avidly.

"Hmmm," he says, "it might work, but I doubt it. Besides, right now it would only make sense if Deaver caught you. If I was the one, your mother would be suspicious."

Her lips purse. "I don't like him."

"Because he's a mage?"

She shrugs. "He doesn't look *at* you. He looks *in* you, like he's watching your mind work. His eyes are really creepy. How could he wear them?" She turns toward him. "Don't they hurt? Doesn't he always know he's got them on?"

"Cybertechnology is very advanced. Some of it's almost as good as the real parts. You can barely feel them. Deaver's only got a little, his eyes. He mostly relies on his magic."

She blinks. "Do you have any?"

"Magic?"

"Cyber stuff."

He nods.

"A lot?"

"More, I suspect, than I know."

She turns back toward the birds, but they've gone. Her eyes focus on the faraway mountains. "I don't want any. I'll never want any. I only want me."

"Sometimes it's not a choice. Like for Deaver. . . and me, a bit."

"I don't care," she says. "I don't care."

Chase knew he needed to fill in those twelve years. He'd heard some stories, read the corporate pages of the tabloids, but wanted to know more. He needed someone who knew where the data could be found and had the talent to get at it. His message ended up in a place where the only reality was electronic. It took a few hours before a response came, and it wasn't from who he expected.

"Church."

Chase looked up, surprised. The telecom hadn't beeped, the voice had simply begun and the face simply appeared. She'd cut through the electronic security of his system like it wasn't there. Her appearance was young and carved from mirrorlike black stone, her eyes two darts of blue neon. The image showed little more than her face and parts of a gently shifting fractal shoreline behind her, but he knew the gown she wore was in the ancient Greek style and woven from the palest orange light. The stylings of her electronic image were perfect. He'd met her once before. He stood.

"Lachesis."

She bowed her head slightly. "You dispatched a message to the Nexus, for Lucifer."

"I did."

"He is dead."

Chase started, and looked away for a second. Another of the old guard dead, another piece of the past slipped away. He felt old again.

"How."

The electronic quaver of her voice did not shift, but he felt a tinge of satisfaction. "It has been reconciled. The individuals responsible have been held accountable."

"I'll want to know at some point."

"Acknowledged. Your transmission indicated you had instructions for Lucifer. I am prepared to execute those instructions in his stead."

He nodded and sat back down more slowly than he'd intended. "I need a full information search on a person, birth name Caroline Tara Villiers. Her father is Richard Villiers, one of the owners of Fuchi Industrial Electronics."

Lachesis' head tilted slightly to one side. The Fuchi name was almost holy to deckers like her. The company built the cyberdeck computer hardware that was the primary tool of her work, and paradoxically, the security software the corporations used to protect themselves against deckers. Fuchi's own worldwide computer systems were considered to be nearly impregnable, a blatant challenge to any decker wanting to test, or hone, his or her skills in illicit data retrieval.

"What are the search parameters?"

"I need as much as you can find about her activities and whereabouts for the last twelve years. But you've also got to be as quiet as possible. Zero feedback."

"Noise is not conducive to continued activity."

"This one's got to be so quiet I can hear a fragging pin drop. I also have a time limit—eight hours for an initial report, with an estimate at that time for your production of a detailed one."

"Acknowledged."

"Also, keep any penetration of Fuchi systems to a minimum. If you've got to do it, do it as a blind behind some other run."

"Acknowledged."

He thought for a moment and then nodded slightly to himself. The information Lachesis turned up would give him more to go on. "That's it. What'll it cost me?"

"There is no charge for this action. The potential challenge is sufficient."

Chase laughed and shook his head. "Oh no, if you're in it just for the wiz, God knows what you'll do before you think you've been duly compensated. How much?"

"Two thousand nuyen worth of random corporate bearer stock now, five thousand negotiable upon delivery."

Chase smiled. "That's better."

4

The next morning, with Lachesis' preliminary report fresh in his mind, Chase stood in a shadowed doorway across from the Caina Hotel, observing its occupants wander out into the morning gloom. The Caina was a flophouse catering to transients and low-income residents of the Lower Westside zone. Most looked like various kinds of wage slaves, but a few of the building's inhabitants seemed to be heading off for seamier occupations.

According to Lachesis, a Cara Deaver was registered in room 407, and was two months in arrears for her daily rent. The hotel computer had her account flagged and noted for managerial attention. Lachesis could have easily changed the account status, but someone on the Caina's staff had already noted it. Cara Deaver was tagged for eviction.

Chase hoped that all the girl wanted, or needed, was

cash for rent and a push in the right direction, but he doubted it. Lachesis' overnight work had turned up a turbulent history for the little girl he remembered. The kind of history girls with her background weren't supposed to have.

A matte-black '48 Ford American pulled up loudly in front of the Caina, and two oversized specimens of street muscle got out. Chase didn't know them personally, but he was more than familiar with their type. Slip them some cash and they were more than willing to act as insurance against, or for, a violent incident at whatever event you might have planned. The driver, wearing mock vintage Euro-Wars battle dress was finishing off a rude joke about trolls and sisters as they got out. His ork partner, similarly garbed but with more street clothes mixed in, seemed amused and appreciative. Neither noticed, or cared, about Chase watching from across the street. They pocketed their sunglasses and entered the building. Chase saw no evidence of weapons, but their field jackets had ample room for carrying light or medium-sized pistols. The odds of them packing anything cybernetic was low.

If the muscleboys were there for Cara's eviction, the Caina's management must be expecting more trouble than a girl her size could usually deliver. Other than the overdue rent, the hotel computer showed no other notations of complaints or problems.

Chase crossed the street and entered the hotel a few dozen steps behind the toughs. His own choice of clothing had proved unusually appropriate: a Texas Ranger military jacket sporting insignia circa the secession of Texas in '35. Displaying such insignia was usually taken as a personal insult south of the border. The Caina's Aztlaner front-desk clerk recognized the patches and scowled as Chase entered. Chase scowled back and gestured toward the stairs. "*¿Yá subierion?*"

The clerk looked him over for a moment, then nodded. Chase grinned, saluted the clerk, and turned toward the stairs. He took them two at a time in case the clerk decided to make more of an issue of the patches. But behind him was only silence.

He'd come to the fourth floor and started to check the room numbers when the echo of voices began coming his way. As the voices grew louder and angrier, he moved forward down the dim, but fairly debris-free corridor. Rounding another corner Chase paused a moment alongside an open door. Voices and light spilled out into the corridor.

A man's voice, angry, probably representing the Caina: "Eighteen hundred bucks is what you owe. I don't care about nothin' else."

"I told you give me a couple of days." It was the voice of a young woman, undoubtedly Cara.

"You said that last week. Like I'm going to believe you now?"

"If she says she's gonna pay," said another man's voice, young like Cara's but wrong for the toughs, "stretch a little, will ya?"

The first man again. "You just jam that. You and your drekhead friends ain't supposed to be here in the first place. I could throw you all out just for that."

"You could try, you fraggin' piece of—" The blow shut the young man up, and from the sound, it also sent him flying. Cara, or another woman, made a noise at the same time and Chase decided to show himself.

The flat was cheap, a main area with kitchenette systems and a door leading to what looked like a bedroom; two smaller doors probably led to a closet and a bathroom. There were more people in the room than Chase had expected: the two toughs, their backs to the door and their eyes on the sprawled youth; an older man, maybe Chase's own age, dressed slightly better than the rest; Cara just kneeling down to help the youth who'd been hit; the kid himself, who looked to be in his late teens and reveling in it; and two boys of similar appearance who were just standing up. They all turned as Chase rapped twice on the door and stepped in.

The two toughs immediately began to size him up, and

shifted position to flank him. The manager scowled. "Who the hell are you?"

Chase shrugged. "I was in the neighborhood, thought I'd drop by." Cara was kneeling next to the boy, who was bleeding from the mouth. She looked up at Chase blankly. He nodded at her and suddenly the color began to rush back into her face. She let go of the kid and began to stand.

"These pukes friends of yours?" asked the manager.

Chase nodded. "One at least." He was looking at Cara, who was standing rigid with her hands clenched together in front of her. She turned toward the manager.

"Could I have a second . . ."

The manager rolled his eyes. "Sure, whatever, but out in the hall. We ain't leavin' this room without the money."

"Sure," she said, walking toward Chase, her gaze locked to his until she moved past him into the hallway. She'd grown a lot taller. Chase looked at each of the toughs once, ignored their grins, and went out after her.

"Look, I'm sorry," she said. "I didn't want to—"

"You need money."

She blinked at him. "Well, yes, I—"

"Eighteen hundred dollars?"

Her eyes widened. "How did you . . ."

"We'll worry about how you're going to pay me back later." He squeezed her shoulder gently and stepped past her into the room. The bleeding kid looked like he was just about ready to get up and do something stupid. Chase cut him off. "Get up and *I'll* knock you down." He turned toward the manager.

"You want eighteen hundred dollars."

"Damn right."

"How do you want it?" He began to reach into his jacket pocket. The two toughs got nervous, but Chase ignored them.

The manager looked at him. "Waddya mean? I want it in money."

"What kind of money do you want? International nuyen? UCAS dollars? Corporate scrip? What?"

"Dollars, for Christ's sake, what do I look like, the bank of—"

Chase pulled an envelope out and tossed it at the manager. He caught it and looked at it, surprised. So did Cara, who'd moved up alongside Chase. "Count it if you like," said Chase, "but get the fuck out of her room."

The manager slit the envelope open and riffled the bills. "If it's not right, I'll be back." He moved toward the door, and gestured the two toughs after him. They followed, but the ork turned as he passed Chase.

"You actually said fuck, how quaint."

Chase snorted. "And you formed a complete sentence; get the *fuck* out." He reached out and slammed the door after them.

The bleeding kid jumped to his feet. "I ain't gonna let no fraggin' grunt badface me." He spit a mouthful of blood onto the carpet as his hand came out of his pocket, clutching a thin switchblade knife. "I'm going to cut that goblin's fraggin'—"

Chase hit him at the base of the thumb, knocking the knife onto the bloody carpet. Before the kid could react, Chase hit him again, hard, in the solar plexus, knocking him back into a chair.

Cara was still standing near the door, wincing at the blow Chase gave the kid. She was tall, only a bit shorter than Chase, much taller than he'd expected. Her hair had gotten darker, or been darkened, and was now cut shorter than it had been the previous day on Teek's security video. She was dressed all in black, wearing knee-high Italian boots, black jeans, a tight shirt with the red and white emblem of the French trash band L'Infâme, and an oversized jacket. She suddenly looked very young.

"You all right?" he asked.

She nodded, and looked down. "Thank you, I—"

"Cara, who's this guy?" It was one of the other kids, who'd suddenly found his voice while the other one helped the bleeding kid.

She looked from the kid back to Chase. "This is Si-mon Church, an old friend of my family."

"Thanks, chummer," the kid said to Chase, "but me and the boys can breeze it from here. We'll pay you once we get some gigs, big truth."

"Glad to hear it," said Chase, turning, " 'cause I expect it—"

"I didn't call you about rent money," interrupted Cara. They all turned toward her as she looked down again for a moment, then back up at Chase. He noticed the gleam of metal below her left ear, just covered by the wave of her hair. "I need some real help," she said.

"Cara, what the hell—" The kid near Chase snapped his gaze back and forth between them.

"Someone wants to kill my father."

Chase stiffened. "You're certain?"

"Someone's trying—?" said the kid.

Chase cut him off. "Shut up, you. Cara, how do you know?"

She fidgeted, looked away and then back. "It's a long story, but I'm sure."

"Do they know?"

"My father?"

"No, the people who want to kill him."

She nodded.

"Then we're out of here." Chase turned toward the boy nearest him, then down at the bleeding kid and the one helping him. "Gentlemen, I suggest you think about leaving too. Odds are trouble's coming, and you don't want to be here when it does."

5

Chase led Cara Villiers out of the Caina by the back door. The three boys started to protest, but were put off not only by Chase's presence and manner, but by Cara's readiness to leave them behind and go with him. Chase doubted if the three would listen to his warning to leave the flat, which bothered him. If he needed to make Cara disappear, they were a weak link: they'd seen her—and him—and had heard her use one of his names. Once he got Cara to relative safety, he'd have to send someone back to pay the boys a visit. Hopefully they'd listen to cash.

"Do you think they're in danger?" Cara asked as they reached the street.

"Depends. I don't know anything about what's going on. Either way, they'd be smart to move on and vanish for a little while." He decided to walk a ways before grabbing transport. Chase wanted to see if they were being followed. A derelict shouted obscenities at his foot as they passed.

She sighed. "They won't do that."

"Oh?" Chase led her across the traffic on Eighth and turned south. They slipped into the human flow and moved with it.

"They're going to be famous." Cara shifted the strap of her bag into a better position on her shoulder. "They've got to be high profile, even if they're not performing. Keep the band's name in the public mind."

Chase saw no signs of any immediate trouble. The rest of the city moved without pattern or seeming concern. "What do they call themselves?"

"Rouge Angels." She walked with her gaze on the ground, her eyes looking everywhere but at him.

"How'd you get involved with them?"

"I met them at the Whisper Gardens. They seemed wiz enough, and maybe had something. They do a retro-acoustic thing."

"Trying to repeat history?"

She stopped walking and looked up at him. He stopped, too, and the pedestrian flow cleaved around them. "You know about that?" she said. There was something in her look, something he couldn't read. Plastic collided with metal a few blocks away. Someone yelled.

He nodded and pointed at the L'Infâme logo on her shirt. "Hard not to. It was in all the media." And Lachesis' report.

"I didn't mean it to work that way." She started to move slowly back into the flow of the crowd. He followed.

"I certainly hope not." He waited for her to volunteer more, but she didn't.

"The hospital says there's now about a forty percent chance the one boy, Gerard, will regain use of his legs without implant surgery." Her head twitched slightly as if she was about to respond, but she didn't. "The Marseilles police have been holding off filing charges against the other, Alain, wasn't it?, until they've spoken with you."

Now she really did stop. The crowds parted again, this time with some grumbling. She looked up at him, her expression easy to read. "Look, it's history, all right? I don't want to talk about it."

Chase shook his head. "If you're in trouble and you want my help, we're going to have to talk about it. And about everything else."

Her eyes narrowed and she began to walk again, then stopped after only a few steps and looked back at him. "Where the frag are we going anyway?"

Chase finished the call, but waited until his telecom security circuits completed the commands that he hoped would make the call difficult to trace, erasing it from the phone company's records. Cara moved about, alternately watching him and examining the artifacts of his apartment. "It's taken care of," he said.

She turned. "Will they be all right?"

Chase shrugged. "Tiger may not be a lot of things, but he's polite. Whether they listen to him or whether someone else gets there first is hard to say."

She looked away and back to some of the paper and

databooks on one of the shelves. She gestured at them.
"I don't remember you being the spiritual type. This is
quite a collection of shamanic stuff." She picked up a
small bracelet woven from twigs and vine and adorned
with stone beads and feathers.

"They belonged to a woman I . . . knew."

Cara stopped with the bracelet halfway down her hand.
She looked at him and then away. "I'm sorry."

"She was killed in an—accident—a few years ago. Like
you said before, history." He entered the kitchen area
and pulled some glasses down from a rack. "Like a
drink? I think it's time we talked about *your* life."

She sat down on one of the soft couches, near where
she'd draped her jacket. "Yes, rum slicer, if you know
how to make it."

"I do. I take it you're planning to pass out early tonight?"

"Don't play daddy with me, all right? I've already had
one man frag that up on me."

Chase worked on the drinks, but glanced up. "Sorry."

She shifted in her seat. "It's all right."

"It sounds cliché, but care to start at the beginning?"

"Sure, just give me a sec."

Chase finished mixing her drink, and his own, and
carried them over. He chose a seat near her, but facing.
He wanted to be able to see her face. She took the drink
and sipped it, licking her lips slightly afterward.

He remembered the series of images of Cara that
Lachesis' report had contained. Spaced just about evenly,
one image passing per year, he could see how the girl—
no, woman—before him had come to be. He could also
see it in the data files, the five runaways after he'd left
the family's employ, and the last one, four years ago, to
the wilds of Europe. She'd honed her independent streak
into such a fine instrument that not even her powerful
family had dared retrieve her when she ran away for the
last time. All the reports revealed Cara Villiers as a young
woman who could take care of herself. And yet she was
here looking for his help.

She took another sip. "About three years ago I was staying with some members of a German radical student group called Neustimme, New Voice. They were mostly Cunningham socialists and fond of sitting around talking, yelling, and slipping propaganda pieces into national datafaxes.

"At one of their parties, I met a guy named Adler, who was a chummer of one of Neustimme's more raddy members. He was older and very charismatic, in a quiet, powerful way. I thought he was interested in me, but now I think he knew who I was." Her gaze had softened as she spoke, and her eyes and words took on a distant quality.

"He became my lover that night," she continued quietly. "He was one of the leaders of Alte Welt, the eco-terrorist group."

Chase shifted and leaned in slightly. Lachesis' report had related rumors that Cara Villiers had radical German policlub connections, but none of the media reports had named names.

"I never participated in any of their actions, but I was always there afterward to congratulate them. They were always careful not to hurt people."

"But they weren't always successful."

"No." Her left hand clenched and relaxed. "Those were accidents."

Accidents, thought Chase, the deaths of innocents, no matter how deliberate, were always "accidents." He knew a lot about those kinds of "accidents."

"Of course," he said. "How did your father get involved?"

"Last year, Alte Welt was involved in a campaign against Hanburg-Stein, a heavy industries corp that was polluting the Eder River and the surrounding town. The problem was that Hanburg-Stein fought back. They hired a group of local criminals to kill as many members of Alte Welt as they could find."

Chase nearly smiled. "You play the game, you live by the rules."

"It was bad," she said. "They knew how to blow things up and all, but they didn't know how to fight. There were maybe twelve people in the group at its peak, but suddenly there were only five. Most of them wanted to get out, to disappear and maybe try to start something again in a few months. Adler wouldn't let them. He'd lost—we'd all lost—some good friends, and he didn't want to let H-S get away with it. But he didn't know what to do."

She was silent for a long time.

"I suggested that they get the support of a rival corporation. We'd turned up some valuable paydata on H-S, but it wasn't anything that was immediately valuable to us. I thought maybe we could use it as collateral to pry something out of the rival corp. Adler agreed."

"He went to Fuchi. He went to your father," said Chase.

She shook her head slightly. "He went to Fuchi, but not to my father. A few days later we were met by a woman, Katrina Demarque. She worked for Fuchi, but not for my father's part of the company. She's an agent for the Nakatomis."

Chase nodded. Fuchi Industrial Electronics was owned by a consortium of three families. Two of them were Japanese, the Nakatomis and the Yamanas. The other third was headed by Richard Villiers, Cara's father. Even when Chase had worked for the family, the relationships within the triad had been tense and volatile. Despite that, Fuchi had become one of the most powerful megacorporations in the world under their joint leadership.

Cara took a deep breath. "I was upset."

"I can imagine."

"I told Adler I didn't want them dealing with Fuchi. But he liked the way Demarque treated him, like he and his organization were important. She claimed that the data we had was actually very, very valuable and that Fuchi was willing to pay well for it.

"It started to feel like I was home again, and I hated

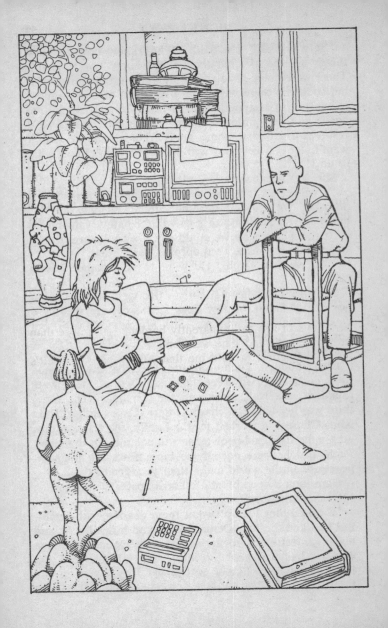

it.'' She closed her eyes. ''I ran away. I don't think Adler really noticed: she treated him well.''

Chase waited, and fixed her another drink. She took it without a word, sipped it, and then continued.

''I went to France for a while; that's where I met L'Infâme. I traveled with them, even sang a little, played some keyboards. They hate the corps and anyone associated with them. They didn't know who I was.

''We were in southern Spain, near Berja not far from the Mediterranean, when I got a message from Nicholas Issan, one of the surviving Alte Welt. I agreed to meet him in Madrid, but when I got there I learned that he'd been killed the night before in a street robbery. His throat had been slashed.

''I went back to Berja and found a letter waiting for me. It was from Nicholas. He'd written it just before he was killed; I think he was expecting it to happen.''

Chase was surprised, but Cara's voice actually got stronger. He'd been expecting her to lose her composure at some point during the tale, but it hadn't happened. Her trials of fire had apparently hardened her more than he'd have expected. She went on.

''In the letter, he told me that Adler and Alte Welt's relationship with Fuchi had become more complex, darker, since I'd left. I wasn't surprised. Fuchi had actually taken over and broken up Hanburg-Stein, and Alte Welt had profited enormously. In the process, however, Adler had sold himself to the company. Again, I wasn't surprised.''

She took another sip from the drink. ''Nicholas' letter said that Demarque had quietly recruited Adler and some of his more radical friends to kill my father while he was in Frankfurt for an economic conference next month.''

''You've got to be joking.''

''I'm not.'' She looked down into her drink. ''I may not like my father, but I don't want him dead.''

''Why don't you just call him?''

''I can't. I don't have access anymore. After he and my mother divorced I made some nasty comments that got repeated in the press. That was when I ran away the last time. The Japanese insisted that he disassociate himself from me. If I couldn't be controlled, then he should let me go. Any messages from me are destroyed without being read.''

Chase stood up and began to pace. ''What about your mother? I heard that she and your father stayed somewhat friendly after the divorce.''

Cara winced. ''I tried, last week in London, but I glitched up. Nicholas' letter said that some of my father's own people would be feeding Adler and his friends security information related to my father's itinerary while in Frankfurt. It didn't occur to me that they might have spies in other places, too.

''My mother was in London on business last week and I went there after the . . . problems.''

''The two L'Infâme boys trying to kill each other.''

She closed her eyes and nodded. ''I told them I was leaving, but didn't want to say why. Alain and Gerard blamed each other, or something. They were wired.''

''Dreamchips?''

She looked up at him. ''What?''

''Dreamchips? BTLs? Better Than Life?''

She looked confused.

''Illegal simsense chips,'' he said.

She nodded. ''Yes . . . I forgot what they're called over here.''

''Go on.''

''I . . . she was in a meeting or something, so I left a message with one of her people. I left my hotel room number. They told me to wait for her call.

''About an hour later I had visitors—a man and a woman. They had guns and forced me outside, but I got lucky. There were some London police rousting a bunch of punks on the corner, so I started to make a scene. They got really nervous and let me get away.''

''So you came here. How?''

''With the help of a friend,'' she sighed, ''but under my own passport codes. I used the last of my money to

grab a transorbital from Heathrow to here. I hoped that
if I moved fast enough they wouldn't have started really
trying to track me yet.''

"What did you plan to do here?"

"My uncle Martin runs what's left of the actual family
business from here. I thought maybe I could get him to
call my father."

"Last I remember, Martin would have hired people to
kill his brother himself. Has that changed?"

She shook her head. "Not that I know of, but I hoped
he might see things my way, and not really want him
dead.''

"Martin's company, Villiers International, has been
trying to build an arcology up in the Bronx for years
now,'' said Chase. "It's billions over budget and years
behind. Strong rumors have it that Fuchi, alias your father, has been behind the sabotage. It's said that Richard
wants to drive his brother out of business so that Fuchi
can buy up the rest of Villiers International, the part
Martin walked away with when he wouldn't go along with
your father's deal with the Japanese.''

Cara looked down. "I hadn't heard any of that until I
got here.''

"There's also another problem. Your cousin Darren."

She nodded. "Yes, but I thought that might be a reason for my uncle to help me. Beyond all the other troubles, I *know* he's mad at the Nakatomis for recruiting
Darren into Fuchi. I thought he might do it just to crash
them.''

Chase leaned against the side of a bookcase. "You'd
be right, except Darren was transferred to Tokyo. He's
going to be running some secret project for the Nakatomis. Your mother's been given his old job as VP of
Fuchi Northwest, as well as staying head of Fuchi Systems Design.''

Cara's eyes were wide. "She's working directly with
my father?''

"Some. The Fuchi Northwest VP pretty much runs the

show, but answers to your father. He's almost always in Tokyo now. Guess he wants to keep an eye on things.''

Her left arm clenched again and she stared at him. ''How do you know all this?''

Chase shrugged. ''I did some research last night.''

Cara slid deeper into the pile of the couch and closed her eyes. ''We could still talk to my uncle . . .''

''Bad idea. With Darren in Tokyo, directly under the control of the Nakatomis, your uncle's been checked. If he gets involved, anything could happen to Darren.''

''But they're brothers.''

Chase sighed. ''That doesn't mean anything Cara. Family doesn't automatically mean friend. You can take that from me, but I think you know it too.''

She pulled her legs up onto the couch, and then under her. She turned slightly to look at him, all the composure she'd held while telling her story gone. ''Then what can we do?''

''We, Cara?''

''Please . . . you've got to help me.''

He thought about it only for a moment; the last twelve years had never happened.

''All right,'' Chase said. ''I will.''

6

The Rouge Angels listened to reason, and money, and were gone from the Caina by early the next morning. Cyanide Tiger could find no signs that the flat was under surveillance, and the band told Cara they hadn't spoken to anyone since she'd left. Chase, however, didn't believe them.

Lachesis' voice was digitally clear over the telecom. For whatever reason, she was audio only. Instead of her face Chase watched the gray morning clouds through the skylight. The only other sounds in the apartment were of Cara's exertions on his multi-use gym in another room.

"Any luck?" he asked.

"I have found two items of immediate worth," Lachesis replied. "The first is that two phone calls were made from the band's flat. Both were local. One was to the Soy Palace. The call lasted three and one-half minutes. I have verified the establishment and have no reason to believe it to be anything other than an Oriental food enterprise."

"Me either; the food sucks. What else?"

"The second phone call was to an Ernesto Gavillon, who works as a music promoter under the alias Ernesto Best. The call lasted fifty-seven minutes. I have found records of numerous calls from the Caina apartment to Ernesto Best over the last few weeks. The records of Ernesto Best also indicate numerous calls to the Caina number."

"Cara," Chase called out, "know anyone named Ernesto Best?"

The gym noises stopped. "Yeah, he's the band's agent." Her voice sounded strained, but Chase wasn't surprised. He'd seen the settings she was using on the gym equipment.

"Did he know you?"

"Only as their manager."

"Thanks!" he uncovered the mouthpiece. "Best is the ban—"

"I heard."

"If nothing else, we can assume they told him Cara'd left."

"You may assume what you wish."

"Thanks. What was the second item of immediate worth?"

"The Caina computer system shows signs of intrusion."

Chase sat up. "Other than your own?"

"Of course."

"Any signatures or style you could recognize?"

"None. The Caina system barely qualifies as such. A

child with a Radio Shack deck could penetrate it without leaving a signature.''

"But you noticed evidence of tampering."

"Subtle, but present."

Chase nodded. ''All right, can you put a watch on my system? I want to know if anyone does any probing."

"I can program a small construct to act as a watchdog. I can also link it to a tag on your telecom account to recognize tampering. Your system's performance will be degraded."

"I'll live with it." He listened to make sure the multi-gym was back in use, then turned away from the sound. "Any word on the detailed report?" he said softly.

"Information is being compiled and re-referenced. I anticipate completion and delivery within eight hours."

"Good. Thanks, Lachesis. I appreciate it."

Dead silence followed.

"Hello?"

"One moment."

He waited.

"You made a telecom call to Great Britain."

"What!"

"Your Manhattan Datacom account shows a message-unit overage charge associated with a call to the Nottingham region."

"Damn."

"There is evidence of a single-source trace that progressed as far as the UCAS-Northeast regional telecom grid before cessation of the call."

"What are the odds?"

"There is a forty-two percent probability, with a tolerance of two point two, that sufficient information was gained to identify your account."

"Any chance of backtracking the trace at this point?"

"None."

"All right. Finish giving me some kind of defense and then contact me as soon as you've got the detailed report."

"Understood." The line went dead without so much as a click.

Chase placed the handset back into the telecom unit as he heard Cara lightly enter the room from behind him.

"Anything?" she asked after a moment.

He stood and turned toward her. "Your friends are probably safe as long as they stay low and quiet."

She dropped down loosely onto one of his couches, her colorless body suit and pale skin becoming almost radiant against the dark leather. She buried her face in a towel for a moment, rubbing away the perspiration. "You really think they may be in danger?" she said, lifting her face to him.

He shrugged. "Hard to tell, but the assassination of a billion-dollar megacorporate official isn't something to be attempted with half-measures. If someone is looking for you, the band is the only link."

She blinked and pursed her lips. "Do you think they'll talk?"

"Odds are they already have." Chase lowered himself onto the arm of a chair across from her. "Your pals called Ernesto Best, and if you asked, I'd bet the spirits'd tell you that they told him you ran off with some joker."

Cara nodded. "Yeah, just the fact that *they* called him, and not me, would tip Ernie—"

A sudden high tone, followed by three loud beeps echoed through the room and cut her off. Chase leaned his head back and took a long, hard breath.

Cara's head whipped around. "What . . ."

A dry, artificial voice cut into the room from hidden speakers. "Building security systems report an unauthorized entry through the rear service entrance."

She stood up and looked at Chase. He stared at the ceiling.

"Building security systems report an attempt to overri—"

Cara looked around and scooped up her dropped towel. "What's happening?"

Chase shrugged. "Someone's in the building who shouldn't be. Probably more than one, I expect."

Her eyes widened and the towel bunched in her hands. "They're after me, right?"

He looked at her. "How could they be?" he said evenly. "Nobody knows you're here. The only ones who might have let anything slip are your band chummers, and they don't know where you are."

She looked at him.

"Right?" he finished.

"I . . ."

"You fucked up."

She flinched. "I had to tell her I was okay: she's the one who helped me sneak into England. She'd have been worried. I didn't tell her where—"

"You talked to her too long. They traced the call."

"Oh, god . . ."

Chase stood up. "You kept everything in your bag like I told you?"

She nodded.

"Grab it and anything else of yours that might be laying around. Check the bathroom. Then come back here."

She did, and met him again in the living room. He was studying a display on one of the telecom terminals. "The security system's been hacked, but there's nobody in it. Damn it, I should have had her secure the building too."

"Her?"

"Later. As near as I can tell, a group's come in the rear entrance and are making their way up the back stairs. The security alarms are off-line so I'm not sure if an alert got out or not."

"What're you going to do?"

"Hide mostly. There's no time to get out. Who knows where they are right now? Here, catch." He flipped her a small object. She missed it and it skittered a ways across the floor before she grabbed it, dropping half of what she'd been carrying.

"It's a lighter . . ."

"Light it and hold it near a heat sensor in the kitchen. Burn the sensor."

She did, searing the plastic, and the automatic sprinkler system exploded water into the cooking area. Cara jumped and barely escaped the deluge. "You drek, why didn't you . . ."

"If the sensor's melted, the sprinklers will stay on until somebody shuts them off. Our drek-for-brains intruders didn't bother to lock out the fire-alarm codes."

"Oh," she said, using her exercise towel to dry off some of her things that had gotten wet. "But shouldn't we . . ."

The telecom display changed, some words flashed red, and then it turned black. Chase sighed. "Well, somebody just opened the security door on this floor, then crashed the whole fragging system. Time to disappear, Cara." He moved across the room and motioned her to follow.

She did, and they stepped up into the day-lit dining area. "Here's hoping they didn't have time to pull the plans for this place."

Cara looked back toward the front door. "Why don't you just . . . I don't know. . . ."

"Shoot it out with them?"

"Well . . ."

"This isn't the sims, Cara." At the room's far wall he pulled a small black remote control from his pocket. "I don't know who they are or what kind of firepower they're packing. Plus, it's been a long damn time since I walked into a fight simply because I wanted to. I try to avoid that sort of thing these days."

As he pointed the device at the largest piece of furniture in the room, a barely audible click came from behind the breakfront, which shifted forward slightly. He reached out and pivoted it away from the wall, revealing the existence of a small dark room. A warning beep sounded from the other end of the apartment.

Cara turned. "What?" He grabbed her arm and pushed her into the hidden room. "Maglock on the front door;

it must be tougher than they expected. Damn well should be.''

Chase followed her in and pulled a lever on the wall. The breakfront closed behind them, sealing with a hiss.

Lights came on. The room was a mere three meters square, and contained only some monitors that Chase began to flip on, two small canisters mounted on the wall, and some weapons hanging on pegs. Cara's eyes widened as she looked at the submachine gun. ''Don't touch,'' he warned.

Images of the apartment began to appear on the monitors. Chase listened to the audio feed on an earpiece.

Cara squirmed next to him. ''Can I . . . ?''

Chase gave her a hard look and then turned back to the monitors. The front door, finally defeated, was opening slowly. A black man in an equally dark long coat brandished a silenced Colt heavy pistol as he pushed the door open and surveyed the room. Cara hissed.

''Recognize him?'' asked Chase.

''Yes, he was in London.''

''Name?''

''I think they called him Victor.''

Victor walked slowly into the room, sweeping the weapon to match his gaze. A red-haired woman in black leathers and a bulky jacket entered behind him. She carried a sound-suppressed Heckler and Koch submachine gun at the ready and covered him.

''They called her Roja,'' said Cara.

''All right, let's see how good—'' He cut himself short as another figure entered behind the woman. Tall and slender, he had the distinctive bone structure and the decidedly pointed ears of the metahuman race of elves. His hair was long, white, and flashed with silver highlights. The elf moved forward carefully, letting his gaze wander over the room, but his eyes had an unfocused look. He kept his hands in the pockets of his gray long coat.

''I think we're screwed,'' said Chase.

Cara looked up at him sharply. ''I didn't see him in London. . . .''

"Odds he's a mage."

She made a noise at the back of her throat.

"I think he's surveying the room with his magical sight, or whatever, for some sign of us or magic."

She put her hand on his arm and he felt it tighten. "Then they'll find us and . . ."

He shook his head as he watched the front two move farther into the apartment. The elf hung back. "This room is supposed to be magically shielded," Chase said. "I paid a lot to have some hybrid bacterium or something sprayed into the surrounding walls. Supposedly a magician can astrally project—or whatever it is they do—something through almost anything *except* living things." He looked intently at the monitor. "I don't completely understand all this magic drek."

"Won't the mage realize the bacteria is there? I mean rats in the walls, maybe, but . . ."

Chase said nothing as he watched the elf mage blink a few times, then begin to move normally. "He's stopped whatever he was doing."

The elf went to join Victor in the main room. Roja had moved off into the adjoining rooms. Victor was looking down at the water-soaked carpet beneath him and then at the spray in the kitchen area. "It would appear that they've gone," said the elf, his voice high, almost musical.

Victor nodded. "Good and bad. We've probably got no more than five minutes before the fire department arrives." His voice had a trace of German accent. "Roja!" he called out. "See if they were stupid enough to leave any clues to where they might have gone."

No reply came, but Chase could hear her moving things around in the other room.

"What are they saying?" asked Cara.

He motioned her to silence, then pointed at another earpiece hanging on the wall. She grabbed it and slipped it into her ear. Chase could clearly see the datajack implanted in her skull near that ear. It was a good one. Expensive and expertly installed.

Victor turned to the elf. "Can you find anything?"

The elf shrugged. "Unlikely, unless they're nearby. There is little to trace. I can try, though."

Chase winced. "Damn." He reached down and touched the pair of small canisters mounted on the wall. He pushed aside a panel cover and placed his fingers on two unlit buttons.

"What're those?" Cara asked.

"CNX II gas. It's nerve gas."

Cara stared.

"It's not lethal, barely more than tear gas, but it makes life hell. We're safe in here, but it should incapacitate them long enough for me to do something."

"How long will it last?" Cara's voice was very low.

"Less than a minute. It's *very* short persistence, breaks down right away, so there's no chance of it getting to the other apartments."

Cara grimaced, her hand tightening further on Chase's arm. "Do you think it's wi—"

Roja's arrival from the other room silenced her. The red-haired woman was smiling. "No worries, chums. I pulled lotsa hair out of the bathroom drains." She flipped a small plastic baggie to the elf. "We can trace them with magic."

Chase smashed his fist angrily against the wall. "*Damn!*" Victor's eyes flicked toward them, then back at the woman. "No choice now." Chase pressed down on the buttons.

The elf held the bag up to one of the windows and looked at the specimens. "I can't tell if it's both of them, or—"

A loud electronic squeal from beneath Victor's coat cut him off. "*Nerve gas!*" he howled. The elf let the bag drop and quickly traced something in the air in front of him. A faint trail of violet light followed his motions. Roja's eyes widened, then snapped shut as her body twitched. She looked like she'd smelled something horrible.

"*Damn,*" whispered Chase. What the hell were they doing carrying gas-detection gear?

Victor stepped around the elf and grabbed Roja as she twitched again and went limp, gagging. The elf finished his motion and snapped his left hand opened. A sphere of misty, violet light expanded quickly outward from it and through the room as a radiant shock wave. The elf turned and grabbed both of his teammates. Victor had a stunned expression on his face. "Help her, Séarlas," he said.

The elf nodded and took Roja from Victor, lowering her to the ground. "The toxin in the air has been neutralized. Now I must deal with what has already entered her bloodstream," said Séarlas. He held his hand over the woman's chest as her body spasmed again and she continued to gag. "How do you feel?" he asked Victor without looking up. The strain was evident in his voice.

"Fine." Victor kept his eyes on Roja. "We must have triggered some security system."

"Perhaps," said the elf.

Chase could see that same violet glow strobing between Séarlas' hand and the woman. Her body began to calm. Chase released his breath.

"Is she. . . ?" asked Victor. His gaze began to roam the apartment again.

"She'll be fine." As the elf lifted Roja up, her eyes were still closed but she grabbed on to his coat with what little strength she had. "We must leave."

Victor nodded and picked up Roja's dropped weapon. He turned to follow the elf, then stopped after a few steps. He grabbed the baggie of hair and darted after his companions, giving the apartment one last look as he closed the door behind him. Chase could see his anger.

Slowly, Chase bounced his head off the wall of the little room just loud enough to make a faint thump with it. Cara watched the monitors for a few moments, then looked up at him. Neither said anything.

"Damn," he finally said, again. "*Poputano.*"

"What?" she asked.

He looked at her. "Fucked up."

"I don't understand. They left . . ."

Chase nodded. "Yes, they left, but they took hair samples with them."

Cara looked at him uncomprehendingly.

"The way it was explained to me was that mages can use pieces of a body, like hair, fingernails, blood, semen, and so on to trace the person of origin. The fresher the better. It takes a few hours, but it's like the finger of God pointing at you from the sky."

Chase glanced at his watch, then pushed up on the lever near the door. There was another hiss, and Cara could see a crack of light appear around it. She held her breath.

"We should be fine; it's been long enough." He swung the breakfront away and stepped into the room. With the seal broken and the door open, they could hear the faint sounds of a fire truck siren. "Time to leave," Chase said.

Cara followed him out, grabbing the pile of stuff she'd carried in with her. "Church," she said.

He turned. She'd stopped just outside the room and was standing there holding her belongings tight against her. She was still wearing her body suit, and Chase could see the fear in her eyes. "They've got magic . . . they're going to kill us. . . ."

Chase wanted to walk over to her, take her in his arms, hold her, tell her everything was going to be fine. She needed him, and he could comfort her. Chase wanted to, but suddenly he was afraid to cross that distance, to take those steps.

Instead he measured his words as carefully as possible. "I won't lie to you, Cara. I don't know what to do. But I know someone who will."

7

"Farraday!"

Chase burst through the doors of the talismonger shop only a few steps behind the wind from the street. He moved quickly into the shop, looking everywhere. Following close on his heels, Cara shut the door behind them. The store resembled an old-fashioned bookshop, except that the shelves were stacked with odd items and artifacts of the occult as well as books. Cara looked around wide-eyed.

"Farraday!" yelled Chase again.

"Up here," came a voice, high and odd.

Chase and Cara both looked up. A man squatted atop one of the high bookcases, his tall, lanky frame crunched tight beneath the ceiling. A row of newly made Amerindian medicine shields hung from the walls near him. Several more, still wrapped in plastic, lay on top of the bookcase in front of him. "I wanted to see who it was before I said anything."

"I'm screwed, my friend. I need your help," said Chase.

Cara gasped, and Chase took a step back as Farraday virtually let himself tip off the top of the bookcase. He didn't move, but his body twisted in flight, end over end, completing the flip just as he reached the ground. He landed on his feet and bent with the impact, the many fetishes and trinkets on his leather vest bouncing merrily. He grinned. His face was long and tight, with oversized dark eyes nearly the color of his short-spiked black hair. A long, thin ribbon of red and gold metal dangled from one ear. "Cat fall," he said, still crouched. "You like it? Bought the spell yesterday; locked it on me right away. Never can tell around here."

"Good move," said Chase. "I've got magic problems."

Farraday rose gracefully to his full height. "Don't we all."

"I think I'm being traced, me and the girl." Cara gave Chase a look as he continued. "An elf mage got hold of some strands of our hair and we're sure he plans to use them to trace us."

Farraday nodded. "Ritual sorcery. Easy."

Chase winced. "Thanks. Just what I needed to hear."

The magician shrugged. "Sorry, I find circumspection morally repulsive."

"Me too, you smelly bag of shit. Can you help me or not?"

"There are things that can be done, yes," Farraday said, smiling. He turned and held one hand up, the index finger beckoning them to follow him to the back. Chase did as he was bid, as did Cara, who kept him between her and the magician.

"Church," she said quietly. "I . . ."

Farraday stopped suddenly and his index finger ceased twitching. "Wait," he said without turning, head tilted slightly. "Where did they get the hair?"

"From the shower drain," Chase told him.

The magician turned slightly, the glint in one eye clearly visible. "Not from a hair brush?"

Chase shook his head. "My hair's too short. I don't bother." He looked at Cara.

"Um, yes," she said. "I use a brush."

The light in Farraday's eyes dimmed.

"But I had it with me; I grabbed it before we went into the secret closet."

Farraday grinned again and gave Chase a speculative look before continuing. "What kind of shampoo do you use?"

"Shampoo?" said Chase.

"Shampoo," repeated Farraday. "Try to stay with me on this. What kind of shampoo did you use?"

Chase stifled a laugh and looked at Cara. "I, um, used what was on my shelf. Ah . . . Chic Clean, I think . . ."

Farraday nodded and smiled wider. "And you, my dear?"

Cara looked at Chase, then at the magician. "Me, too. I didn't have any of my own."

The mage snapped his fingers in triumph. "Then you are, as they say, in luck."

Chase looked at his friend. "As usual, you've lost me."

"You really should be using a natural, herbal shampoo, you realize."

Chase groaned inwardly. "We don't have time—"

"However, the same drek that'll rot your scalp in a few years has probably saved your short-term asses," said Farraday. "Chic Clean is a chemical monstrosity, but in this case that's good. To use a physical specimen as a material link for ritual sorcery, that physical specimen must be as pure as possible. Chic Clean leaves so much residue and pollution in the hair that it'll be a bitch and a half to use it to form the link." Farraday all but beamed.

Chase relaxed slightly. "So then we're safe."

The magician shook his head. "I didn't say that. It'll take them longer, and it's going to be harder to make the link, but they can still do it. If they're good."

"I think we can assume they are."

Farraday's eyebrows went up.

"One of them was carrying a nerve-gas sensor. The mage even had a spell to deal with the stuff."

"Experienced then."

Chase nodded.

"You know who they are?"

"I have my suspicions."

This time Farraday nodded with a slight smile.

"What can you do?" asked Chase.

"I could put you inside a mystic ward. That'll make you harder to trace, but it won't stop them if they're as good as you suspect. Plus, you'll still be local and easily accessible once they do find you.''

"What do you suggest?"

"Run like hell. Get as far away from here as you can. The farther you are from where they think you are, the harder you are to find, with or without the strands of hair."

Chase nodded. "Anything else you can do?"

"I could lock some spells on you," said Farraday, "but ultimately those might prove more dangerous than they're worth. If your enemies do find you, the spell locks will make you incredibly vulnerable."

"I'll take your word for it."

"Thanks. But I can do one thing that'll at least help you get out of the city."

"And that is?"

"Why, the thing I do best, you unbeliever you."

"Ah," said Chase, and Farraday grinned wildly.

With a look of alarm Cara put a hand on Chase's arm but Farraday spoke before she could utter a sound.

"I'm going to summon up the nastiest, bad-assiest spirit of this fine town that you've ever seen," said Farraday, locking his gaze with hers. "And under its protection, you will be escorted out of this fair city."

A short time later they stood in the small alley that ran behind Farraday's shop. At the shaman's request, Chase and Cara had moved some small trash dumpsters and cans to block the alley at either end. Farraday had pointed out that interruptions wouldn't necessarily help his summoning of the city spirit. Chase had asked if they should clear an area in the alley for the ritual, but the street shaman had laughed and said that maybe they should find more garbage and debris to scatter around. It was a city spirit, after all.

Now, they stood waiting for the shaman to emerge from his shop with the necessary paraphernalia. The sounds of the city echoed around them.

"Church," said Cara, the word coming out almost

strangled. Her mouth moved, but no more words came out.

Her intense discomfort was obvious. "What's wrong, Cara?" he said.

"I just . . . I mean, do we have to . . ."

"You don't like the magic?"

She turned to face him, grabbing the shoulder strap of her bag to keep it from falling. "No, frag it, I don't," she said. "Do we have to do it this way?"

Chase shrugged. "We've got magic after us, so we need magic to keep us alive. That's all I know. If our elf and his two friends were right here in the alley with us, I could probably take care of them," he said, shifting the weight of his own pack. "But they could be anywhere, conjuring up God knows what. We need the magic."

She looked down. "I don't like it."

"You never did."

"No, I never did."

"You never liked cyberware, either," said Chase, "yet you got some for yourself."

She reached up and unconsciously touched the gleaming datajack near her ear. "I . . . needed it for the instruments, you know, to trigger them, when I was with the band."

"You know you can play those things manually."

"I . . . needed it. . . ."

She suddenly seemed tense and uncomfortable. She'd stopped touching the datajack, but her left hand had begun twitching. Chase could hear the flexing of the leather glove.

"Look," he said, "Is there something—"

The back door to the shop banged open as Farraday bounced out. He was wearing a long black-and-gray leather coat, lighter-weight cycle boots, gray silk shirt, and the same black vest as earlier. He also had a new, rose-colored stone dangling from a silver chain on his left ear. He looked up and down the alley, oblivious to what he'd interrupted. "Wiz," he said, eyeing the trash

barriers. "Well, time to get down to business." He
squatted down.

The shaman's reappearance had apparently snapped
Cara out of whatever was bothering her. She stared, wide-
eyed, as Farraday pulled various bits and items out of his
pockets and piled them on the ground at his feet. While
she watched the shaman, Chase watched her.

"What are those?" she asked.

"Things I'll need."

She put her hand up to her mouth. "They're toys, I
mean . . ."

Farraday frowned. "Well, of course they are. How else
do you think I can get him to come?"

She giggled as the gray rubber mouse bounced and
squeaked as it hit the ground and ended up next to the
brightly colored circus ball.

"Mister Church," he said, "I assume you have wit-
nessed at least one spirit summoning in your long life-
time."

"Only one," replied Chase, "and it was hermetic magic:
an elemental."

Farraday grimaced. "Brainless creatures, barely
smarter than those who summon them," he said. "This
is very different." He looked up at Cara. "Ever seen a
spirit summoned?"

She shook her head.

"Then I suggest you should stand near Church and
don't do anything unless he tells you. Who knows what
might happen?"

Cara nodded and went to stand beside Chase. She
grabbed his arm again. "What's he going to do?" she
whispered.

"I don't know," he said. "Every shaman summons
spirits differently. It's very personal. Hermetic mages
have tried and true procedures, almost formulas. Shamans have specific rituals, too, but I understand they
make some of it up as they go along based on what feels
right."

She nodded and grabbed him tighter. Without thinking, he reached out an arm and she moved into the shelter of it.

"Now," said Farraday, "I'm going to do this the long way. I could do it all in an instant, but why give myself a headache?" Dropping to the ground, he sat Indian-style in front of the pile of toys. He separated them so that none touched, then reached into his pocket and pulled out a greasy bag.

"What's that?" asked Cara.

"French fries," said Farraday. "Cat just loves Nuke-It Burger fries."

"You've got to be—"

Chase tightened his grip on her, considerably, and she choked back the rest. Farraday's eyes seemed bright, but they weren't focused on anything Chase or Cara could see. His head tilted and began to move in small, jerking motions.

"Ooooooohhhh," he said quietly, beginning to roll the circus ball between his hands. "Little crafty one, eh?"

Cara lifted up onto her toe tips to whisper in Chase's ear. "Is he . . . I mean."

"I assume so," Chase whispered back.

The shaman grinned wider. "Found you, see you, have you, little one. Come here, come here, come to play, come to stay."

The ball stopped rolling suddenly, and the light debris in the alley shifted as if a weak breeze had blown through, but none had. At least none Cara or Chase could feel. Cara gasped.

The ball began to dance about on its own, as if batted by unseen paws. It bounced into the air, fell back down again, only to be tossed back up once more. Farraday laughed. The rubber mouse squeaked. The fries were gone.

A cloud passed across the sun high over head, and its shadow filled the alley. It moved on, but a piece of the shadow remained, caught on something at Farraday's feet. It tried to stream around them and get free, but gradually form overtook it.

Two points of piercing white light turned toward Chase and watched him. Farraday reached out and carefully stroked it, his hand passing slightly into it. It moved against him, blended with his own shadow, and then re-emerged near Cara. She stepped back.

Farraday frowned. "She doesn't really like you."

"Oh?" said Chase.

"Too much poison, she says."

"Poison?"

"Uh-huh," said the shaman. He looked up and Chase could see two thin lines of sweat running down the side of his head. "Both of you."

Cara started and Chase looked at her. Her eyes were riveted on the cat woven of shadow.

"I see," said Chase. "Will that prevent it from . . ."

The shaman shook his head. "No. She'll do it as a favor to me. It just means that on her own terms she wouldn't have anything to do with you."

"Then, please make sure you thank her for that. I mean it."

Chase wasn't sure, but just for a moment it was almost as though he saw a smile deep in the shadow. Then, the shadow streamed away, caught and dissipated by an invisible wind.

The shaman stood up. "You are now under her protection."

Chase didn't feel anything, but nodded anyway. "What does that mean?"

"Spirits like her can do a lot. Most of it isn't direct, but let's just say that within the area of her power she can, um, make things . . . happen."

That didn't really answer Chase's question, but then Farraday rarely did. Chase nodded anyway. "All right. For how long?"

"Until sunset, or until you leave the borders of the city."

"Fair enough." He looked at Cara. "Ready?"

She was still close to him, but watching the ground near where the cat of shadows had vanished. She looked up and nodded.

Chase stuck out his hand toward Farraday. The shaman took it immediately. "I owe you again, my friend."

Farraday shrugged. "Two-way street, chummer. Just make sure you travel back it sometime."

Chase smiled. "I will. I promise."

The two started to walk away, but the magician's call stopped them. "Aren't you forgetting something?"

Chase and Cara looked at him and then at each other. The shaman pointed down.

There at Cara's feet, sitting quietly and matching their gaze sat a small black and white cat. Her eyes reflected brilliant green in the glow of the overcast sun.

"Oh," said Chase.

Chase and Cara set off across the city on foot, the cat apparently sound asleep in Cara's arms. Farraday had recommended they stay on foot, claiming that the spirit could maintain its protection better that way. He also cautioned them against entering any buildings or traveling the subway. Apparently the city spirit's powers were limited to its domain: the streets. Cara wanted to know if the cat needed to stay near them. With a shrug Farraday had told her it was a surprise that the spirit had even bothered to take a form.

Chase was leading them toward the Terminal zone again, but he didn't plan to take any regular train out. Most of the normal exit routes were ruled out by the firepower he'd stashed in his bag before leaving his apartment. It was possible to bribe minor items through the checkpoints, but automatic weapons were a little too illegal for the police to let pass with a wink and a nod.

As they walked he kept his eyes peeled for any sign of pursuit, but saw none.

"I hope you have a plan," said Cara. She shifted the cat in her arms again to lessen the stiffness of carrying it.

"Of a sort," he said, leading her through the stalled traffic at Thirty-fourth and Broadway. The hustle and lights of the city were all around them, but no one paid them any heed. "First we get out of the city. Then we find your mother."

"Oh, good plan."

Chase grinned. "A tried and true one."

"How do we get out of the city?"

"I know someone with a registered car who lives along the Terminal wall at Thirty-fourth and Tenth. We get him to drive us."

Cara laughed. "Just like that?"

"Just like that. Manhattan security's got the train accesses pretty tight, but they tend to be a little lighter at the road checkpoints, especially considering what we'll be riding in."

Cara opened her mouth to speak, then apparently decided to wait and see.

The pearl-white Toyota Elite limousine slid gracefully out of the parking garage and up to the curb alongside Chase. Cara laughed.

"Old hat to you, I suppose," he said.

"What?"

"You must be used to riding in cars like this."

She shrugged. "Not lately."

The door on the driver's side opened and a snazzily dressed ork pried himself out. He placed his cap atop his mop of red hair and walked regally around to the other side of the car.

"Oh, please, Milo, give me a break," said Chase. This was too much.

"Nonsense, sir. For what you are paying you get the full treatment." He executed a station-perfect Japacorp bow and opened up one of the rear doors for Cara. "Ma'am," he said, motioning her inside with one hand, "I believe you will find everything is as you requested. The environmental filters were changed this morning so the air should be perfect for your ride. The

bar is fully stocked, and there is a full selection of apér-
itifs in the cool box for your enjoyment, including some
freshly prepared elaishón with natural vanilla glaze.''

Cara was halfway into the limousine, the cat hanging
languidly from one hand, then stopped. She'd played
along until now, her face shifting into an appropriately
blasé expression, but the ork's last statement changed her
look to utter bafflement. "Elaishón ?'' she asked.

Milo the ork shrugged. "Some kinda elven pastry. It's
got strawberry filling and something else. I'm not sure.
I pick them up special from a dealer uptown when a client asks. They fly them in every day from some bakery
near Eureka in the elflands.''

Cara smiled. "Sounds good.''

The ork shook his head as she slipped into the darkened rear of the limo. "Little too tame for me,'' he told
her.

As Chase climbed in behind Cara, the ork closed the
door and went around the front of the limo. After a moment, his face appeared on one of the monitors near Cara.
He himself was separated from the passenger compartment by an opaque partition. "Where to, sir?'' he said.

"We've got to leave town, but by something other than
the usual routes. Let's see. . . . How about out to Mac-
Arthur?'' Milo nodded and the monitor darkened.

"MacArthur?'' asked Cara. The cat had curled up in
her lap and apparently gone to sleep. Cara was absently
petting it.

"Small airport out on Long Island,'' Chase told her.
"Handles mostly local trés chic traffic.''

"Hence the limo,'' she said.

Chase nodded. The limo pulled out, and the ork turned
uptown at the corner. He skillfully injected the oversized
vehicle into traffic to the blare of only one or two horns.
After just a few blocks, but a great deal of time, Milo
turned west. His face reappeared on the monitor. "I'm
gonna grab the Westside Highway, then head back east
through one of the corp zones. Less traffic.'' Then he

frowned as a thought struck him. "Unless that'll be a problem."

"It shouldn't be," said Chase. "Anybody who's after us may think twice about trying something in corporate territory."

The ork smiled broadly. "My thoughts exactly."

The limo moved slowly cross-town, waiting for lights at each intersection, then waiting even longer for the stream of pedestrians to clear. Finally, the car reached the western edge of Manhattan and turned northward. The drive funneled them quickly uptown, and Milo exited just shy of Fifty-seventh Street in the shadow of the architecturally impossible, DNA-like spiral of the one-hundred-story headquarters of Prometheus Engineering. They moved past the watchful gaze of a pair of lightly armed NYPD Inc. officers and began moving east on Fifty-seventh itself. Cara strained to get a better view of the towering glass and plasticrete skyrakers surrounding them.

The monitor blinked to life again. "Church," said Milo.

Cara looked up at the screen, then over at Chase who had not responded. He was counting the number of buttons on the armrest telecom remote. "Church," she prodded.

Chase looked up, realizing they were referring to him, not the scenery. "Sorry, what?"

"Any idea what the jokers following you are driving?" asked the ork. He guided the limo around a computer-piloted tour bus, with dozens of out-of-town noses pressed against the glass.

Chase sat up and looked out the rear window. "Are driving?"

The ork nodded. "I 'spect so. As we crossed Eighth a Saab that'd been sitting in a parking garage entrance shot out and then slowed in behind us. They're about a block back."

Chase easily saw and recognized the almost nonexistent hood and bubble canopy of a black Saab Dynamit some distance behind them. Cara's pursuers? Perhaps, but already waiting uptown? His mind began to race as he tried to remember which of the megacorporations might have offices in the building over the parking garage. Fuchi Industrial Electronics' primary Manhattan office and one of their major worldwide centers was quite a distance downtown, near the island's tip. Maybe a subsidiary?

Without warning, the tour bus they'd just passed lurched violently to the left and smashed into the front fender of the Saab. The sports car tried to free its twisted nose from the bus' bumper, but the larger vehicle dragged it with single-minded determination across Fifty-seventh. The two collided with a parked Westwind 2000 and together pushed that car onto the curb. The few pedestrians jumped for cover as the tour bus continued on, dragging the Saab, then pinning it up against the Neiman Marcus and Whitton storefront to the accompaniment of a loud shower of glass and metal framework.

Cara's head had whipped around at the sound of the impact. "Jesus fraggin' Christ," she said.

"Milo, slow down a second." The limo braked and Chase strained to make out any signs of movement at the quickly receding accident. The emergency doors on the bus opened and shaken tourists began to stagger out onto the street. Other than that he saw nothing out of the ordinary.

"Go on," he said. The limo increased speed and Chase began to turn away as a lone figure appeared atop the tour bus. Chase could see little of the figure, but had the decided impression that the person was watching the limo drive away.

"What happened back there?" asked Milo as he accelerated the big car to put distance between them and the wreck.

"The tour bus veered into the Saab you noticed," Chase told him.

The ork shook his head. "Hasn't been one of those in a while."

Cara leaned toward him. "What do you mean?"

"The autopilots on those things are pretty fraggin' good. I can't remember an accident like that in a long time."

"Accident," repeated Chase quietly, looking back. The crash was blocks behind.

"What?" asked Cara in an equally subdued voice.

Chase looked at her. "An accident."

"Yeah, an accident."

"What if it wasn't?"

She looked at him oddly. "What do you mean?"

"Where's the cat?"

She grabbed at her lap where the cat had been, but found only her jacket. "He's gone!" She looked about quickly, but saw no sign of the little black and white animal in the compartment with them. "It couldn't have gotten out . . ."

"Farraday said that the spirit could make things happen."

"You don't think . . ."

He nodded. "I hope that was somebody following us," Chase said. "Just in case, we'd better watch what we say until we're out of the city."

Cara nodded, and then stiffened. Chase turned and followed her gaze. Curled up quietly on one of the folding jumpseats was the little black and white cat. It watched them silently through half-closed lids that barely contained the green within.

They sat in silence until the limo crossed the bridge into Queens County. Halfway across the East River the shadow that was the cat melted into the black leather of the seat.

The limo rode on toward MacArthur and a flight to Texas.

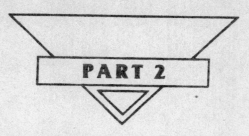

DENVER, VIA DART SLOT

The historic Treaty of Denver, signed in 2018 by the former United States, Canada, and Mexico and the magic-backed Native American Nations (NAN), forever changed the balance of power on the North American continent. NAN, a coalition of American Indian tribes, used mystical terrorism to achieve their demand that the United States government return the lands of western North America to Indian control. The Treaty of Denver outlined a ten-year population adjustment plan that would relocate all non-Indians off lands belonging to NAN. Provisions included the establishment of reservations for non-tribal peoples and corporations, the establishment of Seattle as an extraterritorial extension of the United States, and the division of Denver between the various signatories to the treaty.

> > > Keywords for additional data:

2030—Act of Union—United Canadian and American States Form from the Ashes

2033—Aztlan Reborn—The Mexican Government Falls

2034—On the Brink—Texas Wars with Aztlan

2037—California Free State—Isolation Breeds Secession

2037—The Land of Promise—The Elves Form Tir Tairngire, Separating from NAN

—Excerpt from *Scholastic Hypermedia Release 7: Your North America*

8

Chase bowed his head for a moment, shielding his eyes from the wave of dirt swept up by the helicopter. The craft descended carefully, a ton of high-performance jet engine dangling precariously beneath it. Below them stood two men on the flat-back bed of a half-rusted Gaz-Willys Nomad truck. As the engine dropped to their level, they grabbed it and tossed two hanging guide ropes to two more men standing on the ground nearby. Those two pulled the ropes taut and stopped the slight twisting of the engine. As the expensive cargo stabilized, the pilot lowered the helicopter slightly and worked with the two men on the truck bed to guide the engine safely into its homemade cradle. The truck sagged slightly as the cargo settled into the wood-and-metal braces.

At a signal from one of the truckers, the pilot released the lifting rope. Under his command, the Hughes Stallion copter pitched forward and banked right, accelerating across the nearby open desert. Chase knew if he watched for long enough the craft would be many kilometers away before he finally lost sight of the harsh light reflecting off its metal skin. Here, just northeast of the Texas-Aztlan border, the land was bare, open, dry, and breathtakingly beautiful for all those same reasons.

"Looks like a nice one," Chase's lunch companion

said, dusting the grit-dirt from her blue and black Texas Rattlers cap. "Pratt and Whitney, probably their F604 series." She smiled broadly, watching as the four men secured the engine to the back of the truck. "The fragger's probably thirty years old, but I'll betcha when the boys get finished with it the scragger'll push like she was built yesterday."

"What's it for?" asked Chase.

"Vectored thrust turbofan. Odds are she'll end up as the pusher for *Ms. Mable*." The woman swatted more dirt off her no-longer fashionable three-part ponytail. "Terry and the boys were running her last week when she caught a SAM right on the shield casement. Normally, the fragger would have barely scratched her hide, but the casement let go, the debris shield went, and the turbofan got chewed up."

Becka Trinity squinted at the engine as the flatbed truck pulled clear of the unloading site and disappeared around a cluster of prefab buildings. They'd have been dull and gray and identical in their monotony had it not been for the desert and scrub camouflage netting that covered most of them. To Chase, Becka seemed pretty much the same as the buildings. Superficially, there was little to distinguish her from dozens, no hundreds, of other Amerindian women he'd seen. The same long jet-black hair, the same round face and small eyes that threatened to be swallowed completely in the folds of her weathered skin when she smiled. She'd have looked the same, except that he knew her. She dressed and talked like a veteran of one of the corporate or national Desert Wars teams, and she loved the overpowering roar of a jet engine at full thrust.

She was what they called a "birdie," a fan-groupie who thrilled to the sounds and smells of the powerful, low-altitude military surplus vehicles nicknamed "thunderbirds." Mostly purchased on the shadow market from cash-hungry private armies or nations, the T-birds were modified for speed, light combat, and most of all, smuggling. For many, many years Becka Trinity had been a frequent sight around the camp at Dart Slot, where she watched, and sometimes helped, dozens of small and large T-bird teams prepare for runs into the Aztlan countryside.

Chase watched her and couldn't help but grin. "I take it the *Ms. Mable* made it back?"

Trinity snorted. "Lord, yes. Terry Finch ain't lost one yet."

He nodded and listened to the roar of an engine being tested at low power somewhere behind him where the LAVs were stored and serviced. He could see that she heard it, too, and from her look knew exactly from which T-bird it came. The thought reminded him of what he'd wanted to ask her in the first place.

"Any word on *Rapier's Touch*?"

She smiled and looked at Chase with amusement from under the brim of her cap. "I didn't think you wanted to slop some soy in the sun with ol' Becka just for old times. Damn sure took you long enough, though."

He chuckled and held his hands up in surrender. "You got me, *mea culpa*. As always, I was just using you."

"Damn, I wish."

"Yeah, well, what's the beat? Any word?"

She shrugged and looked off toward the Texas-Aztlan border hidden in the distance. "They shoulda been in yesterday, but I'll bet ya already knows that. Fender told me they were planning to ride the North Branch Channel route up from Muzquiz, or whatever the hell the Azzies are callin' it these days."

"Regular route?"

She shrugged again and looked back at him. "Depends. It ain't an easy route, but it gets ya around some of the nastier sensor nets and listening posts. El problemo is that word is humming that the Azzies are hunting another of their fraggin' revolutionary martyrs north of the Rio Grande, and are doing it in force since that's territory *occupado* and we all know the Texans are looking for any damn excuse to take it back."

Chase pulled off his own baseball cap which was emblazoned with the ancient white-on-blue insignia of the New York Yankees. He let the sun beat down on him unopposed for a moment, then thought better of it. There was a real reason Trinity looked the way she did. "So, it's probably hotter than . . . what? A lizard basking on an exhaust manifold?"

Trinity laughed again and shook her head. "Naw, just hotter than hell, I expect." She looked away slightly, but kept her eyes on him. "Speakin' a hotter than hell, you didn't come down here to check out the old sights."

"Nope. Goin' on a little trip."

Her eyebrows went up. "You ain't gettin' involved in that Azzie civil war, are you?"

"Me? Of course, Senōr Politico, that's me."

"Huh. I seem to remember hearing something from Gordani about you and some Germans—"

Chase quickly brought up his hand and motioned her to silence. He was sure they were alone, but glanced around for good measure. There was no sign of Cara. "You're right, but that's history." His tone got colder. "Dead and buried, you might say."

She winced slightly and looked down. "Yeah, Gordo told me 'bout that. They were nasty fraggers for what they did. Deserved everything you gave them."

"I know, but I don't want to talk about it, and I don't want to hear you or anybody else talking about it."

"It'd only be me and Gordo, I don't think anybody else's been around—"

"Then it'd be you and Gordo. The point is more that I don't want Cara to hear anybody talking about it."

Trinity looked up at him again. "The little girl you came in with?" she asked.

Chase nodded and continued. "Der Nachtmachen is my history," he said. "She's got her own history with some other jokers of a similar persuasion. I don't want her even thinking about any kind of connection between me and people like them. She's got enough justified paranoia without adding more to the confusion."

"I hear you. Nothin' said from now on."

They stood in silence for a few minutes until Trinity was distracted by the growing roar of another set of engines somewhere else in the camp. Chase clasped her once on the shoulder, then moved deeper into the camp, his own clothes blending easily with the ground and the camouflage netting. Except for his hat.

Chase had unintentionally made a lot of noise as he climbed the shallow wooden steps to the plastic house that he and Cara had on loan during their stay at Dart Base. Something had been sleeping in the shade under those steps and it expressed its displeasure at his arrival with a deep growl and the beginnings of some pungent odor. Chase decided not to find out what kind of Awakened monstrosity it was, and all but leaped off the steps and through the door into the building. He slammed the door with a curse, then made a quick check to make sure he hadn't damaged its fragile hinges. He was reaching for a beer in the cooler nearest the door when he spotted Cara, apparently oblivious to his entry.

She was in the main room, really the only room in the small house. Sitting on the floor, back to him, she was rocking slowly back and forth. She was wearing a pair of khaki shorts she'd picked up in Dallas-Fort Worth and a deep-green tank top drenched in sweat. Chase could hear the barest sounds of some words she seemed to be muttering. He didn't understand them.

He left the beer in the cooler, and walked slowly toward her. Her left arm twitched, and her head moved back and forth as though she were watching something on the floorboards in front of her. But Chase saw nothing when he got closer. Nothing, except a small black box no larger than an old paperback book. A thin, twisted double cable of optical wire spiraled up from the side of the case and traveled up near her left ear. Chase didn't need to see the end of the cable to know that it fit neatly into the chrome datajack she had there.

A small wafer of gray was set into the case just above the sparse, flat-panel LCD screen that showed the box's controls. The chip was bare of the usual labels, except for a ragged piece of clear tape on which the word "buzz" had been written with a white marker.

Chase circled around carefully to where he could see her face. Her eyes were open, but unfocused, nearly glazed, and jumping like the end of a loose, high-voltage wire. He could see the quick flashes of a dozen emotions rush across her face: fear, ecstasy, anger, confusion, fear again, and onward. Through it, she held a thin smile, despite the apparent effort of the muscles in her face to change it. Muscles in her neck danced, and a tear swelled in one eye. Her lips were parched. Her own senses overridden, she saw only what the chip showed her, heard, smelled, and tasted only what it was programmed to relate, felt only what it allowed. Her own senses were drowned out by the electronic flood from the deck in front of her.

The simsense deck she was attached to was a Fuchi model, one of the best available. But that was ironic, considering who she was. More clear tape held the bottom half of the case in place; the deck had been altered. Someone had modified its circuits to make it unsafe. Chase figured they'd probably removed the filters and peak inhibitors that were supposed to maintain the signals on simsense recordings within legal limits. With those circuits pulled, there was nothing to protect the user from the raw power of uninhibited sensory input. Days ago, in his Manhattan apartment, she'd claimed not to know what BTL chips were called, but Cara Villiers apparently knew exactly how to use one.

He sat and watched her for some time, listening to the creaks and groans of the cheap house as the unbearably hot midday became simply a hot afternoon. Chase was afraid to turn the simdeck off or to unplug her, not knowing enough about how BTLs really worked. He'd known other users, and had even tried the legal, signal-dampened simchips commercially available, but he knew nothing of the effects of a true Better Than Life. Instead, he sat and watched her for any signs of physical danger.

Just before her left hand lashed out to yank the cable from the deck, her body stiffened and she began a long, sharp intake of breath. Chase jumped to his feet and was ready to move faster than he had in years to unplug her when she did it herself. Though jacked out, she continued to breathe hard as her body compensated for the loss of whatever flood of artificial sensory signals she'd been experiencing. Her eyes had closed as the plug was yanked, so she hadn't seen him. He carefully returned to the corner where he'd been waiting.

She sat still for a time as her body calmed. Finally, her eyes opened, she licked her lips, and reached for the deck. Her hand stopped just short of it as she caught a glimpse of Chase seated in the corner. Looking at him, the fear in her eyes was almost overwhelming.

"How long?" he asked.

She didn't answer, but instead pulled her hand back slowly from the deck.

His legs were pulled up in front of him, knees spread and his feet touching. His arms, hands clasped, rested gently on his knees. From where Cara sat she could see only his eyes past the hands. "How long?" he asked her again from the shadowy corner.

Cara blinked and looked quickly around the room so as not to look at him. She blinked again and her mouth opened as if to speak, but first she reached up and unplugged the cable from her head. Free, it fell to the ground and coiled up into its natural shape.

"How long what?" she said evenly.

"The chips."

She tilted her head. "What about them?"

"Don't play dumb."

Cara actually met his gaze this time. "I don't know what you're talking about." Her eyes had grown hard.

He shook his head and said nothing.

She reached out to pick up the deck as well as a soft red and gray case Chase hadn't noticed before. Cara slipped the deck into the case and put the gray chip into one of the outer pockets. He caught sight of a number of other chips also in the pocket, but all of those were marked with the bright, cheerful labels of commercial simchips. The cable went into its own pocket on the other side of the case. She pressed the cover down and set the case beside her.

"I'm a little surprised," he said.

"About what?"

"*Don't*, Cara, I may not exactly have clinical experience, but I know what I'm looking at."

Her eyebrows furrowed and she tilted her head again. "I told you I don't know what you mean."

Chase shifted his position and let his hands unclasp. "All right," he said. "I'll say it. You're using BTL chips."

"What?"

"We've already had this exchange, remember? You know what I'm talking about."

She glanced over at the case holding the deck and then back at him. "You mean that?"

Chase watched her for some sign of the unease she'd displayed a minute ago. Pulled from somewhere, her poise had returned. He thought that was a bad sign. "Yes, the simdeck."

She surprised him and smiled. "Those aren't what you think."

"Oh?"

She shook her head. "No. Straight legal."

"Even the unmarked one that says 'buzz'?"

She blinked and confusion flashed across her face. "Oh! That's a British compilation chip, from the cable show. It slams you through lots of different things in sequence. It's really a top-wiz—"

"You've developed a twitch already, uncontrolled muscle spasm."

The fear began to slip back in. "I . . . what . . ."

Chase leaned forward slightly. "Your left arm. It twitches sometimes whe—"

A sudden, hard pounding on the thin construction plastic of the door cut him short. *"Church!"* came Becka Trinity's unusually loud voice from just beyond it. "It's show time!"

Chase looked back at Cara as she stood up, grabbing the simdeck case as she did. She was turned away from him. He stood, too, and walked toward the door.

Trinity was standing at the bottom of the stairs, grinning broadly beneath her cap. "Come on. You don't want to miss the works!"

"The works?"

"Fireworks, chummer. Somebody's running for the border, and the Azzies are out to scrag 'em before they do."

9

Cara slipped under Chase's arm before he realized it and bounced down next to Trinity. "Where?" Cara asked her.

The older woman eyed the girl a moment and then Chase. It suddenly occurred to him that Cara looked slightly disheveled and very sweaty. And he was sure that he looked only marginally better.

"They're still a bit off, but Katie's picked up some traffic on the Azzie security channels. She thinks it's a T-bird running north for the border."

"The *Rapier*?" asked Chase.

Trinity shrugged. "No tellin'. Have to wait and see."

Cara shielded her eyes from the sun. "How long till something happens?"

The old woman shrugged again. "An hour, a few minutes. T-birds are fast, honey."

Chase stepped down and closed the door behind him. "So, where are the best seats?"

Trinity smiled again. "Why, right out there," she said, pointing to a small bluff a few kilometers distant. "Grimm's Flat. Some of the camp are already out there."

They rode out in Mickey Dare's pickup truck, a dozen or so of them crammed into the bed. Chase sat next to Cara, pressed up against her side. She spoke to everyone but him.

As Trinity had said, some people were already up there when the truck reached the top of the bluff. The group was stretched out and comfortable in plastic furniture of a type normally found near a lot more water. A small van also sat on top of Grimm's Flat, but it was parked in a slight depression, manmade to Chase's eye, and covered in the same desert camouflage netting as the buildings in Dart Slot. The netting had been lifted up to clear a piece of equipment about the size of a lawnmower and the large, flat black panel that sat atop it, perpendicular and facing the south. Chase was surprised: he'd expected to see a lot of military surplus around Dart Slot, but a fairly new, portable phased-array radar was surprising.

A short, balding man in a bright red shirt slipped out from under the netting. As he straightened up, he adjusted a headset microphone he was wearing. As he blew once into it, the sound came amplified from a speaker hidden beneath the netting. He seemed satisfied.

"Good afternoon, folks. I'm gonna do the play-by-play this time 'cause Wanda's off in DFW. I'll try and do my best."

Some of the Dart Slot regulars nodded, while an even smaller number clapped in approval once or twice. Chase wasn't sure if it was for the speaker or Wanda's trip to Dallas-Fort Worth.

"What we have," he continued, "seems fairly standard. Katie picked up some Azzie air units entering the border buffer zone about twenty minutes ago. She tags them as Aguilar attack helicopters, and they've been loitering since they reached the area. She thinks there are some ground units playing hound for them, but hasn't seen or heard a sign of them."

Chase watched the crowd as the man spoke. They seemed to be listening, at least halfway, though most were watching south toward the border. Chase wasn't sure where it was, but was certain they knew down to the meter. Trinity handed him a beer she'd gotten from somewhere. He thanked her and looked around for Cara, who was standing a few steps away also looking south. She was still wearing only the shorts and tank top.

"You should lotion up or throw on something light. This sun'll cook you," he said.

"I tan. I don't burn." She did not look at him.

"Then tan you will."

"Okay, folks, here we go," said the announcer. "Katie says the beta-line sensor net just went active. The two choppers have dropped low and she's lost them in the ground clutter. No sign of who they're after."

Chase turned toward Trinity. "This happen every time?"

The Indian woman shook her head. "No. Happens more these days 'cause of the civil war stuff, but usually the T-birds slip across real quiet."

Chase nodded. "Why during the day?"

She grinned. "Why not? The tech we got and they got's so good, day or night don't mean a damn thing. During the day, though, the T-bird pilots can use the ground heat to mask their own signature somewhat."

Chase looked over at the speaker, who'd suddenly glanced up and was straining his eyes toward the border. "Missile fire!" he said. "Chopper did a pop-up and took a shot. Target's down in the dirt. No telling—"

Chase caught a barely perceptible flash just at the horizon. People began to stand.

"Choppers are maneuvering. Katie reads three in the air, and has got definite ground traffic." The announcer was obviously hearing more over his headset than he was relating. Chase wondered if it was coming too fast for him to relate or whether it was too technical. The man's eyes searched the horizon. "More air-to-ground fire, rocket pod profile."

One by one, people began to pull optical and electronic binoculars out of bags and pockets. They all watched the horizon.

"Sustained air-to-ground and ground-to-ground fire. The Azzies seem to be tracking whoever it is . . ."

Chase moved closer to Trinity and spoke so that only she could hear. "How many don't make it?"

"Too many."

"Okay, return fire, pretty heavy, tracks like a rotary cannon . . ."

"Could be the *Rapier*," said Trinity.

"Drone launch! At least one drone's in the air. . ."

"Christ almighty, Mike!" came a woman's shout from somewhere to Chase's left. "Whose?"

"Katie says they seem to be tracking the same target as the Azzies. . ."

Chase heard the low cursing and the loud grumbling pass through the crowd. Cara looked at him questioningly. "The Azzies are probably using the drones, not only for additional firepower," he told her, "but to confuse whoever they're after. Too many targets." He looked over at Trinity for confirmation and the old woman nodded. Cara looked back toward the horizon as a series of bright, slightly red flashes reached them.

"More rockets . . . Katie thinks the T-bird caught some air and the Azzies let go at it. She thinks it's still runnin', though."

"Can't see drek," said a kid forward of the group as he scanned the horizon with his binoculars.

"Katie thinks the T-bird's down in the west riverbed, but two of the choppers are moving to cut it off. The third's still hounding it. . . . So fraggin' close . . ."

"You've obviously got the information. Do you ever send any telemetry to the T-birds?" Chase asked Trinity.

"We used to, but about a year ago the Azzies lobbed a radar-seeking missile at us. Fraggin' thing missed, thank God, but we've stopped sending data. Too big a risk.''

Everyone on the bluff ducked reflexively as twin streaks of reflected sun shot over them by a hundred meters or so. The two jets were halfway to the flashes of light by the time their noise reached the bluff. Chase winced and could barely hear the shouts over the sudden noise.

"Texas! Texas!" came a few yells.

"Drek-for-brains a-holes!" came at least one other.

"Ah, two flyers, low and fast. All lit up, says Katie. Locking and tracking.''

"Phantom Fours!" yelled the kid with the binoculars.

Trinity leaned in close to Chase. The noise itself had dropped significantly, but they were all still half-deaf. "Texas Air National Guard jets out of Abilene. They don't like it when the Azzies play in the buffer zone. They don't always get here in time, but we call them as soon as anything starts to show."

Chase grinned. "Anonymously, I would guess."

"Frag, no. They ain't too happy 'bout us being around, but we keep a good eye on the border and keep the Azzies jumping.''

"Uh-oh, the choppers are running. Guess somebody let them know they were less than a klick from the border. Wonder who told them?''

The crowd chuckled and Chase could feel some of the tension draining out of them. He could barely see the two jets himself as they now flew parallel to where he guessed the border to be. There was another flash of reflected light a distance past the jets, but he couldn't make out what it was.

"Yepper, ladies and gentlemen, Katie reports that the Azzie units are in fact moving away from the bord—'' He stopped to watch the horizon and grinned. "Green and clear, chummers. Katie says she has a T-bird grabbin' air in home turf. ETA six minutes.''

There was scattered applause and a couple of whoops at the news. The announcer removed his headset and had turned away when the jets shot overhead again. Chase had been watching them and was ready when they passed, again barely a hundred meters over the bluff, but this time gently wagging their wings. The two fighters cleared the bluff and gained altitude as they sped north.

Trinity tugged on Chase's arm and pointed down below them. "Here she comes," she said, "and I'll bet yer hat she's the *Rapier*."

Chase grinned. "And how do you know that?"

"Hell, how do ya think? Ain't nobody else due in."

10

The *Rapier's Touch* reached Dart Slot a short time before Mickey Dare's pickup, so the low-altitude vehicle was already grounded and powered-down by the time Chase and Cara got back. Its three-man crew was out on the black, radar-absorbing hull inspecting the combat damage as the pickup rolled up. Among them was a tall, powerfully built black man with long braided hair, dressed in beat-up jeans and a brown leather vest. He stood up, pointing an accusing finger at Chase.

"You, sir," he boomed, "owe me money."

Chase shook his head and leaped from the truck to the ground. "And you, sir, have a shit-poor memory."

The black man slid down the sloped, metal side of the T-bird and landed in front of Chase. "No I don't. I bought dinner last in Phoenix."

Chase smiled and walked straight up to him. "Yeah, and I bailed everybody out afterward." Their noses all but touched. The black man had eaten recently.

"That doesn't count," he said and grinned.

"Oh, right, I keep forgetting." Chase grabbed the other man by the shoulders and embraced him warmly, a bear hug his friend returned with several slaps on the back.

Cara walked up behind them. "Better watch it. People will talk, you know."

They both grinned. "Let them, chica," the black man said. "I've kicked a lot more ass than I've—"

Chase cut him off with a shove. "If I might handle the introductions," he said, "that sprawled gentleman is Ryan Blanchard, gunner and tactical ops for this hunk of metal."

Blanchard waved at Cara from the ground. Chase's shove had knocked him into the shadow of the T-bird and he'd decided to stay there.

"Hunk of metal, is it, then?" said one of the two still on the vehicle. A man in his mid-forties, he was just slightly younger than Chase, but thinner and looking more world-weary. "That's not how you should be talkin' about her, all things considered."

"And what might those things be?" Chase yelled up to him, before leaning closer to Cara. "Pete Gordani, pilot," he told her.

"Well, mainly that you're gonna be wanting to hire us."

"Oh?" said Chase.

Gordani grinned. "You sure as hell didn't come wandering down here just to say howdy."

"I might have."

"Yeah, right," said Blanchard, now reclining comfortably against one of the T-bird's wheel guards. It used three wheels, tricycle-style, for ground maneuvering.

Chase glanced down at the black man, then stepped forward, up and over him and onto the T-bird.

"Hey! Watch that!" yelled Blanchard after rolling clear to avoid being stepped on. "That's sensitive electronics you're using as a step ladder."

Chase gave him a look. "Don't give me that crap. It's where the tool box is stored."

"Hey," said Blanchard, "we might have changed something, you know."

"If you did, you should have painted a warning note on it." Chase had reached the top of the wedge-shaped

vehicle and was clasping hands with Gordani, who gave
him a big grin.

Just behind him, partially hidden the whole time by
the weapon hardpoint, was the third member of the crew.
Krista Freid gave Chase a nod and a smile as he stood
with Gordani. "You'll excuse me if I don't shake your
hand, Church, but I'm kinda using both of mine to hang
on at the moment."

"Understandable, given the circumstances. How've
you been?"

"Pretty wiz, considering that half the Aztlan army just
tried to dust us."

Chase smiled and was about to reply, but Gordani
spoke first. "Your social skills seem to have deteriorated
since we last saw you."

Chase looked at him. "Oh?"

The pilot gestured down at the ground where Blanchard had begun talking quietly to Cara.

"Cara," Chase called. "I guess I never finished my
introductions."

She looked up at him and folded her hands across her
chest. "It's wiz. I'll just ignore you sometime in the
future."

"I've already introduced Mister Ryan Blanchard, former conscript in the army of the California Free State
and now gunner and tactician for this bird."

"I already told her that," yelled Blanchard.

"Well," said Chase, "now she's heard it from somebody she can trust."

Blanchard flipped Chase the finger.

"Thank you." Chase pointed at Gordani. "This is Pe-
terson Gordani—"

"Pete is fine."

"Glad to hear it. *Pete* Gordani, as I've also already
told you, is the pilot. He and I go a ways back."

Gordani nodded. "Yeah, I know at least three of the
names he uses."

Cara seemed surprised to hear this and looked at up at
Chase, who shrugged. "I get around," he said.

"Anyway," he continued, "there's one person you can't see from where you are, so you'll have to take my word that it's Krista Freid." Chase leaned over and pointed to the far side of the weapon mount. He started. Freid was gone.

When he looked back it was just in time to see Freid extending her hand to Cara. Though Freid was significantly taller than Cara, much of the intimidation factor was lost by the fact that she was rail-thin. Her long, sharp, face was topped by close-cropped black hair. Unlike the rest of the crew, she wore what most closely resembled a flight suit, though one made of black leather. An interesting choice for the desert, Chase thought.

"Freid is a mage," he said, as the two women shook hands.

Cara dropped Freid's hand and took an involuntary step backward, at which Freid grinned. "I know what you mean," she said to Cara. "Most mages scare me too."

Cara looked uncomfortable. "I didn't mean that . . ."

"Null perspiration," said Freid. "Like I said, I know how you feel." She turned toward Gordani. "I'll leave the bird to you guys and see if I can find the two Richs."

Gordani nodded. "Wiz. Blast their butts over here."

"Done," she said, and with a nod to Cara, walked off toward some of the buildings.

"So," Chase said, "sounded like you guys had quite a ride." He looked down at the *Rapier's Touch* as he spoke. It was covered in dust, with big chunks of dirt and scrub brush caked along its sides. There were clusters of bullet nicks in a few places, too, with at least one significant hit to the rear of the vehicle where a decent amount of armor had been peeled away. The plating had held, though; the armor damage seemed to be the extent of it. The weapon hardpoint they were standing near was another thing entirely.

Chase didn't know what had hit it, but whatever it was had been strong enough to tear through hardened armor and shred the weapon inside. It might once have been some sort of heavy rotary cannon, but now it looked like no more than randomly twisted metal.

"You might say that," Gordani agreed. "Would have been clean and sweet except we ran right over a fraggin' Azzie Land Rover. Until then they knew we were out there, but couldn't pin us down."

"I pelted it as quick as I could, but the alarm'd already gone out," said Blanchard. He was sitting on the edge of the T-bird now, a few steps away from Cara.

"We took a missile in the butt a couple of seconds later," continued Gordani, "which should have hurt us nasty. Lucky for us I was in the middle of a hard turn, which made it hit us at a pretty bad angle."

"What happened to the turret?" asked Cara.

"We came up out of a depression at the wrong time," said Blanchard. "Chopper fired a rocket volley at us. Most missed, but one or two tagged the hardpoint. We were lucky again; I was in the middle of swapping ammo feeds when we got hit. If there'd been live ammo in the turret it could have been worse."

Chase grinned. "Sounds like you used up a lot of karma today."

"Sure did," Gordani agreed. "But we'll make up for it in cold, hard cash."

"What were you carrying?"

Gordani shrugged. "Couldn't really say."

"Got it," said Chase, knowing not to pry further. "How long do you expect to be down?"

"Oh, you're in a rush, I take it?"

"Kind of. Cara and I have to get to Denver."

Gordani's eyebrows went up. "Cara?" he asked, and turned to look at her standing next to T-bird. "The young lady you haven't introduced yet?"

Chase groaned. "Sorry. Gentlemen, this is Cara. I think we'll leave it as simply 'Cara' for now. She and I have to get to Denver."

Gordani looked at Cara a moment longer and she shifted uncomfortably. He turned back to Chase. "Looks like I won't be knowing what my cargo is again."

''Big shock, eh?'' said Blanchard.

Gordani shrugged. ''Most of the damage is easily repairable,'' he told Chase, picking up the thread of the discussion. ''Say, twenty-four hours once the Richs get started.''

''The problem is going to be that cannon,'' said Blanchard. ''It may be tough to replace. How soon do you need to leave?''

''As soon as possible,'' said Chase.

''If anybody around here's got a spare one,'' Gordani said, ''we can have it in about the same time the armor and hardpoint are fixed, assuming you've got the cash to up for it.''

''I do.''

The pilot nodded. ''That'll help. If there isn't one around, it could be drek knows how many days before we can get one. I don't want to go back up against the Azzie with only a pair of medium machine guns and a spitting load of missiles.''

''The Azzies?'' asked Chase. ''I figured we'd go direct across into Pueblo Council lands, through old New Mexico, then ride the Rockies up to Denver.''

Blanchard shook his head. ''You got the last part right, but there isn't any way we're going to use the UCAS-Pueblo border.''

Chase looked from one to the other. ''Why not?''

''Too tough these days. Pueblo's got one of the best security nets out here. Why chance it when we don't have to?''

Gordani nodded. ''We've got much better intelligence about the Aztlan border—where the listening posts and sensors are, and such. Plus, the typical Aztlan soldier isn't as gung ho as those Pueblo border braves; they're not as willing to really trash it out.''

''So what we do is run south into Aztlan,'' continued Blanchard. ''Make it look like we're heading deep, but then swing west, very quietly, and then north again. We'll cross into Pueblo somewhere north of old Las Cruces.''

"But I thought you didn't want to deal with the Pueblo border."

Gordani leaned closer to Chase and almost whispered. "Kinda hard to get anywhere west of here without going through Pueblo."

"I understand that; I've seen a map recently."

"See, it's this way," Blanchard said. "Pueblo and UCAS are friendly, but economics being what they are, Pueblo really frowns on any kind of illicit trading and so clamps down on the border pretty heavy. It's also to control illegal immigration. The western part of Texas is pretty depressed. Lots of people have been trying to sneak across and get work in Pueblo."

"I'm sure that thrills them."

Blanchard laughed. "Chip-truth. So, the Pueblo-UCAS border's pretty tough to punch through. The Pueblo-Aztlan border, on the other hand, is wide open—for us anyway."

"There're pretty heavy forces on both sides of the border, but mostly they're there just to stare each other down," said Gordani. "The Azzies have mostly heavy units, dug in, and fielded with old sensor gear. Stuff's good for noticing a division rolling a cross the border, but not much use for noticing a tiny T-bird running fast and quiet."

Chase nodded. "But what about the Pueblo side?"

"Well, they're not real friendly with the Azzies," Blanchard said, "which means they're more than willing to ignore anything being smuggled *into* Aztlan. The Azzies hate it every time another load of cheap Pueblo electronics hits the streets."

"So they just let you by?"

"More or less." Blanchard looked at his partner. "Unless they have some reason to be looking for a particular T-bird or cargo."

"Will that be a problem?" asked Gordani.

"I don't think so," said Chase. "The people I'm worried about don't have any real pull in Pueblo."

The other two men nodded. "Good," said Gordani,

"then the only other thing we need to worry about is how much this is going to cost you."

Chase grinned. "And here I thought you'd do it for old times' sake."

"Uh-uh, chummer," said Blanchard, shaking his head. "Not as long as you still owe me money."

11

Chase had tried twice during dinner to bring up the subject of Cara's apparent BTL problems, but both times she'd belligerently put off his questions. He knew that the only way he was going to get any real answers would be to pressure her, but he hated to. If Cara's denial of the problem was as strong as it seemed, then pushing her too hard might make her panic and go back to trying to handle her father's problem alone. When they got to Seattle and talked to her mother, he'd try to pass on the word about Cara's problem and also recommend the name of a place where he knew she could get help. He suspected, though, that Samantha Villiers would have more than enough ideas of her own on that subject.

The downtime at Dart Slot had given him time to think. It had surprised him that they'd been able to reach the T-bird base without hassle. Was Farraday right that the hair samples had been too polluted to be of use?

Regardless, if Cara's pursuers, be they her German policlub compatriots or agents of Fuchi itself, suspected that she was heading to Seattle to meet with her mother, they could expect problems.

There were only a few real avenues into Seattle, and a corp with the resources of Fuchi Industrial Electronics could, by flexing only the tiniest bit of its muscle, throw up a net tight enough to catch them. The corp would cover not only Denver, but Phoenix to the south, Minneapolis to the far north, and San Francisco on the west coast, just in case their prey decided to make an end run north around the elven lands of Tir Tairngire. Deckers would have been hired, and tailored computer viruses released into the thousands of computer systems that controlled the transportation hubs of western North America. The word would be out, and the watch on. The team that had shown up in Chase's apartment in Manhattan could certainly qualify as Fuchi-caliber. If the evidence of their training wasn't enough, their possession of a gas-detection system was a clear sign of corporate backing.

Had it been only the policlubbers, Chase doubted he and Cara would face any real problems before actually reaching Seattle. The group looking for Cara had no American chapters. Chase knew about local political cells of Der Nachtmachen, but he'd never heard of any connections between Cara's Alte Welt and his old enemies. For Alte Welt to have any hope of intercepting them before Seattle, the group would have had no choice but to involve Fuchi. Chase had no idea how that particular relationship worked.

After dinner, Cara had accepted an invitation from one of the local boys, a scrawny punker named Gavin, to go hang out with the rest of the base's young people. She'd looked at Chase briefly before accepting, and he'd almost told her no, but something in her eyes said she needed to be away from him. He knew it was because of the pressure over the chips, and that she wanted to be free of his scrutiny.

That angered him. She'd come asking for his help, had agreed to follow his lead, and was now tugging at the short tether he'd formed between them. If she didn't want his help, why come to him in the first place? If she wanted to play the game, she'd have to live by the rules.

He let her go, then followed her for a short distance to assure himself the pair was headed for the shack Gavin had said the base's older kids used as a hangout. He'd stood in the shadows a short distance away listening to the music and watching the shadows beyond the covered

windows until the cold and his own feelings of idiocy
had driven him to find someplace warmer.

Crossing the base he came to an open fire pit that
someone had used to cook dinner, then left to smolder.
Chase decided to remain here; there was something even
colder about the inside of the prefab house just now.

It was still early evening, and the camp was far from
quiet. He could hear the sounds of dozens of trideo sets
blaring dozens of different channels. There was also the
occasional laughter or a sporadic call of anger from
somewhere in the base, and behind it all the intermittent
roar of a T-bird engine and the steady drone of the music
from the kids' hangout.

Suddenly, he caught something short and dark spring-
ing from shadow to shadow between a row of buildings
to his right. Trying to get a better view of it, he let his
enhanced vision amplify the available moonlight as best
its circuits could. He saw nothing other than the shadow
before the glare off the lighter ground and surrounding
buildings pushed the limits of his eyes. Then he lost track
of it.

He wondered why he wasn't worried. Years ago, in a
similar situation, he'd have been on his feet or at least
mentally prepared to act. He felt the press of his heavy
pistol under his arm, knew it was there, but had been
more interested in what the shadow figure might be up
to than whether or not it might be a threat.

Not all that long ago, he'd also have taken more drastic
action if thugs had broken into his apartment. He was
out of practice, but he knew the cyberware in his body
still outclassed nearly everything on the streets. A gift of
former employers. He had no doubt that if he needed to,
he could act, and kill, without hesitation.

Somehow, though, at some point over the last years,
the edge had dulled. That same edge had made him one
of the best bodyguards in the biz. And it was that edge
which had guided him through the blood bath that he
barely remembered as Berlin. He'd moved more as machine than man on those nights, inflicting blind justice

on those who paved their road to political power with the blood of innocents. Specifically one innocent he'd loved.

His body twitched involuntarily, and he fought to drive those thoughts from his mind. It was the past, history. Now was not the time to think about what he'd done and what he'd lost that had driven him to such extremes of violence. He had other matters to attend to now. Other things that needed thinking about. Things that needed calm.

He stood and stretched slightly, wondering how long he'd been sitting by the smoldering fire, lost in thought. The base had grown quieter, but not silent. There were still the laughs, the cries, the engines, and the music, but the long stillness of night had begun to creep its way through the shadows of the camp.

Stepping closer to the fire pit, Chase looked up at the millions of stars spattering the dome of sky. Among them, brighter points moved along straight and even courses. Maybe satellites in orbit, maybe aircraft flying only slightly lower. Maybe other things.

Chase thought about Farraday and again about the magicians that might be using his own and Cara's hair to trace them. If they found him, would he feel their power coming? He didn't know. Magic had spread rapidly during the last ten or fifteen years, and was something he didn't know much about. His own experiences with it were limited. So few had practiced it when he was fully active in the business, at his peak. As the use of magic had been increasing, Chase had been drifting into quieter pursuits.

But he knew someone here who could tell him more. Krista Freid.

He asked around over at the T-bird hangar, and at first no one seemed to know where the *Rapier's Touch* crew was. Finally he learned that Gordani and Blanchard had borrowed Mickey Dare's pickup truck and gone in search of parts for the T-bird's scragged hardpoint. They apparently were also following up a lead on a replacement weapon. He also learned that Freid hadn't gone with them. Someone pointed out her place to him. The lights were on.

Walking up to the camouflaged building, Chase was careful to make as much noise as he could. Unlike the building where he and Cara were housed, Freid's was flush with the ground, not even raised up slightly on blocks or bricks. There were curtains on the windows and a long-abused welcome mat before the door. He stepped up to it and knocked.

"Hang on," came Freid's voice from somewhere within. She opened the door a few moments later and a gust of cool air slipped out and past him as she did. "Church," she said, smiling, but with her head tilted questioningly. "What's biz?"

He returned her smile. "I wanted to ask you some questions about magic. Got a minute?"

She paused a second, then nodded. "Sure. Come on in."

"As long as I'm not interrupting anything . . ."

She made a noise. "Not fraggin' likely. I was just reading." She stepped back and opened the door enough for him to enter. Again he felt the brush of cool air. Chase suspected air conditioning, but couldn't hear the machinery. The layout was similar to his and Cara's place: little more than a studio apartment. Freid's however, had a definite feel to it. Decorated primarily in Aztlan and southwest Amerindian styles, it also had a few European pieces mixed in. Art reproductions hung on the walls, some of them traditional, but most modern. The most prominent item was a tri-dee poster for the dragon Dunkelzahn's retreat and resort on Lake Louise in old Canada.

"Ever been there?" he asked.

"Where?"

"The dragon's place."

She smiled again. "Never. Someday."

"It's amazing, and he's an odd one. He was walking around looking like a human last time I was there. He seemed amused. I think his kind don't have a very high opinion of us humans.''

''Can't say I blame him sometimes,'' she said, watching him.

He moved into the main area and noted the still-active datareader on the couch. Sitting next to it was a small pile of magazine chips. She'd been catching up on the world.

''You seem surprised,'' she said, still behind him.

He turned. She'd entered the kitchen area and was leaning against the counter, watching him. Now it was his turn to look questioning. ''Surprised?''

''By my place. You seem surprised to find it . . . so lived in.'' She pitched the last part like a question.

Chase smiled and nodded. ''You're right. I suppose I never really thought about anybody in your line of work actually having a home. The whole time I ran with Gordo I don't remember him ever mentioning having one. He had a lot of places to stay, but no homes.''

''Not for me,'' she said. ''If I didn't have a place where I could turn it all off, I'd crack. I need a corner that's different than everywhere else. Can I get you something to drink?''

He nodded.

''I'm afraid I've got very little. I haven't had the time to restock.''

''Anything's fine.''

''Water okay?''

He laughed. ''Water it is.''

Freid made them both glasses of water and dropped a lemon-flavored tablet in each. She moved the datareader and chips, and motioned him to sit there. She sat next to him, her legs curled up under her long body.

Chase knew little about her, and was hesitant about revealing too much. The last time he'd worked with Gordani, Freid had been there, but she and Chase had only operated together peripherally. He hadn't intended to tell Gordani, whom he knew far better, anything that the pilot didn't need to know to do his part of the job. But if

there were to be magical problems, he figured that he'd
best alert Freid.

He took a long drink from his glass, put it down on
the table next to him, and looked over at her. He was
suddenly surprised at her beauty. Krista Freid was taller
and of a lighter build than the women who usually attracted him, but there was something about her that he
hadn't noticed before. She was wearing tight black mid-
thigh shorts and a large, oversized pale yellow T-shirt
that threatened to slide down off her shoulder if she
moved the wrong way. Her hair shone and smelled as
though she'd just stepped from the bath. She sat half-
turned toward him, elbow on the back of the couch, head
resting against her hand. She smiled.

Chase took another big drink.

"You said you had some sort of magic problem," she
said.

"Um, yes. I figured you might be able to suggest some
solutions."

"Shoot," she said.

"It's possible that we're being pursued, and I suspect
magic is being used to track us."

Freid's eyes lit up. "To track you? Tell me."

Chase told her as little as he thought he could, relating
only that a powerful megacorporation with good magical
assets might be after them, the events in his apartment,
and Farraday's opinions.

She snorted. "Your friend's a shaman, I take it?"

"Yes. A cat shaman."

She nodded and shifted slightly, dropping both hands
into her lap. "Shamans tend to overrate that kind of
thing. The chemicals would be only the slightest hin-
drance to a mage worth her rate."

"Wonderful."

She smiled again and leaned slightly closer. "I can
check. If they're tracking you, there'll be some astral
evidence. A clear link between you and whomever is doing the tracking."

Chase studied her. She seemed excited by the prospect. "Is there any danger to you?"

"Some, maybe," she said with a shrug. "Depends on what's really going on and how they're doing it. If they're only using a ritual, the danger's almost nil. If someone's actually shadowing you in astral space, a magician or a spirit of some kind, there might be more danger."

"Something could be actually—"

He stopped as Freid suddenly reached out and braced herself against his shoulder. He grabbed her, one hand on her outstretched arm, the other on her far shoulder, as her eyes unfocused and her head dropped forward. He let go of her shoulder and grabbed her chin, just as it snapped back up and a wide grin appeared. She squeezed his shoulder, let go and leaned back. Chase let go of her chin.

"Sorry," she said, "I needed to check quick."

He stared at her. "I don't follow," he said. She seemed very amused.

"It gets a bit technical, but normally there's no danger of someone here in the physical world being attacked by something that only exists in astral space, even if both are in the same room. It's one of the laws of magic, in a way; something in astral space can't normally affect the real world.

"Now, even though whatever's in the room with us can't affect us, it can see us and *hear* us."

"So if there was something here, it would have heard you say that you were going to check in astral space."

She nodded. "And prepared a welcome. Once I shifted myself, or even just my senses into astral space, I'd have become vulnerable. If they were ready, they could have attacked me the moment I shifted astral. By doing it suddenly I hoped to catch them off guard."

"And?"

"And," she said, "there was nothing there."

"No one? No spirits?"

She shook her head.

"No signs of magical tracking?"

She held her hand up. "I didn't say that. I didn't stay long enough to look for that, just long enough to look around."

"So you'll check for the tracking now?"

"Yup, but this time we'll play it a little safer." She stood up and stopped the crawl of her shirt down her left shoulder. "Help me move this coffee table over against the wall."

He stood up, too, then reached down and picked the table up cleanly as she began to lean toward it. "Which wall?"

She stopped reaching for the table, looked half up at him and pointed. "That wall, Samson. Don't worry about dropping it. It's real wood."

"I won't drop it." Chase carried the table over to the wall and gently set it down. The two glasses of half-drunk water barely showed a ripple. He turned back toward her and watched as she rolled up the large Aztec-pattern throw rug that dominated the room. Beneath, painted in near-shining metallic colors, was a double-ringed circle drawn around a triangle. Other geometric shapes, symbols, and designs were drawn between the two rings. Freid reached down and touched the circle, and instantly it seemed that some invisible light played across the designs. Chase couldn't see the light, but the metallic paint reflected it nonetheless.

"Now," she said, "since this is active I don't want you crossing it or stepping into it. It's an inscribed circle. If you're being tracked magically, the circle's properties would interfere with the tracking. They might not notice if they weren't paying attention, but I don't want to take that chance."

She stepped into the circle and dropped down cross-legged at its center, within the triangle. "While I'm in here, I'm protected against things in astral space. They'll have a hard time attacking across the circle's boundary.

"If there is a spirit following you, and I missed it when I checked astral space a minute ago, it might decide to come after me physically instead of challenging me astrally, where in some ways I'm slightly more powerful.''

Chase was surprised. "Physically? I thought you said things in normal space were in no danger from things that exist only in astral space?''

"Right. A spirit, like an elemental or a watcher, is a dual being. It can exist in either place at one time. Its choice. It could be waiting and watching in astral space for me to astrally project so that it can drop into the physical world and go after my defenseless body.''

"Now, wait just a minute.''

She grinned. "Yup, as they say on the trideo, that's where you come in.''

"I can't deal with a spirit. I mean, how in the hell could I hurt it?''

She shrugged. "Punch it, kick it, it doesn't really matter. All that matters is that you're trying to harm it. Not only might you harm it, but if your will is strong enough, you'll slow it down long enough for me to take some action. See, because it's a dual being it still has a presence astrally even when manifest in the physical world. It'll still be vulnerable to me, assuming I get the chance to do something.''

Chase moved up to within a step of the circle and pulled out his heavy pistol. The moment he grabbed it, the weapon sensed the presence of his hand and activated the cyberlink circuits in the grip. Those sensors matched up with another set hidden beneath Chase's palm and wired into his nervous system. He felt the warm flow from his hand that told him the circuits were engaged. A small targeting dot appeared in his field of vision as the cyberware in his head translated the positioning data the weapon fed through his hand and up his arm. The dot showed him, within barely a millimeter of error, exactly where the pistol was pointed. Other readouts appeared in his eye showing the status of the weapon's safety, which was on, and its current ammo load, which was full, sixteen rounds. With the weapon now linked and in sync with his already wired and hyped-up nervous system,

Chase was ready. He realized that this was the first time since the whole thing had started that he'd actually drawn a weapon.

"Will this do?" He let her clearly see the heavy Colt Manhunter pistol, but was careful to keep it pointed away. He didn't like the sight of the targeting spot near her.

"Um," she said, "it'll work, some. See, when you attack the spirit you're using your will, your desire, to attack and damage it. It's you against the spirit. The gun's a tool, a symbol, that acts as your surrogate against the spirit. Yes, you aim, but the bullets themselves have no will of their own. The effect is lessened. If it's you attacking—your own hands, your own blows—there's nothing interfering. You strike with your own will."

He looked down at her for a moment, weapon still pointed clear. "You know," he said finally, "I haven't the faintest idea what you just said."

She laughed. "That's okay. If something shows up, you can hit it with the gun, just don't shoot it."

"Now, wait just another minute."

Again she held up her hand. "Quiet, please, I'm going to go astral." As she finished speaking, the muscles of her face and then the rest of her body went slack. Her body seemed to remain upright only by its own instinctive balance. Her lips parted slightly and she exhaled a long, slow breath.

As Chase watched and waited, he carefully scanned the room, his cybernetic low-light vision turned up to bring the area to near-daylight levels. He watched for movement, listened for noises, anything that might betray the presence of a spirit. He saw only the room and heard only Freid's breathing.

Then her breathing changed, losing its rhythm with a sharp gasp. Instinctively, he brought his pistol up and around toward her. The dot centered on her forehead for just a moment until he saw her eyes blink and her jaw begin to work slightly. He kept the weapon moving and brought it up to a rest, pointed at the ceiling.

Freid stood up and brushed herself off. She stepped

out of the circle, stopping within arm's length. She blinked a couple of times, then smiled.

"Well?" he said.

"Nothing."

"Nothing?" he said.

"Nothing. As far as I can tell nobody is tracking you in any which way."

Chase cybernetically commanded the gun to power itself down to conserve the battery, then holstered it. "I'm surprised," he said.

"Oh?"

He nodded. "We were nearly ambushed trying to get out of Manhattan, and I'm pretty fragging sure the only way they could have found us was through magic. I assumed they'd kept up with us."

"They could have lost the trail."

"Maybe," he said, running one hand across his chin. He was surprised at the layer of stubble he found there. With all the anxiety over Cara this morning he'd forgotten to shave. Cara. "Damn. We'd better check on Cara."

Freid's eyes narrowed slightly. "The girl you were with?"

"Yes."

She seemed to take a moment to absorb that, then shook her head with a light smile.

"What?" he asked her.

She looked back at him, her head dipped slightly and still holding the smile. "Oh, I've just been trying to figure out if you've really got a problem or if this is just a very complex come-on."

Chase started. "No . . . I mean . . . I'm sorry I gave you the wrong impression."

She smiled a little wider and Chase saw amusement begin to dance in her eyes. She stepped closer to him and reached out, draping her arms across his shoulders, her hands loosely clasped behind his neck. "Don't worry about it."

He reached up and gently took her arms just above her elbows. "Look—"

"Where's your friend?" She clasped her hands tighter, and Chase felt them begin to press against the back of his neck.

"With Gavin and some of the other kids. They went to that shack, I don't know—"

She interrupted him again. "Put your hands under my shoulders."

Chase took a deep breath. "I'm not sure—"

"Like this." Freid took his hands and placed them farther up, under her arms. He wasn't surprised by the tautness of the muscle he found there, nor the softness.

"Don't let go," she said, lowering her voice. "I'm going to check out your friend. Hold me up."

Chase started to say something to stop her, but the muscles in her face relaxed too quickly and her head leaned forward, eyes unfocused. "Damn," he said, supporting her sudden weight.

He pulled her limp body against his side and supported it easily with one arm. With his free right hand he pulled out his heavy pistol and let all the circuits engage. He wasn't sure if it would help, but he wanted it out.

Freid's head rested against his shoulder and her breath was slow and regular against his neck. He watched the room, and her, and wondered what to do next. He thought about laying her down on the couch, but knew from the few mages he'd worked with that they didn't like to be disturbed once they'd begun astrally projecting, so he didn't.

Every few minutes he thought he felt her body stiffen slightly, but nothing further happened. He could read the time on the display of her music system. Much more time was passing than when she'd checked him.

He waited and watched. Her body seemed to shift closer to him.

A car horn blared somewhere in the base, and he heard the distant crash of what could have been metal barrels. He decided to put her down, and she stirred.

Her breathing changed, and she opened her eyes, first allowing him to continue to support her, but then standing on her own. She stayed close and let him half hold her. "What is it?" she said quietly.

He took a half step toward the center of the room, and she came with him. "Noises. A crash of some kind."

She smiled. "Billy Finn was trying to steer his truck past the junk piles as I was coming back. He didn't seem too sober."

"Still . . ."

"The base is safe, Church. You shouldn't worry."

"It's my job to worry," he said. "What about Cara?"

"She's clean; no sign at all of anybody tracking her."

"Really?"

She punched him lightly. "No, I'm lying."

"I take it she was all right."

"Well . . ." Freid looked down and kicked at the edge of the rolled-up carpet. "She wasn't in any danger, but she was certainly venting some serious frustration."

Chase tensed slightly. "Oh."

She placed her hand on his chest. "Hey, relax. I said she was fine." She looked up at him. "Are you two just friends, or . . ."

"She came to me because she needed help. I worked as a guard for her family when she was little."

"Ah," said Freid. "Well, she's gone off with one of the techs, a real ganderer named Willie. I found them by listening in on some conversations. She was apparently quite aggressive. Gavin's not happy."

He looked down at her. She was still standing very close. "Oh."

"Yeah, she was working him over pretty good." She grinned. "Not that he was complaining, mind you."

"I see."

"You know, it's tough for a mage to just wander in on something like that. All the emotion just resonates through astral space. It's tough to ignore."

"Really." He felt her hand, still on his chest, press harder against him and begin to slide downward.

She looked down and watched her moving hand. "It gets to you."

He let her words hang for a moment, then took the plunge. "Anything I can do to help you get over it?"

She giggled. "Well, for starters, you can put that gun away."

12

Blanchard winced at the unholy sound coming from the power plant of the air-cushion vehicle parked a dozen meters away. He shook his head and turned back to Chase. "I don't know what their problem is."

"She sounds way out of tune," said Chase.

"Yeah, and even a tech-wiz like you can tell that. Willie's been working on it for an hour. Something must really be out of whack."

Chase leaned back against the warm hull of the *Rapier's Touch*. "Which is he?" He put up one hand to block the early morning sun and its reflection inside his aviator glasses.

"Willie? The one with the blue bandanna on his arm." Blanchard pointed at the cluster of technicians near the raised engine hood. The one he'd pointed out was shaking his head and recalibrating a pocket-comp. "Why?"

Chase shrugged. "His name came up last night."

"Oh, yeah, I heard something about that."

"Oh?"

"I hope there won't be any problems."

"About?"

Blanchard rolled his eyes. "Come on, chummer, don't do me like this. Willie and the girl."

"Just checking that we're talking about the same thing," Chase said, glad he hadn't jumped to a different conclusion. "Sorry to disappoint you, but it's just business, and we're friends."

Blanchard actually seemed relieved. Chase imagined

the T-bird's gunner hadn't been looking forward to a socially stressful run. "Wiz," he said.

Metal clanged against plasteel somewhere behind them, and Chase turned to see Gordani garbed in a flight suit similar to Blanchard's coming around the rear of the T-bird. Behind him, the two technicians he'd seen inspecting the vehicle were arguing. The two, one insanely tall, and the other, of about the same weight but half the height, had been working on the LAV all night. Gordani seemed pleased.

"Everything shipshape, Captain?" asked Chase as he approached.

"Yeah, seems so," he said, rubbing a hand through his stubby hair. "Fragged if I know how they do it."

Chase looked over his shoulder at the repaired, freshly painted turret halfway to the rear of the T-bird. From its front protruded a long, slender gunmetal barrel. Chase recognized a sophisticated gas-vent and flash-dampening system at the end of it. "What is it?"

"Maxwell chain gun. It's actually aircraft ordnance, but what the hell?"

"Where'd you find it?"

"One of the choppers over at White Base a few klicks up the road got trashed a couple of nights back. I wasn't sure, so I checked, and sure enough they still had her chain gun and needed cash bad."

Chase turned toward Blanchard. "How's it compare to the old autocannon?"

The black man shrugged. "Well enough. It's lighter caliber, but has a higher rate of fire. It's also less bulky and lighter overall, so the turret'll track better. I was a little worried about the anti-air servos, but the two Richs seemed satisfied."

Chase nodded and noted Gordani looking around. "Seen Freid?" he asked.

"No," said Blanchard. "I slipped a note under her door last night, so she knew we'd be prepping before seven. I didn't want to bother her. She sounded preoccupied."

"I haven't seen her either." Chase had learned about the T-bird's morning departure from that note and knew that Freid had seen it.

"Great," said Gordani to his gunner. "I hope she got enough sleep."

Blanchard shrugged.

Chase resisted the temptation to say more, wondering instead where Cara was. When he'd returned to their quarters barely a few hours ago, she was sleeping restlessly against one wall. Blanchard's note to them had been left conspicuously on Chase's blankets. Cara had seen it, and knew he hadn't been there.

Her movements had awakened him just after dawn. She was stuffing some clothes into her bag and zipping it up when he stirred. He could tell she'd heard him, but didn't look over.

"Take my bag to the T-bird," she said. "I'll meet you there." She stood up and left the bag on one of the chairs. What little light there was from outside blinded him as she left. He could feel the day's temperature rising already.

Before he carried the bag over, Chase had checked to see if her simdeck case was there. It was, as were the chips. He didn't think she'd try running away without them.

Gordani's voice intruded on his thoughts. "I've checked with Katie and she says Azzie activity's been real low this morning. She thinks most of the units that bothered us yesterday pulled back south of the Rio Grande sometime last night."

"That'd be good," said Blanchard. "We ain't got enough chain-gun ammo to be playing too many games."

Gordani nodded in agreement. "Here comes Freid."

Chase looked up and caught sight of her rounding one of the larger buildings that doubled as a makeshift hangar. She was wearing the same black leather flight suit he'd first seen on her yesterday. Chase no longer worried how she stayed cool in it; it was the same way she kept her quarters comfortable: magic. He'd learned a lot about that last night.

Cara was with her, walking alongside, hands thrust in her pockets and head down. She'd picked up a tan army jacket somewhere. Freid seemed to be saying something to her, but Chase couldn't hear the words over the protesting engine of the air-cushion vehicle. Cara glanced at it once as they passed, but Willie was half-buried in the engine housing. She looked down again, nodding at something Freid said. The mage patted her on the shoulder, then quickened her already long stride.

"Morning, guys," she said, coming up to them. She smiled at each one, seeming to hold Chase's gaze for just a moment longer. It was hard to tell behind the dark glasses she wore. "Everything running?"

"Wiz and clean," said Blanchard. "I think you've been teaching the Richs a little sorcery on the side."

Freid laughed. "They'd rather eat snake." She hoisted her bag over one shoulder. "Well, let me stow my gear and grab the databoard."

"Yell when ready," said Gordani.

She nodded and headed off toward the access hatch. Cara was walking toward them, wincing against the light.

"Don't worry," said Blanchard, laughing. "It's pretty fraggin' dark inside the T-bird."

Cara almost seemed to smile. "Good."

Chase started to ask her if she'd eaten, but a sudden voice in his ear stopped him. It was soft, quiet, breathy, and seemed to be made from the wind. It was Freid's voice. "Don't worry," the voice said. "I spotted her while I was out running this morning. Something's gnawing at her. I couldn't find out what, but I don't think it was you."

As nonchalantly as he could, Chase turned and tried to find the source of the voice. Freid was nowhere in sight, having already stepped inside the T-bird.

"She's got a bit of a wisher for you, though, so I wouldn't tell her about us last night," Freid's voice went on. "She thinks you stayed out because you were angry.

Apparently she's used to the guys she likes being temperamental jokers.''

Chase scanned the body of the LAV for an open window or port, knowing that to work a spell on him she must actually be able to see him. The only exception to that was the special magic of ritual sorcery, but that took hours to prepare. He saw nothing, no openings of any kind.

"Confused?" she said. "Look at the top of the turret."

He did and saw the glint of coated, non-glare glass seated deep inside a small device set atop the turret. As he watched, the whole device rotated slightly.

"Optical targeting system. It's my eyes outside the T-bird while we're running. Because it's pure optical, no cameras, I can cast magic through it."

"Church."

Chase turned in response to Blanchard's voice. He wondered how long the gunner had been trying to get his attention. "Sorry," he said. "Thought I heard something."

"Yeah, my voice yelling in your ear."

Chase chuckled.

Cara was looking at him a little oddly and seemed to want to say something, but Gordani unknowingly cut her off. "I want you and Cara here to pay close attention as we pre-flight the T-bird. Most of it'll mean nothing to you, but I want you to hear the names of things and listen to what we're doing. If something goes wrong, it could save your butt."

"I guess I should tell you I don't know anything about one of these things," Cara confessed. "I can barely work a telecom."

"You can program a synth though, right?" asked Chase, hoping his choice of words didn't sound too much like an attack. "You told me you played keyboard."

"Well, yeah, but . . ."

Blanchard smiled. "Little difference in some regards. Don't worry. You'll do fine."

Cara smiled slightly at him, then turned toward Chase and tried to smile a little more.

Chase heard Freid's voice again, but this time it was her real one and it was coming through the external speakers.

"Okay, chummers, let's run through this. I got a date in Denver and I plan to keep it."

Chase laughed and remained standing next to Cara as the crew went to work. Lost in thought, she seemed to be a million miles away.

13

Chase leaned over and helped Cara adjust the position of the bulky headgear Blanchard had given her. She was having trouble with the friction straps that were designed to keep the gear on the wearer's head no matter what happened. The helmets were heavily padded to protect the head, and contained a headset and microphone combination that linked into the T-bird's internal communications system. She and Chase were seated on single-person, removable padded couches back near the cargo lockers.

Freid sat in a similar seat, just forward of Cara, but hers also had a control panel on each arm pad. Through them, she could operate various optical and electronic targeting and tracking systems to locate a potential enemy. Freid also wore the same basic headgear, but hers had goggles linked via fiber-optic cable to a kind of periscope on top of the main gun turret. Chase had learned that there were two other optical ports, as she called them, on the vehicle, both along the centerline, one forward and one to the rear. Using her armrest controls Freid could swap the visual feed to her goggles between any of them.

If she chose, and if Blanchard agreed, she could also slave any of the *Rapier's* weapons to her optical sensors. Though the opticals were not as sophisticated and effective as the high-tech electronic sensors Blanchard commanded, she could engage additional targets if necessary.

At her command, the chair swiveled, and Freid looked at Chase and Cara through a small optical camera mounted on the goggles. The goggles covered nearly her whole face and the optical lines connected to the camera. "Ready?" she said loudly over the thrum of the LAV's power plant.

Cara nodded slightly, obviously intimidated by what was going on.

"I think so," Chase said. "Any last-minute changes?" Though both he and Cara wore headsets, Gordani hadn't yet connected them into the comm network.

Freid shook her head. "No. Gordo's been talking to Katie at the radar and she says everything is pretty quiet. She also thinks that one of the other bases has launched a run carrying medical supplies south toward Monterey. We'll hold off and let them get some distance before we head out."

"How long will that be?" asked Chase.

"Not long," came Blanchard's voice over the comm net. Chase saw Cara flinch and manually lower her set's volume. "They're already over and in, so we're just waiting to see if they set off any of the sensor lines or pickets. If they do, we go under the cover of the distraction. If they don't, we go anyway."

"Got it," said Chase.

Blanchard's position in the vehicle was directly in front of Chase, but slightly farther forward than Freid's. He sat on a small platform raised a step above the main floor of the cabin. His own light-acceleration couch reclined even further than Chase's or Freid's, giving him enough clearance for the suite of video and data display monitors in front of him. They were there for emergencies, as was a similar set near Freid.

Blanchard himself was cybernetically connected to the

weapons and sensor system. Every piece of data the sensors obtained was fed directly into him. He was aware of it, and processed it at the speed of thought. The weapons responded to him in the same manner, quick and deadly. The system told him everything he needed to know about the vehicle's movement, the wind conditions between the T-bird and the target, the barrel condition of the chain gun, its ammo status, and dozens of other pieces of data that affected the shot. He knew everything he needed to know.

Gordani was not visible, seated out of sight in a black plastic cocoon at the farthest point forward of the tight cabin, barely five meters from Chase. Called a rigger tank and just slightly larger than a coffin, the cocoon completely isolated him from the rest of the vehicle. It was sound-dampened to prevent distraction, and in it Gordani sat suspended on a bed of body-temperature gel-cushions that gave him the sensation of floating. He was rigged into the vehicle like Blanchard, but he was almost exclusively concerned with steering the *Rapier's Touch*. The sensor feeds he received cybernetically were his only eyes and ears to the outside world. For all intents and purposes, he *was* the T-bird while rigged into the vehicle's systems. The sensors told him what was around him, the internal systems fed him continual updates of its condition, and the vehicle's control systems responded instantly to his thoughts. It was only that level of control that allowed the vehicle to fly at nearly six hundred kilometers an hour only a meter or so off the ground.

Chase knew they were moving, following a complex, distracting, pre-run holding pattern on the Canadian American States side of the border. The vehicle's path had been carefully planned to conceal the T-bird by taking advantage of the natural and manmade terrain in the area. If the Azzies happened to be expecting a run, the less they knew about its initial course the better. The T-bird's path followed a section of the Aztlan-CAS border forty kilometers long.

Gordani's voice came over the comm net. To Chase

the voice had the same odd, distorted sound as had Lachesis' days ago. That wasn't surprising, for in some ways the differences between a rigger and a decker were minor. Both experienced an artificial reality. For a decker like Lachesis it was the Matrix, designed to bring a degree of reality to the artificial world of computer networks and data. Gordani's was made from the hyper-realistic data flow of the T-bird's internal and external sensors. Both rigger and decker were at their best when reality was filtered for them.

"Looks like we're green. The other run should be well clean of the border sensors by now, and nothing. So we go." The sound of Gordani's voice reminded Chase that Lachesis' detailed report on Cara was probably ready and waiting. He'd have to read it in Denver. Maybe he'd even see her personally.

The *Rapier's Touch* lurched slightly, knocking him to one side. He noticed that Freid and Blanchard's chairs seemed to compensate automatically; there was barely any movement from either of them.

Adjusting the position of her headgear slightly, Cara smiled slightly and leaned toward him. "Do you think it'll be rough?"

Chase started to reply, but Blanchard's chuckle cut him off. "Naw, it'll be slick," he said, and Chase remembered that the headsets were voice-activated. "Assuming they don't notice us."

Cara rolled her eyes and tried to make herself more comfortable in the chair. She was strapped in using a standard cross-x upper-body harness, a design that was effective but uncomfortable.

Chase felt the T-bird's power plant increase its output and the resulting acceleration as they eased into a left turn. The video monitors near Freid showed bright Texas terrain blurring as they sped past. For the first time, Chase noticed the row of hanging souvenir toys above the monitor row. He chuckled to see Freid moving her head side to side as she panned through the optical port she commanded. She smiled slightly as he watched, then rotated her chair to face forward. Did his watching distract her on some level?

Gordani's electronic voice cut through his thoughts. "Ladies and gentlemen," he said, "welcome to Aztlan. I hope your passports are in order."

The first problems came a little more than half an hour after they entered Aztlan. They'd passed easily through the permanent sensor lines; the crew knew where they were and how to avoid them. It was the unexpected things deeper in-country that would be a danger. The first word was Blanchard's announcement over the comm net.

"I've got what looks like a DEW craft at nine thousand meters, bearing two-eight-nine, heading one-nine-seven, relative."

Cara glanced questioningly at Chase. He reached up and toggled his microphone off the network before responding. He didn't want to distract the crew.

"DEW craft," he said, "defensive early warning. Basically a plane with air and ground-search radar. Not as sophisticated as the regular EW craft, but dangerous enough. If it spots us, it can direct other units to our general area. A regular EW craft could pass on telemetry information that units with that capability could use to attack us from a long distance. Even kilometers away. They wouldn't have to see us as long as the EW craft could."

Cara'd listened to him without commenting, and when he was done she turned away to look at Freid's monitors. Chase suspected she was scared. He knew he was.

The *Rapier's Touch* traveled for several hours at reduced speed to cut down on their electromagnetic and acoustic signature. Anything that could be done to reduce the chance of the DEW craft spotting them was done. Gordani took Chase's and Cara's microphones off the comm network to cut down on any unnecessary chatter and electrical signals.

Twice, the DEW craft changed course in their general

direction, and Blanchard thought it might have picked up something worth investigating. Twice Gordani changed their own course to see if the plane matched them. It didn't.

They continued on, leaving the Aztlan patrol plane behind.

Four hundred kilometers in from the point where they'd crossed the border, Gordani turned the T-bird west.

"We may be in luck," his artificial voice said. "I've been monitoring Mexican Free Radio and they're reporting that Aztlan forces are going head to head pretty heavy with one of the rebel armies way east of us, south of San Antonio."

Chase nodded. "That makes sense. There's a lot of support for the revolutionary factions in the occupied Texas areas."

Cara looked at him. "There are still Americans there? I figured they'd have left by now."

"Most have," Chase told her. "A lot, though, don't want to leave their homes. Some figure Texas will eventually win back the area—"

The T-bird lurched suddenly to one side, tossing Chase and Cara about in their seats. Something large flashed by on one of Freid's monitors, and then they were past it.

"FRAG!" Gordani yelled. "What was that! Somebody tell me what that was!"

Chase could see something, maybe a vehicle, receding quickly in Freid's rearview monitor. As he watched, the image grew as she triggered magnification lenses into place.

"I read it as a truck. Two tons, maybe," came Blanchard's voice. Chase heard a faint mechanical noise over the roar of the engines: the main turret was traversing to the rear.

"Jam them!" said Gordani. Blanchard's back-up data screens flashed angrily as he enacted the pilot's command.

"Confirm truck," said Freid. Her optical image had

stabilized some, and the camera was tracking the truck
even though Gordani was putting them through heavy
evasive maneuvers. Cara was doing all she could to avoid
being beaten senseless against her chair. Chase's more
powerful muscles had him braced and secure now that
he knew what to expect.

"One truck, standard size, about a ton and a half. I
see crew. And passengers. Soldiers."

"Hit 'em!" Gordani barked again.

Chase could barely make out anything on the blurred
and jittery monitor, but Freid's analysis made sense. The
truck seemed to be parked on the side of the road. He
could make out figures, many of them, climbing out the
back of it. Then suddenly Freid's body moved oddly. She
spoke, and there was a blue-white flash of magical energy at the rear of the truck. The soldiers coming out of
the truck fell to the ground as though they'd been hit with
a bat; a few even fell back in or fell out face-first onto
the dusty ground. The canvas back of the truck shredded.

The monitor flared again, this time to pure white before the systems compensated for the glare of the missile
launched from the rear rack. It sped toward the truck,
and was lost from sight as the T-bird changed course
again. The optical cameras tried to reacquire the truck,
but it was hidden by intervening terrain. Nonetheless,
Chase clearly saw a flash and an explosion just beyond
some rocks as they completed a turn.

"Hit!" exclaimed Blanchard.

"Status!" came Gordani.

"Can't tell. Too much in the way," the gunner replied.

Gordani again. "Freid?"

"Checking!" she yelled, and Chase saw her hands
move in tight, practiced gestures, her head turning this
way and that as if she were looking for something. Sweat
poured out from under her goggles. Chase glanced at the
monitors and saw only blurred ground. Whatever she saw
wasn't on those monitors. Cara too stared at the monitors, her face ashen.

"The truck is scrap," Freid said, strain evident in her

voice. "Some of the soldiers are still alive, but only one
or two seem up and about. I count maybe five dead outside the truck."

"Can you do anything?" Gordani asked.

"Negative. I don't have line of sight."

"Frag it to hell!" the pilot said. "Blanchard, it's your
call. Tell me what you want."

"We're jamming," Blanchard said, "but that means
that if the Azzies are looking this way we're lit up like a
skyscraper. Turn us back in. I'm going to pop a drone."

Gordani cursed again, but Chase felt the LAV turn
quickly to one side. Some mechanism clanged in the wall
to the right of his head, and one of the few dark monitors
at Freid's and Blanchard's stations burst to life. At first
it showed sky, nearly cloudless and spinning overhead,
but then it stabilized as the camera dipped toward the
ground. The Aztlan landscape glared brightly in the midday sun as the camera's image systems struggled to balance the bright ground and the brighter sky that still filled
part of the picture.

"Drone's away!" yelled Blanchard. The *Rapier's
Touch* carried two remote-piloted drones, one in a covered rack on each side. The right rack, the one that had
launched, carried a short-duration, solid-fuel winged
drone that was more like a rocket than a small aircraft.
It was designed to do just what it was doing: carry a
video camera quickly to something the T-bird wanted to
see. A single, small electric motor controlled the drone
while it loitered over the target, but its flight time was
very limited. It had one weapon, the equivalent of an
assault rifle.

The left rack carried a much heavier combat drone.
Designed to fly along with the T-bird, the combat drone
mounted a pair of light machine guns and its own onboard autopilot and targeting system. Blanchard could
command it directly, or give it a general order that it
would then carry out to the best of its dog-brain ability.
The combat drone was very expensive and used only as
a last resort.

"Over target!" Blanchard yelled again. The drone's video feed was coming over clear on the monitor near Freid. The truck was on its side and burning. A complete ruin. Two figures could be seen moving near the truck, trying to drag injured or dead comrades clear of the wreckage. The camera zoomed in to one of the soldiers. He seemed to be alternately talking into, and banging on, what could only be a handset radio.

"Damn," continued Blanchard. "There's at least one radio."

"I confirm," said Freid. "Can't tell if it's working."

"Roger that," replied Gordani. "Take them."

The drone suddenly dropped low and fast, but kept itself centered on the men. There was no way to tell how far away they were; the level of magnification in use wasn't displayed on the monitor when the gun fired. Chase saw only the telltale plumes of dust and blood rise up around the soldiers. The drone shot over the wreckage and then began to work its way around.

"Again," said Freid.

The drone turned hard, and the burning truck came quickly into view once more. Blanchard angled it clear of the plume of smoke and brought it in for another pass. On the screen Chase could see a soldier crawling for the truck. Even though it was afire, it still offered some degree of refuge. Dust burst up from the ground near him, his body jerked, and he stopped crawling. The drone continued on.

After a moment, Freid spoke. "That's it."

"Roger, angling for drone retrieval," said Gordani.

Chase felt the LAV slow as Gordani turned the vehicle away from the drone and allowed it to catch up. He'd match its speed and then Blanchard would land it back on the rack, ejecting the now-useless solid-fuel booster just before he did. Then, Chase surmised, Gordani would open up the throttle to get them as far away as possible from wreckage.

Though they'd jammed any radio alerts, the dark plume of smoke winding its way into the sky spoke loud and clear, one of the most ancient of all warning signs.

14

Cara wasn't hard to find: there were only so many places where she could be inside their temporary shelter.

The capture net had malfunctioned as they'd tried to recover the drone, and both the drone and the rack were damaged. They'd continued on for some time with the rack open and the drone jutting out from it because Gordani wanted to put the burning truck as far behind them as possible. As night approached, Blanchard detected no signs of pursuit so they decided to ground the T-bird for repairs. After landing the craft into a space between two large outcroppings of rock, they made camp.

Chase walked around within the camouflage tent that covered the vehicle in its entirety, masking both its silhouette and its heat from possible observers. The thermal covering also created an almost-comfortable warmth. Blanchard was working on top of the T-bird, methodically repairing the drone rack. Gordani was alternately inside and outside the *Rapier's Touch*, trying to rig the electronics for something Chase wanted to try. Chase had offered to help, but the pilot had politely refused, seeming to take the offer as a personal challenge. Freid had been sitting inside too, periodically projecting herself astrally and surveying the area for pursuit. She'd been the one to suggest that he talk to Cara. Chase had also noticed that Cara continued to be upset following the one-sided fight with the truck, but he'd been reluctant to attempt a talk ever since their confrontation over her chips.

She was seated on a small rock half, jacked into her simdeck. Chase froze and watched for a moment, but

this time her body language was different. She seemed
tense and excited by what she was sensing from the chip,
but the stress Chase had observed the day before was
absent. He moved forward carefully, until close enough
to see that the chip in the deck was one of the brightly
labeled commercial ones he'd seen in her bag. He was
torn between whether to leave her alone or to risk another
confrontation when she reached down and poked the disconnect switch. She blinked a few times, and Chase could
see the traces of barely formed tears glinting in the shafts
of the crew's work lights. Then she breathed in sharply,
her body shaking once, spasming, before its natural
looseness returned. She turned and looked over at him.
In her eyes he could read nothing.

"What were you chipping?" Chase asked, trying to
keep his voice even. He didn't want to set her off.

She shrugged and pulled the chip from its slot. *Against
the Hive,* she said. "Euphoria's last one."

"Any good?"

She shrugged again. "Could have been more realistic,
I suppose, but the action stuff and the effects were wiz.
The ending is kinda rough to take, though."

She was looking at the chip in her hand and turning it
slowly, end over end. "Something bothering you?" he
asked.

She didn't answer, just continued turning the chip and
looking at it.

"Okay," Chase said finally. "Blanchard told me we
should be ready to go again in about an hour. I'll be
inside if you need me." He turned and began to walk
toward the rear of the *Rapier's Touch.*

"Did they have to die?"

Chase turned sharply at Cara's words. They weren't
quite what he'd expected. "Who?" he asked, but then
knew the answer. It should have been obvious.

She looked away, but he could read coldness and anger. "The soldiers."

"Unfortunately, there was no other choice."

"No other choice?" The tone of her voice rose with her gaze. "We could have let them *live*."

"And if they had, *we* might be dead right now."

"*Might* be dead. They definitely are."

Chase took a step toward her and held out his hands. "Look, there's no point in arguing this. What's done is done."

Her mouth tightened and she shook her head. "It's that easy for you to just let it go? What about their families? Don't you care—"

Chase cut her off, letting his own voice rise. "Of course I care. I regret every death I've ever been connected with. Do you?"

Cara had been about to snap out more angry words, but his last comment stopped her. She blinked.

"You seemed to deal pretty easily with the 'accidental' deaths caused by your friends' political statements." He took a step forward, his hands clenched now. "Do you think about them, Cara? Do you think about those 'accidents' dying, suddenly and for no reason they could imagine? Do you think about their families?"

Cara blinked at him again, and her mouth worked silently as her face danced with emotions she couldn't entirely control. Chase knew he should stop, knew he should let it be, but he didn't. There were things about who Cara Villiers was and had done that ate at him. He'd ignored them for the girl she'd once been. Ignored them until now.

"Have you ever thought about those families hearing that someone they loved had survived the explosion, might even have survived the fall to the ground, only to drown, to *asphyxiate*, in the chemical foam that had been spread there to save her life?"

He raged at her, though his voice was barely louder than a whisper, his face almost pressed against hers. She'd stiffened as he leaned in, her eyes wide and frightened, but could not move.

"Do you ever think about the fact that she couldn't unbuckle the seat belt because her arms were broken? Do you think about her mouth being so filled, so choked, with the foam that she couldn't sing her songs of power? Does it bother you that her beloved Eagle, her fucking totem, let her die falling from a fucking plane, from the fucking sky, so that a bunch of buttholes could make a point to the airline about the construction of a new terminal near an eco-safe zone on a different continent entirely?''

As the words had run away from him, he saw something settle in her. Something he'd said had connected and her face lost some of its fear. The fright was still there, but now it was backed by what could have been understanding. Her left arm spasmed, her hand flexed, and she pulled it to her lap and held it there. The energy fled from him, and he glanced away. His own body was stiff, almost shaking, as its artificial portions sought to do what they'd been built to do: remove the threat, stop whatever caused him such pain. The source of the pain wasn't here, though, and he hadn't been there when it might have mattered. He looked down, away, then took a step back, trying to regain control of himself.

She took a deep breath. "I . . . I didn't know," was what came out first. "It wasn't us. They never . . .''

He didn't bring his face up, but his eyes locked with hers. She seemed almost calm, much more controlled than he, but her skin had blanched nearly pure white. "I know," he said. "Do you think I'd have helped you if I'd believed you were even remotely responsible?''

Cara looked away, said nothing.

He stood up and focused on controlling his breathing. He'd let his anger dominate him, something that hadn't happened in a long time. There were times when letting it happen was necessary, but this certainly wasn't one of them.

"I kill only when I have to," he said, "and by god I carry every single death with me. Just say the word and we'll stop now. I'll take you wherever you want to go, and that will be the end of it.''

"And my father will die. . . .''

"Maybe. Maybe his guards will stop it, maybe one of them will do it. Maybe a lot of things, Cara. The question is, is it worth it to you? Can you live with doing what has to be done?"

She was quiet for a while, almost long enough for Chase to take that as her answer. Then she turned and looked up at him. There was that something in her eyes again, that something he couldn't name.

"Yes," she said finally. "I can."

15

Gordo looked at Chase out of sunken eyes. Leaning into the shaft of white light from the reading lamp over Freid's position, his already thin face looked almost skeletal. The long fingers of one hand played absently with the stubble on his cheek. "What the frag was that all about?"

Chase looked back, away from his datadeck, which was attached to a notebook computer, and wired to the T-bird and the small satellite dish set up on the desert floor. "Old anger, misplaced blame and all that shit." He shifted slightly to stop the small ache that was beginning to set in from squatting.

Gordani nodded. "Is there going to be a problem?"

"On the trip?"

The pilot nodded again.

"No." Chase sighed. "At least I don't think so. Things'll probably stay quiet for a while." He looked at the liquid-crystal display of the small computer. A flashing blue cursor demanded his attention. "God knows I don't have the energy anymore."

"Look, I know who she is," Gordo said.

"Oh?" Chase let his gaze wander slowly over to the other man.

The pilot smiled. "Don't even *try* to start scamming me, chummer. I know it ain't my damn business, but I'm just letting you know that Death comes knocking, I know what the biz is."

"That makes one of us."

"Church, I'm serious."

Chase nodded. "I know you are, but it's not your deal. Besides, if Death has a bigger gun than me, maybe you don't want to know about it."

"Maybe, but I think you'll get the job done. And when you do maybe you can put in a good word with her father, and then make sure the word works its way down to whoever it is that doles out Fuchi's freelance assignments. We'd be mighty pleased. Who knows? Maybe Blanchard would even give you a pass on that dinner you owe him."

Chase laughed. "I'll think about it. Now, let me sit there."

"What? You need to sit to think?" Despite the jab, the pilot slid out of his seat, dropping into the one Cara had occupied earlier.

"No," Chase said, "but I do need to get some circulation back in my legs."

Gordani's eyebrows rose in mock surprise. "You mean to tell me you've still got your own legs?"

"Yeah, and if you'll let me work on the biz you don't know anything about I might let you keep yours."

The pilot stood as tall as the T-bird's low ceiling would let him. "Hey, no problem, it's only my fragging LAV. I'll just go and sit with Freid, if I can find wherever you threw her out to. I could use the warmth."

Chase ignored the last part. "You do that. I'll fire one of the guns when I'm done."

"Great. I'll let Blanchard know so he's not too surprised." Gordani worked his way to the rear of the vehicle and out the rear access door. He closed it behind him, but not completely. If something happened, he wanted to be able to get back in fast. Chase didn't blame him.

Chase reached out and pulled the dataline cable from

its pouch on his datadeck and uncoiled it. He connected one end with his own datajack, and the other with the deck itself. He willed the piece of microtronics to life.

Instantly, a menu of choices superimposed itself in the air before him, fed directly into his mind by the datadeck's simsense circuits. It was only visual at this point.

He commanded the deck to validate its connection to the portable computer, initiate the satellite-tracking programs in its memory, and position the satellite dish at the most appropriate target. The databanks told him that the satellite was a Pueblo Infonet VII in geosynchronous orbit over Phoenix. According to the records it normally handled educational traffic to and from Pueblo schools in outlying areas. He suspected that it also carried transponders to handle more covert traffic, but he had no use for those. Besides, they were probably protected by many of the same systems that protected the more sensitive, ground-based Pueblo government systems. Chase didn't want to frag with any of that. The relatively low-band width educational channels would serve him well enough even though they'd be unable to handle a full Matrix interface. He'd have to resort to an icon interface, which he would cybernetically command through his own deck. An interface was still an interface, however, and in case of trouble he'd lose precious nanoseconds as the system worked through it. Chase commanded his deck to link up with the satellite.

The link was nearly instantaneous, but Chase could sense the lag in the connection procedure between his system and the satellite. He'd forgotten about this distance-and-processor lag and had never run the Matrix while having to deal with it. He was suddenly pleased he wasn't running full Matrix. The cumulative delay between the interface and the satellite would have been enough to throw him off completely. An experienced decker, someone like his former teammate Lucifer, or even Lachesis, would have no problem. He, however, was nowhere near their class. The satellite's onboard routing system responded and the words hung in the air before him.

> > > > > [Welcome to the Pueblo Education Services Information Network. Please input your passcode now.] < < < < <

He dropped his hands to his lap and used his deck's cybernetic link to issue commands. The keyboard on the personal computer would only have slowed him down more. He initiated a program he'd won nearly a decade ago in a private game of blackjack in Atlantic City. It might be ten years old, but the program had been custom back then and so Chase didn't doubt it would be up to the task now.

The program spoke to the satellite, lied and cajoled it into believing he was some poor, sick child calling in from home for the day's assignments. The system gave him entrance.

Chase commanded his program to again fool the system into giving him unrestricted access to its capabilities. As he suspected, the satellite had a secret system, but his program was smart enough not to try and deceive those circuits. Instead, he routed his signal to a ground station in downtown Phoenix and hooked into a long-distance telecom line. In his mind he dialed Teek's number in Manhattan.

The number rang, and he initiated one of the trace-detection programs his deck held in memory. It appeared as a small window hanging within his field of vision, just next to the status readouts for the deck and the connection. It flashed **CONNECTING:::NO TRACE DETECTED** in cool blue letters. If anything changed, he'd be ready.

Fed to him by the deck, the number rang again clearly in his head, and he mentally tensed. He expected some surveillance on Teek's line. Whoever his enemies were, he figured they must have discovered his connection to Teek by now. The moment someone answered, the trace would engage and Chase would be ready to trigger his own programs to stomp on it.

The line's dead sound changed and became an open hollowness. "8219," Teek said. Chase didn't answer. He waited.

LINE ACTIVE:::NO TRACE DETECTED

"8219," his friend's voice repeated.

LINE ACTIVE:::NO TRACE DETECTED

"Hello?"

LINE ACTIVE:::NO TRACE DETECTED

Damn, thought Chase, as he mentally toggled the system to accept voice input. "Teek, it's Church."

"What the hell? You using one of those other phone companies again?"

"No, it's just a strange connection. But I haven't got time to talk. Anything going on concerning me or that I should know about?"

A moment's pause, and then, "No, nothing that I've heard."

"You're sure?"

"Yes, very. Want me to ask around?"

Needlessly, Chase shook his head. "No, don't bother. But if you do hear anything, send it to this electronic mail address. Ready?"

"Ready. Go ahead."

"D-E-N dash five-three-zero-three-zero-eight-six-two passcode CAVER, all capitals, and put an end code of Priest on it. I'll get it."

"Hey, I recognize enough of that to know you're walking straight into Hell."

"Or Heaven, as the case may be. I look on it as rather appropriate."

"Good luck. Next one's on me."

"Deal." Chase commanded the system to disconnect, then stared at the blue letters flashing in his mind. Nothing. No trace had been detected. Had Teek found it and dealt with it? Had Lachesis? He shook his head and resolved to think about it later.

He sent his attention back to the running telecom program and fed it an access number not all that different from the one he'd given Teek. This time, he primed the system to accept a visual signal and reproduce the image within his sight. He himself wasn't generating any image, which would be a slight to the intended receiver, but such was life. He hadn't the time to rig in a video pickup to the system just to avoid stepping on some virtual toes.

Chase terminated the trace-detection program; there would be no traces on this number. No one dared. The trace-detection program's visual window faded from view only to be replaced by another, this one filled in completely with black. Chase spoke as soon as the connection was established.

"I seek entrance," he said.

A voice responded from the black. It sounded grim and cold and held nothing of life. Even through the interfaces and filters, Chase felt himself shiver slightly. "Speak and be judged."

"I seek Lachesis."

There was a pause. "You are incomplete. You cannot enter here."

"The datapath I'm using can't handle a Matrix signal. If Lachesis is there, tell her that Priest wishes a word with her."

"Priest." The word came out slowly, stretched out to the breaking point. "You did not come to the funeral."

"I did not know of Lucifer's death until Lachesis told me a few days ago. Otherwise I would have been there."

"I am denied you. I cannot prove you are who you say you are."

"I understand. If Lachesis is there, have her enter the connection. I can prove it with her."

"She is not here."

"Do you expect her to return?"

"Eventually."

"Then tell her I'm coming. Tell her I'll see her in a few days."

"Your flesh is coming here, Priest?"

"Yes."

"He will be pleased."

Chase felt his body tense. He would go to Denver; there was no way to avoid it. For all that had come before, and in spite of all that had passed since, he would have to see him.

"Tell him I'm coming." Before the voice could answer, Chase reached up and pulled the cable from his datajack, instantly severing the line. He sat there and listened to the muffled sounds of Blanchard working on the T-bird's hull.

Denver. If he was going to be in Denver, he'd have to see Shiva. He had no choice.

16

The *Rapier's Touch* bucked for a moment in a sudden gust of crosswind and then responded to Gordani's stabilizing commands. Chase found his mind endlessly preoccupied with his forthcoming encounters in Denver when he should have been mulling over Cara's problems instead.

Cara Villiers was in her own world, too, tuned out from the interior of the LAV and intent only on the music and accompanying video feed from her simdeck. Chase had been casual about trying to get a look, but he was reassured to see that the simchip in the deck was yet another commercial one, a recording by her old friends L'Infâme. He watched Cara occasionally during the trip

north, but she continued to stare blankly at the cabin's
far wall. Every so often her left hand twitched. Mostly,
though, Chase thought about Denver.

Only when Gordani's voice awakened him from a light
doze did Chase realize he must have fallen asleep. "Make
sure you're strapped in good. We're coming within sensor range of the Aztlan-Pueblo border units and may have
to do some jockeying."

"Roger." Chase leaned over and visually checked
Cara's straps. They seemed tight enough; he'd helped her
fasten them when they'd left the temporary camp just
before dawn. She'd thanked him, but hadn't said much
else.

Blanchard's voice came over the headset. "I've got
high-band sensor echoes in the foothills, bearing four-
seven degrees, about seven klicks."

"Read that," Gordani responded. "Freid?"

Chase glanced over at the mage, whose back was to
him, and caught her nod. "On my way." She shifted in
the chair, rotated it toward her console, and visibly relaxed. Her eyes closed and her breathing slowed.

Chase watched her monitors and the terrain that her
astral form was presumably now flying over. She'd tried
to explain what the world looked like from astral space,
but he still couldn't picture it. Try to imagine the world
as if the only light was the light that came from within,
she'd said. The more alive something was, the more light
it gave. Imagine that texture was emotive, and not tactile.
Imagine that physical presence was defined by how close
it was to its natural form. The more refined, the more
manufactured, the less tangible—

"Confirm definite KS-band radar sweep," said Blanchard. "The signals are getting stronger, so either we're
in an area where the reflections happen to be focusing,
or the chopper's moving this way."

"Roger," Gordani replied. "Prepare to jam. Wait for
my word."

Chase carefully reached out to touch Cara's leg. Startled, she jumped and turned to him wide-eyed.

"There may be problems. You might want to jack out."

She blinked rapidly, then reached up to pull the cable from the datajack. Her eyes focused on him. "What? Did you say something?"

"There may be problems."

She nodded and quickly stuffed the simdeck and cable into her bag. Blanchard's voice came again as Chase helped her stow the bag under the seat.

"I've got a second active source almost directly ahead. Suggest you alter course to three-two-seven," said Blanchard.

Chase felt the T-bird change its heading before Gordani replied. "Roger, heading changed. I'm either going to have to slow down in this terrain or else trigger the ground-imaging radar to handle it."

"Slow down. I'll bet dinner that whatever they are has passive detectors too."

"Roger. Slowing down."

The T-bird decelerated through a shallow turn and Chase felt himself pressed lightly against the acceleration harness. He could see the first rays of sun beginning to appear across the ground. The sky was already light enough that the T-bird's automatic sensors had deactivated the low-light video systems.

"Church?" It was Gordani.

Chase reached up and reactivated his headset. "I read you."

"What's Freid doing?"

"Um, as far as I can tell, she projected astrally just after you last spoke with her."

"Can you see her?"

"Only the back of her head." Chase turned toward Cara, who'd been listening in on her own headset. She nodded and leaned to her left to get a better view of the mage's face.

"Uh," she said as Chase reached out and activated her microphone, "this is Cara . . . um . . . she looks tense, sweating. . . . I can't really see her face, though, with all the gear.''

"Drek!"

"Church . . .'' Chase was looking at Cara when Gordani spoke, and from her expression he thought she might have suddenly been disconnected from the intercom. She looked at him, puzzled, and tapped her headset to confirm it. ''We may have a problem . . .''

Chase shrugged at Cara, then turned to have a look at Freid. He noticed a slight jerk of the mage's shoulder.

"I take it you're armed," said the pilot.

"Yes."

"The girl said Freid looks tense, like something was happening. If she got ambushed out there in astral space, we might be in danger. While her astral body's in astral space, she's creating a link between there and here. It's like a pipe or a conduit. Somebody in astral space could toss a spell down that pipe and detonate it right here.''

"Oh, great."

"So, chummer, you gotta watch her. If she starts freaking out, or things seem really bad, or if magic energy starts leaking out of her, you've got to geek her, fast.''

Chase stiffened. "What?"

"You've got to kill her. It's the only way to protect us. Freid knows.''

Chase stared at the back of her head and counted the beads of sweat running from her hairline and down her back. Four.

Blanchard's voice cut in, quiet and controlled, but Chase could sense the tension in it. "Gordo's right. You've got to be ready to do it. Usually I keep an eye on her when she's astral. We haven't had a problem yet, but . . .''

A new line of sweat began on the mage's neck and trickled quickly to join the growing stain just below her collar. Chase remembered her smell. Her left leg lashed out and thumped against the control console.

"All right," he said, eyes turning away from Freid

and toward Cara. She was staring at him, fear growing slowly on her face. He wondered what his own face betrayed; surely not calm anymore. He reached under his jacket and let his fingers slide over the hilt of his heavy pistol. He felt its warmth as soon as the grip settled into his palm. The weapon's status information appeared superimposed over Cara's face. He drew the weapon and brought it up to point at the back of Freid's head. The red targeting spot obediently centered there and waited, flashing. He braced the weapon with both hands. Cara brought up one hand to cover her mouth. Better she should cover her eyes, he thought.

"I'm ready," he said over the intercom.

"Good thing," came Blanchard's voice, "'cause we've got definite trouble. I've got three active sources, two are terrain echoes, but the third is vectoring inbound directly ahead. It's airborne. Easy money says they're looking for us."

"Frag!" said Gordani. "We stay cold for as long as we can, then we see how much heat they can handle. Get the search radar ready."

"Search radar to hot standby. Enabling weapons."

"Roger."

Chase, looking past his pistol and the targeting spot, could see the terrain clearly on Freid's monitors. The sun was up enough to light almost everything, but there were still deep shadows. He hoped some would be large enough to hide the *Rapier's Touch*. Something dark stood out against the sky for a split second on the forward monitor.

It was Blanchard who spoke. "Target, bearing three-five-eight, course two-five-one, speed one-five-zero. Heat profile roughly matches a light attack chopper, probably Cuervo type. Forward-looking active sensors only and full thermo passives. Single forward minigun, right and left rocket pods, and a missile rail on each load wing."

"Track her passively if you can," came Gordani's reply.

"Roger."

Gordani spoke again. "Church, anything different with Freid?"

"Not that I can see." Chase glanced over at Cara, who shook her head. Apparently Gordani had put her back in the link.

"Roger, let me know."

An alarm siren screamed in the tight cabin, and Chase felt the T-bird immediately slam into a hard right turn. The cool green of one of Blanchard's monitors had begun to flash red. The gunner spoke.

"We're painted! KS-radar locked and tracking. I've begun jamming."

"Let's see how big their *cojones* are today," Gordani said. "Blanchard, engage at will. I'm coming off the deck."

Chase tightened his grip on the heavy pistol as the dull throb of the T-bird's engines rose to a deafening roar. The ground on Freid's monitors dropped away as Gordani brought the LAV up and into flight. Data and graphic displays flashed to life as the *Rapier's* own sensors went active and began hunting for targets.

"Confirm, three targets, light attack class," Blanchard said. "Two are out of position. Engaging the local target."

Chase watched the monitor displays shift as the main turret traversed. Suddenly, the LAV's chain gun began to fire. Chase could see the bursts of smoke from the firing quickly swept away on the wind, followed immediately by a series of sharp flashes in the distance as the rounds struck their target. He couldn't see the helicopter itself against the high rock formations behind it, but the flashes and sparks of the rounds impacting marked it clearly. Light, flame, and smoke blossomed suddenly from the sparks, then were lost from view as the turret rotated to set up for the next target. Gordani slammed the LAV into another hard turn as ground views filled the left-side monitors.

"Confirm one target down. Enemy One is moving—" Blanchard stopped for a moment, his normally calm voice suddenly taking on an edge. "New target, emitting KS and LR bands. Where the frag did she come—*Launch!* I have multiple launches inbound!"

The *Rapier's Touch* accelerated even faster, and Gordani banked her hard and then down as he tried to evade the incoming missiles by bringing the T-bird closer to the ground. Chase heard Cara shriek. He glanced at her and saw she'd pulled her legs in close and was covering her head with her arms.

The LAV banked again. "Two incoming," Blanchard reported. "ETI twenty-eight seconds. Full jamming, blowing flares."

The rear monitor lit up as the flare ejector fired a series of mini-rockets. A fraction of a second after clearing the tubes, they erupted and burned with a white light hot enough to nearly blind the cameras. With any luck, the missiles were tracking the T-bird's heat signature and would be distracted by the flares.

"No luck. Missiles still tracking," said Blanchard. "They're homing on the chopper's radar. Show her our tail so I can use chaff."

"Roger."

The LAV turned again, and in the left monitor Chase saw two points of light bank after them and continue to close. The T-bird rocked slightly, the interior cabin echoing with the sharp sound of metal on metal.

"We're taking fire!" Blanchard shouted.

"Do it!" Gordani yelled.

More mini-rockets fired and exploded immediately, spreading a bright curtain of metallic debris between the *Rapier's Touch* and the new helicopter that was using its own radar to guide the missiles. The T-bird slammed into a hard right turn, hoping to use the chaff and the terrain to break radar contact long enough to lose the missiles.

Chase saw Freid's head pitch to the side against the movement of the LAV. He was having trouble keeping the gun trained on her.

"*Drek!*" howled Blanchard. Chase had only enough time to see a flash on one of the monitors before the missile struck. The thunderous explosion slammed him sideways as metal shrieked and tore directly above him. One of the panels in front of Freid, and something behind Chase, exploded in a fountain of smoke and sparks. The T-bird, bucking from the impact, scraped hard against something along its left side. Chase was thrown again, his outstretched hands slamming against the structural support alongside him. The cybernetic contact with his weapon winked out as it bounced from his hands and struck the floor, sliding to a stop a few steps away.

As the T-bird dropped, Chase was thrown upward and then down again into his seat as the vehicle bounced along the ground. Freid began a slow, mournful wail, and Chase saw her begin to thrash against her restraints. The cabin seemed to grow brighter as her hand slapped at one of the hanging toys, snapped its cord, and tossed it to the floor.

Letting his cybernetic reflexes take over, Chase smashed the palm of his hand against his restraint's quick-release buckle and threw himself forward toward his heavy pistol. The slower buckle held him for a moment, then let him go. He hit the cabin floor faster than he'd expected as the T-bird rose again, its engines straining to gain altitude.

Flat against the floor, he reached out to grab the weapon. The cybernetic link engaged, haltingly, as he rolled onto his back and braced himself, one foot shoved against the base of Freid's seat, the other against his own. He pulled the weapon up as Freid's toy hit the floor and bounced away into the shadows.

She was almost howling, her hands pawing at her headset and the collar of her jump suit. The cabin *was* brighter. Chase felt sudden heat and commanded the weapon's safety off as its targeting spot focused on the side of her head. Her hands suddenly clenched into fists and she screamed as a haze of red grew around her.

The T-bird banked hard into another turn and at least one missile leaped from its rack. The barrel of his heavy pistol was less than a meter from her head as more rounds struck the T-bird's hull and ricocheted away. Hearing the sounds, Chase suddenly realized that at this range his pistol's armor-piercing slug wouldn't stop when it hit her. It would continue to travel, through her, and then into the electronics. Then, maybe, it would stop. If not, it would ricochet madly in the tiny cabin. He hesitated.

Freid strained forward against her harness, and her head snapped back. The red haze of energy suddenly seemed to flow back into her and her hands spasmed opened. *"Christ!"* she screamed and collapsed limply against the restraints.

Chase jumped up, and grabbing the back of her chair, pulled himself to her. Now standing, he could hear the steady stammer of the LAV's chain gun firing. He holstered the pistol and pushed some of the optical gear away from her face. Freid looked as though she'd just taken a severe beating. Her entire face was one huge bruise, blue-black, swollen, and ugly. She blinked at him with horribly bloodshot eyes. She grabbed at his arms and he saw that her hands were bruised in the same way. All over her body the capillaries in her skin had burst. She started to manage a slight smile for him, but then realization hit. Her gaze snapped to the monitors.

Chase kept one hand firmly gripped on her shoulder as support for them both, bracing the other against the monitor bay's support brace. Freid reached up and slipped the optical goggles back into place.

"Gordo," she said. Chase couldn't hear the response; the cable connecting his headset to the intercom had snapped when he'd lunged for his gun. "I'm back." Her voice was weak, barely audible above the roar of the vector-thrust engines and the occasional stammer of the chain gun. "Give me targets."

Chase looked over the monitors that were still working and saw nothing but rushing ground and the quick image of a white trail of smoke across the sky in one of the views.

"No . . . no . . . ," she said, and thumbed the joystick control built into her chair's armrest. The image on

one of the monitors shifted quickly and centered on a
hill. The image stabilized as a helicopter crested it. Chase
recognized the design as an Aguilar, Aztlan's premier
attack helicopter type. If he remembered the trideo show
he'd seen on modern combat aircraft, the copter was agile
and packed a high-grade sensor package and a broad as-
sortment of weapons. Its one weakness was its light armor plating, the designer having traded protection for
maneuverability. The Aguilar passed over the hill, and
as its nose dropped, rockets exploded from launchers on
each of its stubby weapon load-out wings. The *Rapier's
Touch* moved clumsily, but dashed behind a rock out-
cropping, dodging the unguided missiles.

Chase heard the roar of another missile launch from
the T-bird, and saw the bright flare of its solid-fuel engine light up one of the monitors. It sped toward the
Aztlan helicopter. Points of light leaped from the attack
chopper as it spit flares to distract the missile. It was the
same technique the *Rapier's Touch* had tried earlier, with
no success. This time, though, their own dumber missile
was fooled by the new sources of heat and turned toward
one, exploding harmlessly against the scrub desert floor.

A targeting cross hairs had appeared on the monitor
showing the pursuing helicopter, and Freid was franti-
cally pushing console buttons. The cross hairs flashed
urgently. "Nothing," she said into her microphone.
"Secondaries are out."

Chase saw muzzle flashes and smoke from the chain
gun, heard the rounds hitting the T-bird. Something
punched through the cabin wall not far from Cara, then
buried itself in the emergency storage locker. Still curled
up tight in her chair, she didn't even seem to notice.

Chase looked down and scanned the controls in front
of Freid. The console displays gave manual readings on
most of the T-bird's weapon systems. The chain gun's
ammo load was getting perilously low, and Chase had no
idea if there was a secondary ammo source. The gun
fired again.

Gordani was leading the Aguilar on a winding path a

few meters above an old, dried-out river bed. Any loose debris not scattered by the passing of the heavy vector-thrust LAV was whipped by the ground-effect of the helicopter. No other pursuers showed on any of the monitors or the intermittent radar display, so Chase assumed they were either far out of position or else had been turned into burning wrecks.

A small panel on the display caught Chase's attention. "The drone," he said.

Freid heard him and shook her head. "The combat drone's jammed in place. I guess we got hit. . . . It's not going anywhere."

"What about the other one?"

"Gun's too small. It'd barely scratch the paint."

"Would they know that?"

Her head snapped up. "Gordo, did you hear that?" she said into her microphone. She paused, then reached for the cable dangling at his side. "You're off-line." She grabbed the cable end and plugged it into her console next to her own cable. The T-bird banked hard again, and Chase heard a faint scraping along the left side.

Gordani spoke in his ear: "Hear what? Somebody better have a brilliant idea, quick. We're gonna be shootin' blanks in a second."

Chase adjusted his headset. "The drone. *We* know it's not much, but they don't. All they'll know is that the meanest-looking missile they ever saw is heading their way."

"They'll just jam us," Blanchard said over the intercom. "They haven't covered those frequencies yet, but . . ."

"Let's see how fast they think," came Gordani. "Blanchard, take over the chain gun. Hold the last of the ammo. Freid, I know you're hurtin', but we can use whatever you can give us."

She nodded and Chase squeezed her shoulder. "You've got it," she said.

"And Church, can you remote-pilot the drone?"

"Well enough, I suspect."

"Let's do it. When I yell, pop the drone."

The *Rapier's Touch* turned again, and seemed to drop a few meters. Chase lost sight of the Aguilar on the monitors, but he was more concerned with the controls Freid was quickly pointing out to him. She assumed he knew how to use them, so she just pointed out their location. Fortunately, she was right, mostly.

"Here we go!" said Gordani. Chase felt the T-bird gaining altitude as the blurred sides of the riverbed dropped away on the monitors. The Aguilar was there, maybe a thousand meters out and running parallel.

"Pop it!"

Chase reached for the button, but Blanchard's cybernetic command was far faster. The drone's rack cover slammed open, and Chase heard the drone roar from its mounting. On the monitor showing the drone's point of view Chase saw only sky, so he eased the small joystick forward. Regardless of its actual orientation, he'd be pushing the drone toward the ground. The horizon and then the ground slid into view, and Chase caught the edge of the Azzie chopper as it slipped from sight. The solid-fuel booster on the drone kept it flying at a constant speed, and Chase began to swing it around toward the Aztlan helicopter.

Gordani spoke in Chase's ear, "Church! Come at her from the front! Everybody else get read—"

More rounds slammed into the T-bird's hull, but Chase tried to ignore them as he commanded the sluggish drone. It was built for speed, not maneuverability. He was suddenly concerned about getting the drone anywhere near the fast, agile chopper.

The chopper appeared on his monitor as it pulled up to avoid a piece of the broken terrain. He was behind it, but faster. A thin stream of oily smoke waved in the air some distance ahead of the chopper. It was the *Rapier's Touch*, and she was smoking. Not bad, but it was enough to let the helicopter keep her in sight.

"Gordo," Chase said into his microphone, "you're going to have to keep it straight for a minute."

"Frag your minute. Just do it!" yelled the pilot.

Chase cut the corner on the helicopter's course, and then it quickly slipped from view off the monitor. A second later the drone overtook the T-bird. The smoke was coming from the left-rear thrust port, which showed signs of heavy damage. Most of the LAV did.

Chase rolled the winged drone and pushed it hard toward the ground. The desert floor rushed up, an incomprehensible blur of brown, tan, and sparse green. The image stabilized and Chase brought the drone's nose up to slow it. The Aguilar banked through a turn in the riverbed and came into view. Knowing they would be ineffectual, Chase triggered the drone's small machine gun, hoping they'd at least see the muzzle flash. Bright flares ejected from the helicopter as it suddenly pulled up, headed for the sky. Chase pulled up after it, keeping it directly ahead of him. He felt the T-bird's engines surge as they too gained altitude and turned, hard.

Suddenly, darkness appeared, flowing like a great wave in the air in front of the helicopter. Beside him, Freid gasped at the strain of her magics. The helicopter darted to one side, but couldn't avoid the sudden dark cloud. They passed through part of it, slipping in and quickly out again. Chase pulled the drone around it, catching sight of the chopper again on the far side. He was nearly on top of it, meters away

Chase started as the *Rapier's Touch* was filling the rest of the monitor, leaping into view a few dozen meters to the far side of the helicopter. The chain gun blared at pointblank range. The main canopy shattered and the Aztlan chopper twisted violently in flight. Chase saw a flash of whirring metal and then nothing as his monitor exploded with static. Metal howled and shattered just outside, barely audible over the engines. The LAV lurched suddenly, tossing Chase against the far side of the cabin. His shoulder smashed into a brace.

The T-bird rolled in the opposite direction, and he was flung forward against the back of Freid's chair. Loose cases and supplies knocked free from the storage lockers bounced around him and across the console. He wrapped his arms around the mage and the chair, and felt her grab and hold them in place. A vibration began somewhere to the rear.

The engine was whining, a terrible metal-on-metal noise that only seemed to be growing. The T-bird lost altitude and Chase felt it lurch as it fought against Gordani's mental commands. The wild pitch of the engines dropped suddenly as they were throttled back and the LAV's flight stabilized. Freid's grip on Chase's arms loosened. He looked up as she pushed the goggles clear of her face, which was bruised, battered, and streaked with sweat. She smiled. "Did you hear him?"

Chase shook his head and shifted his feet to better brace himself. "No, I lost the cable." He tensed himself, prepared to hold them both though the coming battle.

She squeezed his hand and he could see the glaze of sleep coming into her eyes.

"Welcome to Pueblo," she said.

17

Chase kept the window open and let the cooler night air fill the room. Noises entered, too, the sounds of a city that could not sleep. He understood.

Denver.

The *Rapier's Touch* had just barely managed to slip across the Pueblo border when most of her avionics began to fail. Through sheer skill, Gordani kept the T-bird airborne as Blanchard bravadoed their way past the Pueblo Forces lines. Lucky for them, their high-profile kill—on the military sensor net anyway—had earned them a degree of respect from the defensive forces posted there. Blanchard's radio conversation had ended with a chuckle and an unseen grin, and they were allowed past.

Gordani nursed the T-bird another hundred and sixty kilometers north, before grounding her near a small camp known as Keane's Corner. Here they could get limited repairs for the bird and some basic medical attention for Freid. The mechanic cum paramedic living at Keane's Corner was reluctant to do much for her beyond superficial treatment of her few external injuries. Hearing that she was a mage had made him just a little nervous. He also knew enough from his training to realize that the medicines and treatments usually administered to a "normal" person were more dangerous to a magician. A mage's nervous system, wired tight from the workings of magic, was far more susceptible to harm from chemicals and pharmaceuticals than a mundane's. That would limit the possible treatment and, thus, Freid's recovery.

With the help of some local herbal inducements, she slept in the cushioned hammock they set up for her all the rest of the way to Denver. Chase manned her position as best he could, quietly thankful that they weren't going to have to put up any further resistance.

Cara became nearly hysterical during the running fight with the Aztlan forces, to the extent that she had still not regained control even after it was all over. Refusing the strong dose of tranquilizers that the paramedic offered, she did accept the help of more conventional administrations. Chase made several attempts to speak with her, to which she responded politely, but he could see in her eyes a well of dark emotions that the violence of the previous days had churned up. Unable to bridge the chasm between them, he ended up helplessly walking away from conversations that dribbled away into uncomfortable silences. Maybe help for her was best left to the experts they'd find in Denver.

Cara had brightened as they approached the outskirts of the city, the T-bird swinging to the west but within sight of Denver's southern leg, which stretched precariously down to Colorado Springs. The multihued points of city light seemed to call to her and she actually joked with him slightly as they watched the lights passing on the monitors.

Now, in his cheap hotel room, Chase heard the pops of firecrackers, maybe even light gunfire, coming into the room from the streets. He shifted in his chair and adjusted the sling that held his right arm relatively immobile. He'd barely realized it at the time, but a shaft of metal had sliced into his shoulder and nicked a bone during those last few moments in Aztlan. It cost Chase a few hundred extra nuyen to buy the silence of the clinic doctor who treated him and Freid. He didn't want his friends to know that the wound was only to the flesh. Normal bone would have chipped from the impact of the metal, but that part of his shoulder had ceased being natural two years after Cara had been born. The doctor was amazed at his healing rate, predicting that Chase would have full use of the arm within a day or two.

They'd booked into two adjoining rooms in a Cozy Inn on the fringes of the Confederate American States sector of town. The *Rapier's Touch* crew had a long-standing financial relationship with a point of entry official in that sector and so the LAV had entered the city across the CAS border.

Cara and Freid were asleep in the other room. Gordani and Blanchard were staying with the *Rapier's Touch* as it underwent necessary repairs in one of the vehicle barns on the city's outskirts. Freid was too hurt and exhausted to maintain the edge she'd need in that barely civilized corner of the city. Her comrades had asked Chase to take her into town with him for a while. He agreed immediately, triggering Cara's apparent disapproval. She'd walked off by herself, cursing under her breath but still audibly.

It was Cara, however, who offered to share a room with Freid. Girls with girls, she'd said. Chase had wondered what she thought the alternative was.

The telecom beeped, and he answered it on the second ring. "Yes?"

"Priest," came a woman's voice, synthetic and crystal clear.

"Lachesis. That was quick."

"Your message was received, and the allusion to your location insufficiently obscure. You must be more careful."

"I'll keep that in mind. Do you have the other information I asked for?"

There was no reply, only the dead, clear quiet of the line.

"Lachesis?"

"I am still here. I am weighing the tone of my reply."

"You don't have it?"

"The information you requested has been compiled and correlated, the little there is. I, however, do not have it."

"You don't?"

"No. He does."

Chase felt cold, either from a sudden breeze or his own reaction to her words. "I understand."

When she spoke again Chase almost heard a trace of the human somewhere behind the electronic persona. "I feel I must apologize for the unintentional violation of the confidentiality of our agreement. I honestly do not understand how he found out about the nature of my data searches."

"He has his ways. I do not hold you responsible."

"Thank you."

"I take it he wants to see me?"

"Nothing of that nature was stated or implied."

Chase chuckled. "Yeah, he knows I'll come. Tell him, Lachesis. Tell him I'll come."

"If he knows you'll come, then I do not need to tell him."

"No," Chase said, almost to himself. "I suppose not."

After finishing with Lachesis, Chase knocked on the door to the adjoining room. He heard movement, a muf-

fled noise that might have been a voice and then the sound
of the door latch. He was surprised; he hadn't heard it
lock. He was even more surprised to find Freid standing
there.

"Hoi," she said, leaning against the frame of the half-
open door. The light from Chase's room spilled past her
and across Cara's sprawled form. She was asleep,
sprawled at an angle across the bed, wrapped tight and
twisted in her sheets. Freid glanced over her shoulder as
the younger woman shifted slightly and made some noise
Chase couldn't decipher. Freid stepped toward him,
gently closing the door, but not shutting it all the way.

"She restless?" asked Chase.

Freid nodded and ran a hand through her own disheveled hair. The rest she'd gotten since Aztlan seemed to
finally be helping. Her face was still reddened and her
hands still slightly blued from the bruising, but much of
the visible damage had faded faster than Chase would
have expected. He'd been in enough fights to know that
the kind of bruising she'd taken usually needed more than
a week to fade.

Freid sat down on the edge of Chase's bed. "I talked
with her a little bit, but she's holding everything in. I'm
not sure why."

He nodded. "There's something going on in her head,
but I can't figure it out," he said. "But that's just what
I've got to do."

Freid shrugged helplessly, and Chase saw her eye the
room's built-in refrigerator. "Can I get you something?"
he asked. "A drink? Room service?"

"Just a drink would be fine. Whatever they have that's
closest to water. Nothing sweet."

He stepped over to the fridge and quickly rummaged
through its contents to see what it might yield. He flipped
her a plastic bottle filled with sparkling liquid. "There
you are. The most expensive bottle of water you'll ever
have."

She laughed, saying, "I'll savor it," then popped the
cap and took a long drink. Chase sat down again near

the window and watched her. She was wearing the long, oversized T-shirt she'd pulled out of her bag earlier. He was surprised and amused at the images of Dalmatian puppies scattered all over the shirt, staring innocently at their beaming parents. He wondered where she'd gotten it.

She recapped the bottle and looked at him. "Mind if I ask you what's going on?"

"I told you back in Dart Slot."

"Look, I know biz is biz and what I don't know can't hurt me and all that drek, but could you tell me a little more of what you're up to?"

He glanced out into the night for a moment, then back at her. "Why do you want to know?"

She shrugged. "I just do. Maybe I can help."

"You probably could, but that won't be necessary."

She looked down and Chase could see her lips tighten. "You seemed concerned enough before to ask me."

"I'm still worried, but not overly. I think what you said that night was right."

"I think you're lying."

Chase stared back at her.

"Look," she said finally, "I can appreciate your concern, and I'm flattered, but I do want to help." She paused for a breath. "Gordani told me about Cara."

Chase cursed. "Wonderful."

"Who the frag am I going to tell?"

"I know you won't tell anyone," he said wearily. "I'm just cursing whoever else Gordo might have told."

"Only me and Blanchard. That's it. He had to tell us," she said.

Chase leaned forward. "Okay, he told you about her. Did he fill in the rest?"

She looked at him quizzically. "The rest?"

"This is the scenario. I'm escorting Cara Villiers down the middle of what could be the start of the biggest corporate civil war anybody's ever seen. Fuchi's always been known to field the best company men and to stage the best covert ops. They were among the first to start deploying full mages as a standard part of their combat teams. If the families that run the company go to war, God only knows where the security forces will hit, or even who they're allied with now.''

Freid was staring at him, listening. He could see her taking in everything he was telling her, then analyzing it, piece by piece. He was beginning to suspect that she had a sharp mind along with everything else she had going for her.

''And if what Cara says is true, that's exactly what's happening. The Nakatomis, at least, are backing an attempt to kill her father, who owns and controls the Villiers faction of the company. Bang. Instant schism.''

Her eyes widened. ''I can't imagine that leading to anything particularly pleasant.''

''Exactly. The race would be on to control Richard's slice of the corp.''

''Wouldn't that depend on how his will read?'' she asked. ''They wouldn't automatically gain control of his shares, would they?''

Chase shrugged. ''Don't know. Maybe not, but there's a whole other spin that starts up if her father dies. Suppose his corporate shares are hereditary? Who gets them?''

''You tell me.'' There was a growing gleam in her eye.

''Four possible people, to the best of my knowledge. Martin Villiers, her uncle, but he was opposed to the merger of the Villiers family assets with the Japanese from the beginning. I can't see Richard bestowing his shares on his brother.''

''Could he have written a death rider in?''

''What do you mean?''

''You know,'' she said, '' 'In the event of my tragic and violent death my will is null and void and all shares go to my brother,' or something.''

''A poke in the eye from beyond the grave? Martin would pull the Villiers' assets out and leave the Japanese high and dry, so I think the Japanese would want to make sure that Richard dies peacefully, of natural causes.''

"Assuming they know what his will says."

Chase snorted. "If the Japanese are anywhere near as paranoid and fond of, um, 'tactical intelligence-gathering' as Richard was when I worked for him, they *know* to the jot what his will says. Besides, it may be part of the corporate agreement."

She nodded. "Who else?"

"Well, there's Martin's son, Darren, Cara's cousin. He's actually an employee of Fuchi, but in the Nakatomi camp, or at least under their control. Risky, from Richard's point of view. Maybe he hopes Darren'll come into his own. Who knows?"

"But, as you say, risky. Next?"

"The more likely candidate, Richard's ex-wife Samantha."

"Ex-wife?"

"Uh-huh. They divorced about six years ago, but she's a card-carrying member of the corporate structure in her own right. Her background's scientific management, and she was head of the Fuchi Systems Design group out of Seattle for the last seven or so years. Then, not long ago, she was named the new vice president of Fuchi Northwest, replacing Darren Villiers, who's been transferred to Tokyo."

Freid shook her head. "I'm starting to remember why I enjoy T-bird running."

"Allegedly, Richard and his wife remained on fairly amicable terms after the divorce. They were never a particularly loving couple when I worked for them, very distant to each other. I suspect it was a political marriage, of sorts. Arranged by themselves. At least that was my take on a few oblique exchanges I happened to overhear now and then." Chase suddenly became aware of the volume and tone of his voice. He threw a quick glance toward the partially closed door.

Freid followed his gaze, then raised her hand toward the room, curling her fingers as she did. Her mouth moved, but Chase couldn't make out the words. After a moment she turned back toward him. "No, she's out. Doing some rough dreaming, but out."

"Could you tell what she was dreaming?"

"No," she laughed. "I'm not *that* good."

"Hmm," said Chase, thinking again about Cara and the source of her problems.

"Anyway," Freid prompted.

"Yeah, anyway . . . from the way I heard them talk on a couple of occasions, Cara must have been an unwelcome accident. Richard, I don't think, was pleased at all, but Sam wanted—Samantha insisted on carrying the baby to term."

"Did Cara know?"

"Oh, I'll bet she did. She was a smart one, even at eight."

"Did her father get over it?"

"No, not really. I'm sure Cara sensed that even if she didn't understand the reason. Samantha tried hard, very hard, to be a good mother, but it just wasn't her style. She was too much a corporate manager."

Freid glanced at the adjoining door. "What do you think are the odds that he left her some or part of the company?"

"She was number four on my list. The question would be, why?"

"Guilt?"

Chase considered that for a moment. "Guilt is not one of the emotions I associate with Richard Villiers."

She nodded. "Which basically leaves you with nothing."

"Right, just confusion that stresses the fact that I'm very unclear about who exactly the players are in this game."

"But you think they've got to be Fuchi, right?"

"No. According to Cara, the hit against Richard was supposed to be carried out by some German radical policlubbers. So they could be the ones after us. If we're lucky, it's them, anyway."

"Less worried about some policlubbers than a Fuchi combat team, eh?"

"Damn right. I've dealt with policlubbers before, a group very much like Cara's friends, in fact. They're full of sound and fury, and don't give a damn about anything beyond their version of the truth. Politically naive, socially deficient, morally bankrupt, psychologically unstable, and more than willing to kill the defenseless to prove their superiority. No, I'm not worried about their kind. I've handled them before."

"Sounds like it."

Chase found himself leaning forward in his chair, hands clenched into fists. When he suddenly remembered where he was, he found Fried staring at him, slightly wide-eyed, tensed and quiet.

"Damn," he said. "Sorry." He stood up and walked over to the fridge.

"Raw nerve, eh?"

He nodded, then changed his mind about the drink. He turned back to her. "Look, I've got to meet with some people and see what I can find out. In Manhattan, Cara and I were nearly ambushed by a group that practically reeked of being a combat team, but I didn't recognize any of them or their style. They could have been mercenaries, a wise move if the Fuchi security division was uncommitted, but I need to know. There are people here who might be able to discover their identities."

She nodded and stood up, too, pulling at her shirt to straighten it out. "Need back-up?"

He laughed. "No. I like you too much to inflict those people on you. I'm going into the data haven."

"*Into* the data haven? You mean into the Matrix?"

"No, I mean *into* the data haven. Me, meat-body, flesh-head. I've been there before."

"So what do you want me to do?"

"Guard Cara. Watch her, don't let her out of your sight. And if she'll talk to you, see if she'll tell you anything she won't tell me. You know, 'girl to girl'."

Freid smiled. "I think I can handle that."

Chase grabbed his heavy jacket off the bed. It was warmer than the weather dictated, but he wanted the armor plating in its lining just in case. It would also conceal his Colt Manhunter and its quick-release shoulder rig. He pulled them both on.

"There's a certified credstick in my black bag that should be untraceable. Use it if you or Cara get hungry. Room service, if you can."

"Got it."

"I should be back before lunch."

Freid nodded and sat down on the bed.

He started to leave, then turned back for a moment. "Oh, and there's a Heckler and Koch submachine gun in the black bag, too. Just in case."

"I think I'm up to taking care of myself."

Chase grinned. "Yeah."

He'd just started through the doorway, when she stopped him this time.

"I guess this means I'm helping out, huh?"

He glanced back at her. "I guess," he said.

18

Chase decided to walk the seven or so blocks from the hotel to the high-speed rail link that would take him south to Colorado Springs. The night air was crisp and clear, a welcome product of the near-continual breezes that had swept the city year-round ever since the signing of the NAN treaty. Many people blamed the change in air currents and the overall warming of the local climate on Daniel Howling Coyote, founding father of the Native American Nations, and his fellow Ghost Dancers. They said that the weather changes were due to the Ghost Dancers' use of powerful weather magics during their weeks of brinkmanship with the old United States. Like most truths, however, no one knew for sure.

The maglev train line veered from its seeming attachment to Intercity 25 for a short time to make its pass through downtown Denver. Chase caught the train where it ran along Speer Street and the barely moving Cherry River. He boarded along with a band of young, raucous French-Canadians who made crude jokes about him and the other Denverites on the train, never even considering that he might understand their tongue. Twenty minutes later the brightly lit finger of Pikes Peak passing to the west told Chase that Colorado Springs was moments away. On disembarking, he thanked the young gang from Québec for the entertainment. "It's not every day you get to see people so good at making fools of themselves," he said in French.

Inside the steel and sterile rail-link station he found a telecom stand. He dialed, the line connected, and then he was greeted by silence.

"This is Priest. I'm here."

More silence before the reply finally came. "Come then. You are welcome at the gates." Chase shuddered again at the cold, inhuman voice he'd first heard over the satellite link. Before he could respond, the line went dead.

He was lucky. An electric autocab sat waiting near the station. Inside, he called up a datamap on the information screen and touched his finger to the destination. Instead of the usual acknowledgment and cheerful greeting, the cab refused the address. Its voice was pleasant, bland, and female.

"We're sorry, but the Spring Service Corporation cannot authorize this vehicle to enter that location. Please choose another."

Chase sighed and stabbed his finger against the screen at a point a little south of the large blank space he'd first chosen. Any nearby street would do.

"Thank you for traveling in a Spring Service cab!"

Chase grunted, and the cab pulled out into a nearly

empty Colorado Avenue with an annoying electric whine. As the city passed on either side of him, Chase was pleased to see most of the old buildings still standing. The Treaty City being what it was, he was always expecting to hear that terrible violence had swept it. Denver was divided up among six governments, the United Canadian and American States, the Confederated American States, Aztlan, and the Sioux, Pueblo, and Ute Nations, each with its own laws and dancing in constant opposition to each other. Being a servant of six masters made it a sure thing that the city of Denver neither slept nor played well.

The criminal element controlled much of Denver Territory, doglegging from Boulder, through Denver proper, and then down a long stretch to Colorado Springs. They used its strategically advantageous position at the center of the Native American Nations as a base for anything and everything. Anything a body wanted, he could find it in Denver. Weapons, people, technology, information. Name it.

It was for information that Chase was now headed toward Colorado Springs. Here at the northern edge of the Pueblo-controlled sector was the most vital source of secret information in North America. It hadn't been created there, but it could be *located* from there. Built quietly on abandoned government land in the days following the fracturing of the U.S., it grew in secret to become a massive web-work of hacked computers and wild technology that no sane person could ever hope to comprehend. It became a mecca of sorts for those who preferred the dynamic, volatile world of the computer Matrix to flesh and blood. Originally formed as a techno-utopia and named the Denver Technological Cooperative by its founders, it was now more commonly known as the Nexus. In the data haven there, and the ones like it scattered about other parts of the world, data could be bought, sold, or found for any price, in any form. All you had to do was ask. It was, however, unheard-of to ask in the flesh.

Chase left the cab, and his arm sling, on Woodmen Road, the closest destination the vehicle's programming would accept. From there he walked the rest of the way, north along Intercity 25 and under the raised tracks of the maglev. He'd seen his destination—dim masses of dark buildings, quiet, open land now overgrown, and the broad streaks of a long-abandoned runway—rush past as the train had begun its deceleration into Colorado Springs.

Coming up to the smashed gates, he eyed the piles of wrecked cars and trucks just inside. The place's few defenses would be no more than a nuisance to any trained military or security force, but to date no one, not even the Pueblo Council with their billions of words on tech law, had dared pass the gates. No one wanted to risk the data haven's wrath. One worldwide computer crash was enough for a century.

He ramped up his low-light and thermographic vision and spotted a few pockets of warmth scattered among the cold metal of the cars. He guessed these to be video cameras and sensors, but he waited. The voice on the phone had said he was welcome at the gates, but nothing about once he was inside.

Finally, a small, lithe figure slowly approached from around the remains of a rusted fuel truck. By the other person's size, Chase placed him in mid-adolescence. The boy was too tall and too thin for a dwarf, which meant he could be either elven or human. Chase figured human. When the figure got close enough, Chase discovered that he'd been right about the age and the race, but wrong about the sex.

She was wearing a battered and torn technician's jump suit, but military-style boots. Her dark hair was short and cut unevenly, unprofessionally. A pair of light-amplification goggles hid her eyes but gave her the same kind of vision he obtained from his far more expensive cybernetic systems. He thought she might be Asian.

She cocked her head. "Identification?" she said, her voice flat, unemotional, and artificial. Chase heard just the faintest touch of a Japanese accent that she was strenuously trying to suppress.

"My name is Priest. I'm expected."

"Wait," she said.

And he did, for a few minutes, before a sudden flare of white light from one of the junk piles focused on him. He threw up a hand in front of his face to block the light as the systems in his eyes fought to compensate before permanent damage was done.

"Lower your hand," the girl said.

He did and stood squinting. "Got a good look yet?"

"You are confirmed," she said. "Stand by."

The light went out.

"So, where did you run away from?" he asked after a few moments.

Her head jerked slightly, but she made no reply.

"It's okay," he continued. "I'm not here to take you back. I've already got enough problems with another girl who's not much older than you."

She still said nothing, but her mouth worked slightly.

"Can I guess?"

She stared at him.

"San Francisco."

This time her whole body jerked in surprise and her mouth opened slightly. He'd guessed right. Before he could press her further, the controlled roar of a truck engine silenced him. It took a moment for the vehicle to appear as it wound its way through the maze of trash that led to the gate. When it finally arrived, roof-mounted search lights blaring, its appearance confirmed Chase's suspicions. An old, multipurpose light military transport, it had been painted flat black, with broad slabs of wood bolted to its front and rear. The Hummer ground to a stop just inside the gate, and a tall, thin figure stood up through the truck's custom sunroof. Despite the darkness, the glare, and the San Diego Padres baseball cap, Chase could tell that the man was an elf.

"You are Priest," he said. "Your access has been approved."

"And?" said Chase.

"You may enter the Nexus. He is waiting."

When Chase climbed into the vehicle, they blindfolded him with a motorcycle helmet whose faceplate had been blinded with spray paint. Chase had only gotten a glimpse of the Hummer's other occupant as he mounted, but the words scrawny and nervous jumped to mind. The vehicle actually went out the gates to make its U-turn, and then headed back in, winding its way through the junk.

Finally, the winding stopped and the Hummer gained speed as it hit a main road. Chase tried to remember what that road was called. He knew that it became Academy Boulevard and headed down into Colorado Springs just outside the gate where he'd been, but what it was called inside the grounds eluded him.

The ride was rough, probably a combination of the road's poor condition and the questionable driving skills of the scrawny man. This road stretched for a few kilometers before reaching the cluster of buildings that housed the actual data haven and its inhabitants.

"So, I hear you had some problems with Shadowland being compromised in Seattle," Chase said. The Nexus distributed a great deal of its publicly disseminable information through locally controlled, mobile computer bulletin board systems. Called Shadowland, the system could only be accessed by those who knew its daily electronic location. Via the board, fed from Denver, one could download chips full of data, scuttlebutt, and conversation that regularly made the governments and corporations howl, hence the system's mobile nature. Chase had heard from local friends that the Seattle Shadowland system had apparently been infiltrated by corporate agents who'd erased some volatile data, tossed a rather nasty virus back toward Denver, and then killed the maintainers of the system.

Chase waited for their reply, but none came. The Hummer continued on.

"So, how about them Nuggets, eh?" he said.

The truck began to brake, and Chase thought for a moment that he'd crossed that treacherous line hard-core technophiles had about sports, but when it sped up again he realized that they'd simply reached the first of the few turns they'd make to reach the center of the haven.

The Hummer turned again, again, and again, the last time clipping a curb before finally stopping. Chase reached up to remove the helmet, but thin hands stopped him. "This wasn't necessary last time," he said.

He heard a sharp intake of breath, and smelled the long slow stream of fetid exhale. To admit an outsider in the flesh was obviously odd enough to them, but to have one suggest this wasn't his first time might have been blasphemy. The Hummer's side door opened, and Chase felt himself carefully pulled out. Then he felt a hand on his elbow, probably the elf's, guiding him forward and up a short set of stairs. A door opened, and he was hit with a gust of air that reminded him all too much of a locker room. They walked him through a door, and then down a longer flight of stairs.

As they passed through another door, Chase had the distinct impression that a larger group was moving along with him now. He heard noises around him, muffled voices, occasional laughter, the crackle of static, the hum of electronics.

Another door, and more stairs. Now he was certain he was in the midst of a pack. Through a door, down a hallway that echoed noisily with the sounds of dozens of feet. Then the procession stopped. He heard a muttering and the swipe of what could have been a magnetic pass-card. An odd security measure, he thought, in a place where an outsider would be immediately recognized as out of place. The click of an electronic lock, the opening of a door, and the pack moved him forward.

The acoustics here were bigger, for Chase sensed the air flow of a larger room and heard the pack fan out. His ears picked up the distinct sound of electronics and the steady whine of a video monitor.

For the first time in nearly twenty minutes, he clearly

heard a voice. "Oh, Christ Almighty, get that damn helmet off him," it said.

Chase started, and then quickly assisted the pairs of hands that worked to remove the helmet. He knew the voice, it was the one he'd been expecting, but there was something wrong with it. The timbre was off, the tone too low. It had come through speakers and been artificially generated.

The helmet finally off, Chase looked around the room. Maybe it had once been some sort of large conference room or classroom. Now, it was empty except for the dozens of cheap, archaic metal folding chairs that filled it. Wires and cables ran everywhere, weaving their way along the floor and across the ceiling. Single strands hung down and swung lazily over the chairs, while other lines were draped casually across the backs of others. He was guided forward by a tall, redheaded boy with near-glowing opal cybereyes, and led to a chair at the center of the room. These chairs were better, but only slightly. Maybe they'd been taken from an office.

The red-haired boy was now joined by others: males, females, whites, blacks, elves, Asians, orks, and Hispanics surrounded Chase and the chair where he now sat. They were all young; a few were older than Cara, but most were younger. They wore clothing of all styles. Some were dirty and unkempt, others fastidiously clean. Some looked him boldly in the eyes, others seemed barely able to summon the will power to be in the same room with him. Most smiled, a few frowned, and one, a bald black girl of about fifteen, cried. The others ignored her.

They circled him, in and among the chairs, and waited.

"Um . . . ," Chase said, and a hand from behind him held out a thin fiber-optic cable with a standard connector on the end. Chase took it carefully, noting the frayed covering where the connector met the cable. "Thanks."

A voice behind him, a new one, said, "He's waiting for you."

Chase nodded and carefully inserted the connector into

his datajack. It clicked into place, but then nothing happened. He started to turn around. "I don't think it's—"

And then the room exploded into a dazzling dance of millions of neon fireflies, cutting off any more words.

19

The transition took Chase by surprise. Whenever hard core deckers were involved, he always expected a sudden and spectacular interface sequence as the simsense signal overrode his own sensory data and pulled him into the artificial, virtual reality of the Matrix. He wasn't ready, however, to see the young red-haired boy's head become a neon sand sculpture whose molecular adhesion was suddenly lost. Nor was he ready to see every person in the room, and the room itself, explode into particles of light in the same manner.

The lights fell away from their original form, and then soared upward again to join with the others and swirl about him. Faster and faster, brighter and brighter, a great roar grew with it, drowning out even the sounds of his heartbeat and his own thoughts. He reached for the data cable, intending to pull it clear and jack out to end the rising madness, but found he had no arms, no physical body, no existence. Chase looked down at himself just in time to catch the last pieces of light that had been his own body dance away to join the prismatic swirl.

As he felt himself being dragged into it, he screamed, then fell hard against the white marble. He felt its coldness seep quickly into him. He dug his fingers in against the stone, starting a sudden rush of pain from their tips. He stopped screaming and opened his eyes.

He was in an arena, a coliseum perhaps, constructed of brilliant white and pink marble. It was huge, monstrous, far larger than any of the real super-stadiums he'd ever seen. From his view at ground level, the center area seemed flat and featureless and ended against a high wall. Above the wall were rows of benches, room for thousands, rising upward at an incline. They were empty.

Chase rolled over and faced a deep blue sky through which ran ripples of purple and cyan. A cool breeze washed over him. He shuddered. It wasn't real, he told himself. It was all created in a computer. It's not real. . . .

"Mikael, *tovarich*?"

Chase rolled his head toward the voice and saw, finally, the man he'd come to see. Tall and lean as ever, but with a presence no flesh body could ever muster, the man stood a short distance away. His hair was short, layered, and as fine as spun silk. His features were those Michelangelo had failed to perfect in stone, and his clothing was sharp, black, and perfect. And he was young. As young as Chase could ever remember him.

"Fuck you," Chase said.

The man's expression had been almost a frown, and it did not change. "I'm sorry. Are you all right?"

Chase pulled himself up into a sitting position and found the attempt far easier than he'd expected. "I'm fine. Finally getting your revenge?"

"No. That was inexcusable," the man said. "Pardon me a moment." The man looked skyward and said, quietly, "Bash."

For a moment there was nothing, and then the air next to him shimmered as another man formed there. He was unnaturally tall and emaciated, the bones of his face covered by only the barest hint of skin. He wore an archaic mourning coat three sizes too small, and wild red power danced in his eyes.

"Shiva," hissed the newcomer through clenched razor teeth.

"Cut the drek, Bash," said Shiva. "What the frag was that all about?"

Bash turned his head only slightly, but Chase felt his gaze. "He's to blame. I wished some compensation."

"Blame?" said Chase.

Shiva cursed and flexed his black leather-gloved hands. "You had no right. He is a guest here, by my word."

Bash laughed, a quiet, clipped chuckle. "You are not in charge here. By *my* word he was to be punished."

"To blame for what?" asked Chase.

Shiva met Bash's gaze. "You wish to match words? You want to see whose voice rocks the heavens more?"

Bash laughed again. "No, no," he said. "That would be bad for morale, wouldn't it? Besides, it might resolve something. We wouldn't want that, would we?"

Not real, Chase remembered. Everything that he was seeing and sensing was being generated on the Nexus' computer systems, a system that responded to his own cybernetic commands. Chase extended his artificial senses inward to see what kind of hardware or programming he had at his disposal. He didn't know much about decking or computer programming, but figured he could hack together at least a minor something that would get Shiva and Bash's attention. But there was nothing to be found. As far as he could tell he wasn't connected to an actual cyberdeck, but was only being fed the simsense signal. Still, there had to be some two-way communication—he was, after all, a participant in the virtual reality, not merely an observer—but he couldn't find the connection. He stood up.

Shiva looked down and shook his head. "He and I have things to discuss." Chase felt an odd sensation and started to say something, but didn't get it out in time.

"So we'll be leaving," Shiva continued. Chase felt himself suddenly drawn toward Shiva, who seemed to be receding. Chase turned to look at Bash as Shiva reached out an arm toward the taller man. A ball of quicksilver and lightning grew in Shiva's palm, and he tossed it to the suddenly wide-eyed Bash. "Merry Christmas."

Chase felt himself spin away from Bash and into the darkness of Shiva's clothing. For a moment, there was nothing, and then the shapes and forms of a high-tech chrome and black metal office resolved into existence around him. Shiva was already seated behind the massive silver and black desk that dominated the room. Behind him was the unbelievable Matrix vista of the inside of the data haven, the heart of the Nexus. Brilliant geometric constructs and shapes of all sizes representing the massive amounts of computing power hidden within its walls circled a single point of near infinite darkness. Ignoring Shiva and his bemused smile, Chase moved closer to the window to get a better view. Not real, he repeated again.

Blinding lances of light, massed packets of data, intermittently connected the orbiting constructs with each other and occasionally with the dark center. The bursts of light accelerated as they grew closer to that black heart, becoming long, thin shafts and then finally vanishing as they were absorbed in the all-consuming darkness. Chase could see figures moving through the spaces between the systems; deckers in their various electronic personas all showing a healthy respect for what lay at the center. Chase had to get away; it was almost more than he could stand. Sometimes, it was impossible to believe that nothing in the Matrix was real. The images, the feel, were too *right*.

Chase said: "That isn't . . ."

Shiva shook his head. "You should know better, but it is an intimidating rendering. It's the repository of all the information that passes through here, compiled and compressed for storage. A black hole of data, if you will. Every request and every result obtained," he continued, "is filed away there. And it's all retrievable."

Chase turned toward him. "Retrievable by whom?"

Shiva shrugged. "I will admit access isn't equal. Power has always revolved around who has access to what."

Chase nodded and lowered himself into an unusually comfortable and plush chair. He leaned back and closed his eyes. "How much do you know?" he asked Shiva.

"You are guarding Cara Villiers. Data correlation indicates connections between her, you, Fuchi International, and certain German corporate and antisocial concerns. History repeating itself?'' Shiva said.

Chase shook his head. ''No. Different set of buttholes.''

Shiva looked at him steadily. ''There are things, I take it, you need to know.''

''Lachesis has been gathering information for me.'' Chase snapped his eyes open. ''Which you probably already know. She told me you knew about it.''

''I know what her search parameters were, but not the results. She was not able to tell me.''

''What do you mean, wasn't able to tell you?'' Chase was watching him carefully. A few hours ago Lachesis had said that he, Shiva, had all her data.

''You really don't know then?'' asked Shiva. When Chase didn't reply, Shiva shifted in his seat and continued. ''It's what Bash was going on about. Lachesis got burned a few hours ago. She was making a run against Fuchi, at your request apparently, and got lined. There's neurological damage, maybe permanent, but she's alive.''

Chase stood up and walked back to the window and focused his stare on one of the orbiting computer systems clear of the black data hole. Something was wrong, but Chase knew he had little choice but to play along. Here, in the Matrix, he was at Shiva's mercy. ''I explicitly told her *not* to go into Fuchi. Which system did she try and run?''

''Seattle.''

''She should have known better than that.''

Shiva shrugged. ''It's what her kind live for. I don't lay blame on any side. Deckers like Bash, however, see it differently.''

Chase looked over at him.

''The way they see it, you dangled the Fuchi involvement in front of her as bait. You have Fuchi connections, they say, why didn't you just get the data?''

''I see.''

''They don't know the whole story.''

''Do you?'' Chase asked.

"No. Nor, do I suspect, do you."

Chase nodded. "You'd be right. Too much of it makes no sense. I was hoping that Lachesis would turn up something. I take it her deck got burned?"

"Total loss."

"Does anybody know about any back-ups she might have kept?" Chase asked him.

"There were no back-ups."

Chase shook his head again. "You'd think she'd have played it safer than . . ." He glanced outside at the data hole, just for an instant, and then back at Shiva. He'd play along, but that didn't mean he'd have to play it safe. "But you said every request, and every result, is stored away in there for retrieval."

"I did."

"Then if Lachesis used the data haven's systems—"

"She did."

"—the data should be stored away in there."

"You're correct."

"So . . ."

Shiva's eyes shone. "The problem is that it is *not*. The data was diverted before compression. It's not in the main memory core."

Chase stared at him. "The haven's been compromised?"

"Perhaps. Hopefully, it is merely one individual with questionable loyalties."

"Damn."

"Exactly so."

Chase dropped back down into the chair. "Well, that points everything back at Fuchi again."

"Oh?"

Chase nodded. "Somebody is after Cara. Fuchi made sense, except it didn't feel like them. Fuchi's internal intelligence is *good*. I should know, I had to deal with them enough."

"Times change."

Chase shook his head. "Fuchi's still on top. If their

intelligence people were letting them down, they'd be slipping by now.''

"Which leaves?"

"Alte Welt. Cara's old friends. It looks like Fuchi-Nakatomi hired members of Alte Welt to kill Villiers when he's in Frankfurt next month.''

"Ah," said Shiva, "pieces drop into place. She found out. Then Fuchi-Nakatomi found out she knew, and now, presumably, wants her dead.''

"Except that if it was Fuchi after her, there should be more evidence of it," said Chase. "There was an incident in Manhattan, but no proof beyond circumstantial that it was Fuchi. Since then, nothing. No pressure at all."

"Which implies that it's Alte Welt. They're fearful of telling Fuchi, perhaps?"

"That's my guess, but I doubt Alte Welt could have agents here in Denver.''

"You'd be surprised where we hail from," Shiva told him. "There are quite a few Germans here, of all types and kinds.''

Chase nodded and stared for awhile at the slowly changing gray patterns of the walls. He hadn't noticed the motion before. It was soothing. What kind of game was Shiva playing? Should he confront him? How much of the old anger remained?

"Could Der Nachtmachen be involved?" Shiva asked after a moment.

The statement surprised Chase. Why would he bring up Nachtmachen? Chase shook his head. "They're castrated. I barely ever give them a thought anymore.''

"I doubt they're as dead as you think.''

"The organization is active, cheap local politics, but it's just a dead body thrashing. The heart is gone.''

"It's been thrashing for some time now.''

"Look, Veitman is dead. So are Lieber and Kaufmann. Who's left?"

Shiva stood up and moved over to the window. He

stared directly into the darkness. "No one who was involved when you were. Even Steadman is dead."

"Oh? Falling out later?"

"Of a sort. He was assassinated in Hamburg a few years ago. It is believed that the person who ordered the assassination also killed Shavan, shadow-liege of The Revenants policlub, a few days later in Seattle."

"News to me," said Chase, and then after a moment, "Seattle?"

Shiva turned away from the window, but did not look at him. "Shavan was there to work the tail end of a deal with Saeder-Krupp."

Chase stared at him. "Holy shit." This was all very interesting, but what was the point?

"The deal did not go down. She was stopped before it could. Rumor has it that she was opposed by another interested party that did not want Saeder-Krupp extending its power."

"Fuchi . . ."

"No." Shiva shook his head. "Not Fuchi. Not a corporation.

"Saeder-Krupp has the distinction of being the only known megacorporation owned and actively run by a great dragon."

"Lofwyr."

"And apparently," continued Shiva, "even dragons can have brothers, if that word is even entirely accurate."

"You've lost me."

"The information is sparse, but indications are that Shavan's deal to use Saeder-Krupp money to back The Revenants was opposed by another dragon, one Alamais, allegedly Lofwyr's brother, who wanted to keep the two groups from reaching a deal."

"As if Saeder-Krupp doesn't already wield enough power in Europe."

Shiva smiled. "That, I believe, was the point. Saeder-Krupp is one of the backers of the Pan-Europa Restoration plan that would restore the political borders from

before the wars in the thirties. Alamais apparently likes
things the way they are: nice and chaotic.''

''Sounds like he should be running a policlub,'' said
Chase.

Shiva shrugged. ''Dragons seem to be running just
about everything else.''

Chase shook his head. ''Jesus. What a fragged-up
world.''

Shiva said nothing, but shifted in his chair again.
''What about Alexi?'' he said finally.

Chase started. He was surprised Shiva would bring that
up. He had expected that they would tap dance around
their past history just as they always did. ''Alexi?''

Shiva nodded. ''Could he finally be coming after
you?''

''From the dead?'' said Chase, incredulous. ''Sorry,
but I haven't read about any resurrections recently.''

Shiva's eyes widened slightly. ''Then you don't
know?''

The room felt colder. ''Know what, Gennedy Pole-
mov? *Know what?*''

''Your brother is alive.''

''That's impossible.''

Shiva stared at him.

''You were there, damn it. You saw what I did.''

The other man nodded. ''I was there, and I would have
agreed with you.'' He sighed. ''Except that I've seen
him.''

''You've *seen* him?''

''Yes.''

''Where? When?''

Shiva shook his head. ''I cannot say. But he is alive,
and now a magician.''

Chase couldn't believe what he was hearing. ''A *magician*? Look, what the fuck are you trying to do here?
You can't expect me to believe any of this.''

''Believe what you will. I'm simply telling you that
Alexi is alive.''

Chase leaned back in the chair and stared at the other

man. What he was saying was impossible. Alexi was
dead. Chase had seen the gunfire tear into him and had
watched as his body flipped backward over the rail and
into the water. Weighed down by his combat gear, it had
quickly sunk. Nothing could have saved him at that point.
Nothing.

"The magician part is a nice touch," Chase told him.
"It's the only way the whole story could work."

"No matter how it sounds to you, all I can say is that
Alexi is alive, which raises the strong possibility that he
is the source of some of your problems."

Chase shook his head. "No. Regardless of whether or
not my brother is alive, he's not the cause of this."

"You're sure?"

"Very," said Chase. "None of this could have any
possible connection with him. Remember, I'm involved,
but it's not directed at me. If Alexi were coming after
me, he'd be in my face. I'd know about it."

"Yes, he always preferred direct confrontation."

"Right to the end."

Shiva looked up at Chase. "I wish I could tell you
more, but I have certain obligations—"

Chase held up his hand. "Then don't. When all this is
over I might be back. Then I'll expect some answers, but
right now I need something else."

"And that would be?"

Chase thought for a second. No, there was too much
about what his old comrade was doing that he didn't understand. He cut the list of favors he was going to ask
for down to one. "Travel passes, three of them, out of
Denver, across NAN, and into Seattle."

"Travel passes."

"Yes."

"How mundane."

"And that's exactly the way I'm trying to keep it,"
said Chase.

20

The big room was empty when Chase's senses finally became his own again. More time had passed than he'd have liked as he and Shiva had sat and talked, raising ghosts best left to rest. The conversation had turned to the things they'd done and the people they'd done them with. Shiva knew more about their fates than Chase, which wasn't surprising. Counting Alexi, they were the only three of the seven still alive.

Finally, they'd parted as they always did, uncomfortably, and almost silently. Shiva did promise to have someone continue Lachesis' research and to keep Chase apprised of her condition. Chase thanked him, but knew somehow he'd never see those results. Had Fuchi gotten to his old friend? Was the Nexus not as impartial as claimed? Or was it something else?

Just outside the room, two deckers waited for him. One was the red-haired boy, the other an ork who smiled as Chase stepped through the doors. The redhead looked away.

"Bash," said Chase.

The decker glanced back at Chase, but said nothing. The ork, however, chuckled.

"We're leavin', and guess what?" he said with an even bigger grin.

"What?"

The ork hefted his prize. "You get to wear the helmet again."

Leaving the data haven and the staring girl at the gate, Chase thought of what little he knew and had learned. Something about it all was *wrong,* a feeling that seeped deeper into him every time he reviewed the little he had.

It was a puzzle that had the *wrong* pieces instead of pieces missing. His meeting with Shiva had only made it worse.

He drove the Hummer onto Intercity 25 and took it north without concern. Whomever it had belonged to, wherever it had come from, Chase knew that within minutes it would be the registered and legal property of the identity on the credstick locked into the ignition slot. It was one of three newly forged credsticks that he'd been presented with halfway through his blind exit out of the haven. The Hummer had been Shiva's idea. It even had a full tank of fuel.

Chase almost had second thoughts about taking the credstick IDs and the Hummer, but Shiva seemed to be relieved, despite his pretense, that Chase had ultimately asked for something so simple. Chase thought there was a decent chance that no matter what else was going on with his old friend, the IDs would be secure.

He noticed the changing colors on the distant horizon and realized that his dealings in the haven and his long talk with Shiva must, in reality, have taken far less actual time than it had seemed. Another benefit, he thought, of a world where even talk occurs at the speed of thought.

He entered Denver proper along Intercity 25, exiting at Broadway. From there he took the Hummer cross-town and approached the hotel from the south. The front of the building was just catching the morning sun as he rounded the corner, promptly letting out a curse at what he saw.

There, in front of the hotel, were two men. Tall and lean, they wore long dark coats and looked far too alert for the hour of the morning. They were waiting and watching for him said a gnawing feeling in his chest. But they were amateurs, local talent. He drove on past them, casually glancing away at just the right moment. One of them continued to watch the light truck, but the man's gaze moved on as Chase slowed and signaled to turn.

They were playing an obvious game, and Chase decided he was willing to play by those rules.

Chase parked the Hummer just out of sight of the watchers. He got out, leaving the credstick inserted and the vehicle running. It was worth the risk. Pulling his Colt Manhunter from its shoulder holster, he began to walk back toward the hotel. The silencer, normally kept safe in its own little sheath on the holster, snapped cleanly onto the barrel of the weapon. He felt the gun's growing warmth as status messages flashed across his eye. It was ready. As he rounded the corner, he kept the weapon tight against his side, where it was buried in the folds of his coat. There was still a chance the two watchers weren't connected to him at all, but Chase doubted it. This was a situation he should have expected, been prepared for.

Sloppy, he thought. He was around the corner, halfway to the hotel steps, when one of the two noticed him. The goon's body stiffened, and he turned toward his partner. Chase continued on. The first looked back toward him as the second began to speak into something in his hand. A weapon, an Uzi III, street-drek hardware, cleared the first goon's long coat. The flash of a laser sight caught Chase's eye. The rest of Chase's body caught up with his cybernetic reflexes.

Chase pivoted the pistol at his side and brought the barrel up. The bright red targeting dot whipped across his vision and settled on the second goon. His mouth opened to speak, and Chase put a bullet in it. The man's head snapped back in a quick cloud of blood, and Chase kept the target dot on him and fired a second bullet through his chin.

Not sure what had happened, the first goon turned to glance at his partner. While he did Chase was walking toward him, putting rounds into either side of the man's chest.

The hotel's glass front doors opened, and four figures stepped out: Victor and Roja, the human man and woman from Manhattan, another man, and a stunned, will-less Cara Villiers. Seeing the second goon fall, Victor's eyes widened, scanning the street. Ducking below the line of cars, Chase reached for the first goon's Uzi, which had clattered to the ground.

He heard movement, people beginning to run, and Cara begin to scream "Nooooo. . . ." Then came the sound of a punch, hard and expert, and the whoosh of suddenly expelled air.

Roja came around the car directly in front of the building, firing her submachine gun, but Chase had already rolled back toward the curb. Her rounds hit the first goon's body and she began to turn toward him, keeping the trigger down. Chase fired, the gun low to the ground but angled up, catching her in the thigh. She yelled, and her gun jerked up from the recoil and sprayed high over him. She fell and glanced off the hood of the car as her leg collapsed under her.

Chase stood, the Uzi in one hand, his own pistol in the other. Cara was free and running toward him, wild panic on her face. Her two kidnappers were moving to either side, Victor to Chase's left and the unknown man to the right. They had their guns up and aimed at him, but they didn't shoot. They were afraid of hitting Cara.

Chase fired both weapons. The Uzi fired blindly, his arm jerking uncontrollably from the recoil. But Victor ducked. The unknown man took a round in the chest from the pistol linked to Chase's brain, and staggered back against the glass. Behind him, seen dimly through that darkened glass, Chase made out a running figure, his arms rising above him. The elf mage. Chase fired at him through the glass. The heavy rounds pierced the glass, creating a huge spiderweb of cracks that filled the window. Chase couldn't see if he'd hit the mage, but an alarm began to sound in the hotel. For once he thanked corporate security.

Cara reached him and slammed against him, gasping, but he was braced for her. "Freid?" he said, watching the front of the building for signs of the elf mage. When Cara didn't answer, he looked at her and saw the answer burning in her eyes. He understood, and he felt it settle in him.

''Go!'' he said, pushing her in the direction of the corner. At first he thought Cara wasn't going to obey, but then she began to run. A noise and a motion caught Chase's attention, and he turned to see Victor rising from behind a car, heavy pistol held before him combat-style. Chase fired the Uzi blindly again, putting more rounds in the car than anywhere near Victor, but again Victor ducked. Roja moved, and Chase pointed the weapon toward her, but did not fire as she crawled to the curb, her gun left abandoned.

He began to run, following Cara, but keeping the Uzi pointed back toward the hotel. Suddenly, Victor rolled out onto the street and came up firing. Two rounds passed close by Chase, one scoring his coat. He returned fire with the Uzi, but only one round spit out before the clip emptied. Chase darted into the row of parked cars and heard at least two more rounds impact against them. Cara was just ahead of him as he reached the corner. She looked back, still panicked.

''The Hummer!''

She dashed to it and opened the door on the driver's side, throwing herself into the truck. Chase reached it just as her feet slid clear, and he turned, expecting Victor to be close behind. He was, almost. Chase spotted him running on the far side of the parked cars, almost to the corner. Seeing Chase standing there, weapon raised and waiting, Victor threw himself to the ground. Chase's two rounds shattered a car and a store window beyond him.

Chase jumped into the Hummer and slammed his foot down hard against the accelerator. The light truck leaped forward, smashing and scraping against a parked car before Chase got a hand on the wheel.

Through the rearview mirror Chase saw Victor stand and aim his pistol at the back of the truck.

Before he could fire, Chase had turned the corner, and the Hummer was no longer in sight.

Cara was curled into a ball next to him, weeping, but right now Chase was more concerned with getting clear of the hotel. He took the Hummer as far north in Denver as he dared before hitting the Sioux Council border. He'd considered going northwest into Boulder and then crossing into Pueblo Corporate Council territory, but the Pueblo border crossings were tighter and more likely to pick up on their forged credsticks.

He stopped at the northern edge of Commerce City, a bare kilometer from the border crossing. Cara was still crying, but she'd begun to regain control of herself during the drive. When Chase reached out to lay a hand on her shoulder, she turned suddenly and grabbed it, pulling herself across and against him. She began to cry harder. He wasn't sure what to do and so just let her cry. ''It's okay,'' he said softly again and again, brushing back her hair with fingers that smelled of gunpowder.

After a time, she quieted and pushed carefully away from him. Her eyes were red and swollen and her hair matted where it had picked up her tears. She tried to untangle the strands and he helped.

Finally, she looked at him. ''Are you okay?'' he asked. She nodded, but didn't look too sure.

''I'm sorry, Cara, but I must know what happened.'' Looking away, it was a few moments before she spoke. ''I was asleep, but somebody pulling on me woke me up. Whoever it was knocked me onto the floor and put his foot on the back of my neck. Somebody, the woman, said, 'Don't move. We're not going to kill you.'

''I looked across the floor, and Freid was there. She looked hurt, there was some blood or something. . . .

''I . . . she was . . . They'd pulled a pillowcase over her head, I don't know why. The elf was cursing, yelling, he kicked her. The man, the one who was standing on me wanted to know where you were. I couldn't tell him; I couldn't breathe.'' She was crying again.

''The elf shot her. He pulled out a gun and shot her. I . . . they made me get dressed. They took me downstairs, they said a car was waiting. I couldn't . . .''

Chase reached out and pulled her close again. ''It's all

right. You did what you could, what you were supposed
to do.''

"I couldn't stop them."

"I know, I know," he said. "I understand."

She finally calmed again, and under their forged identities as father and daughter, Chase and Cara crossed
from Denver into the lands of the Sioux Nation. Driving
tirelessly day and night, the Hummer's autopilot brought
them within sight of Seattle a few days later.

PART 3

SEATTLE, 2053

Though no longer the fair playground it was in the twentieth century, Seattle is a vital and vigorous city. Today's Seattle sprawls from Everett to Tacoma, encompassing sixteen hundred square kilometers along the coast of Puget Sound. It remains an outpost of the United and Canadian American States. Hemmed in by the Salish-Shidhe Council nation on three sides and the Pacific Ocean on the fourth, Seattle is an active port city and still very much an important gateway to the Orient.
—Excerpt from *Fromor's Guide to the Northwestern American Continent: 2051*. Reprinted with permission.

"We don't have any social problems here that a few thousand troops won't solve. Know where I can find some?"

> —Marilyn Schultz, Governor of Seattle,
> during an interview on the local
> news program "Sound Bites"

21

He'd been staring at what little of the Renraku Arcology he could see out the restaurant's south windows. Some of the structure was blocked by intervening buildings, but there was virtually nothing in Seattle that could completely hide the arcology's 320 floors. The giant building, ninth largest in the world, had been constructed over an area once known as Pioneer Square, a centerpiece of Seattle's former life.

Now, it was the site of a building more than a kilometer tall that commanded the attention of all, its base covering some fifty-six square blocks. Some parts took their influence from the macroglass and chrome school of modern architecture, while others seemed to hearken more toward the master builders of ancient Egypt.

Chase, though, cared about none of that. His eyes and his thoughts were focused on the slow, precise shifting of the green-gray glass on one side of the building. Many of the arcology's windows contained special light collectors that channeled sunlight into the deeper, almost citylike reaches of the building, and then out the far side to illuminate the part of the city that would otherwise have been in the arcology's literal shadow. From that side it was impossible to look at the building, and Chase often wondered if many of Seattle's citizens had picked up the habit of averting their eyes out of almost religious awe. For Seattle, the arcology and her owner, Renraku Computer Systems, were a kind of economic god.

He'd almost achieved the level of attention he needed to perceive the minute shifting of the glass panels when the maître d' appeared at his side.

"Sir."

Chase blinked a few times and returned his attention to the restaurant. It was high tide, and a sea otter made faces at patrons through the restaurant's rear wall, which was entirely of glass. The patrons tried to ignore it.

"Sir."

Chase looked up, and then down, into the face of the dwarf. Though sans the customary beard, the man nevertheless showed the rounded, pouty features of his metahuman ancestry.

"I'm sorry to disturb your thoughts, sir, but there is a young lady at the door who says she is here to meet you. A Miss Janet Jane."

Chase smiled. "Yes, I've been waiting for her."

The maître d' nodded, but then shifted uncomfortably.

"A problem?" asked Chase.

"Well, yes, sir. You see, it's her appearance . . ."

"I'm afraid I don't understand."

"She, um . . . Well, sir, you see, we have a dress code."

"Ah," said Chase. "And she doesn't meet your standards."

"That's correct. I'm sorry to cause this—"

Chase held up a hand. "I understand. In this case, however, you're going to have to make an exception."

The dwarf stiffened slightly. "I'm afraid, sir, that our policies cannot simply be—"

Chase cut him off again. "Is Mr. Bjeland in?"

"The owner?" said the maître d', suddenly realizing what was happening. "I'm afraid he is not here at the moment."

Chase nodded, pulled a pen and small notebook from his pocket and scribbled down some numbers. "Here is

Mr. Bjeland's portable telecom number. He's never without his phone. Call him and ask him about your dress code. Tell him also that Mister Michael Dengeo says hello."

The dwarf stared at the paper and seemed to recognize the number. Chase saw his already wrinkled brow furrow as he considered his options. Finally, he said, "I'm sorry, sir. I did not realize you were a friend of Mr. Bjeland's. I will escort the young lady in immediately. I do apologize."

Chase waved him off. "Don't apologize to me. Apologize to her. She doesn't like to be late to a meeting."

The dwarf nodded. "Of course, excuse me," he said as he hurried off. To hide the smile on his face, Chase turned to look at the otter, who'd been joined by another. He watched them dance and play with each other, occasionally bouncing off the glass wall, much to the concern of the patrons nearest them. They obviously knew nothing of the history of the Gray Line restaurant and the fact that the glass wall was not merely a simple window, but was actually made of hardened ballistic plastic. In a botched holdup a few years back, a stray shot had created a flood of water that claimed twelve lives. The owner had vowed that history would not repeat itself.

Only a slight rustling announced her presence. When Chase turned back to the table, she was already seated opposite him. Leaning back in her chair with her hands thrust deep into the pockets of her glossy black leather jacket, she gave him a grin. "There's a reason, you know," she said, "why I like to pick the meeting place."

Chase had suggested the restaurant; he was fond of its interesting menu of elven and Salish cuisine. He suspected that Janey was familiar with it, too, and had chosen her clothing to protest his veto of The Big Rhino, an ork eatery with a raucous atmosphere a few blocks away.

Her leather jacket was stylish, with lots of straps and buckles and had probably been custom-made in Hong Kong. The black jeans probably hadn't been tailored, but they fit like they were. Chase knew that her black, knee-

high boots with their delicate silver filigree and chrome
spike heels were. None of these should have barred her
entrance, however, so Chase figured it must have been
the red silk and lace brassiere revealed by her open jacket.
Janey was staring at him, wide grin intact, daring him to
say something. Beyond her, Chase could see the mâitre
d' apparently explaining the situation to an elven woman
Chase took to be one of the managers. The woman didn't
seem pleased, but it was also obvious she would not cause
any more of a scene.

Chase's gaze wandered back to Janey. "Nice jacket,"
he said. "Is it new, or did you let an old one out?"

"No, I've always had it. You just never noticed before."

"Damn unlikely," he said.

She shrugged. "So what kinda drek are you gonna
take me swimming in this time?"

Chase picked up one of the electronic menu pads and
flipped it toward her. She grabbed it from the air a few
centimeters from his fingers. "Drek?" he said. "Oh,
nothing serious. Just standard fare."

She tipped her tousled blonde head back and laughed.
"Jesus fraggin' Christ, you *have* gone corp. The last six
suits I did deals with said the same thing."

"Did you believe them?"

"Oh, yeah, just like I believe the elections aren't as
fixed as my cat."

"Good. Well, order something that'll take the kitchen
a while to cook. What I've got for you is a long tale of
soured relationships, runaway teens, love-crazed rock
bands, murder, magic, assassinations, butthole politics,
terrorism, Fuchi Industrial Electronics, and a possible
corporate civil war."

Janey didn't even bat an eye. "You're right," she said.
"Standard fare."

Chase's elven dish of *se'-shepetra* was excellent, even
with the duck being a little gamier than he liked. Janey
wasn't as fond of her baked *ahal'eaish* and salmon, but

she wasn't complaining. After leaving the restaurant they walked cross-town, and uphill, eventually turning north toward Denny Park and the safehouse where Chase had hidden Cara.

Chase was observing the city, noting the subtle and not so changes since his last visit a few years back. Janey's attention was inward, mulling over the story he'd told her.

"Fuchi should be all over you," she said.

"I know. I didn't ask Shiva directly, but I assume he'd have told me if there was any word out about Fuchi looking for Cara or me." Then, again, Chase thought, maybe not.

"Shiva?" she asked. "Is he, or she, a decker? I'm not familiar with the name."

"Sorry, that's a part of the story I skimmed over. He's a decker of sorts, works out of the data haven in Denver. Old friend of mine. He, um, checked into things after the decker I'd been working with got burned in the Fuchi system here in town."

"Do you know which one?"

"Which system?"

She nodded, and Chase shook his head. "No, not a clue."

"Jack mentioned that he thought something had happened, or was happening, at Fuchi. Their systems design network is apparently on continual alert."

"Samantha Villiers, Cara's mother, runs the design shop."

"Didn't she get promoted?" Janey asked.

"To head of Fuchi Northwest, but she's still managing design."

Walking on, Chase spotted an elf watching them from the seat of a big, black motorcycle down a block to their left. Janey noticed the bike and Chase's attention at the same time. "Chummer of yours?" she asked.

Chase nodded. "Kind of. The Ancients are protecting Cara."

"The Ancients? You've got to be kidding."

"They owed me a small favor. Plus, I'm paying them," Chase said.

Janey was staring at him. "I'm surprised. There've been problems with the Ancients. I'd have thought their entire leadership had turned over since you were last in town."

"It did, but there were enough who remembered."

They walked another block, Janey lost once more in thought before she said, "Look, I'm in, but under two conditions. First, you take me to see Cara Villiers."

"Already doing that. We're halfway there."

"Second. We get more help."

Chase grinned. "That's why I called you, Janey."

The house on Dexter, just north of the monorail, was old and getting shabby. The moment they'd entered the Denny Park area, Janey had begun to show the same hyperactive tendencies Chase remembered from the last time they'd met. Her gaze darted over every part of the street as they moved deeper into the elven district and he felt the attention of the whole neighborhood centering on them. A block short of their destination, an elven girl rode up and paralleled them in the street. That meant that the local people had relaxed. The word must have gone out that the Ancients said the intruders were all right.

They reached the house, where two elves sat lounging on the front steps. Their green and black gang colors were barely noticeable, but Chase imagined they'd show up like a beacon if the neighborhood was wrong.

Inside, he and Janey were met by a tall, platinum-blond elf with short-cropped hair and dark green and black riding leathers. As they entered he was speaking in hushed tones with another, smaller elf whose face had a look of concern. The taller elf turned toward them.

"Janey," said Chase, gesturing toward the tall elf, "this is Falchion. He is a lieutenant, I suppose you could say. Janey's going to be working for me."

Falchion gave a slight grin. "Janey Zane. Well, well, it all just gets bigger and bigger."

Janey said nothing, only nodding to the elf in greeting. Chase suddenly wondered if there was more behind her reaction than just professional detachment.

He turned his attention back to the elf. "Is there some problem?"

Falchion snorted. "Fraggin' right there is. Step in here." He pointed to one of the side rooms. When they entered, Chase figured it must once have served as a living room, but it was now empty and bare except for a few unlabeled crates.

Janey was last in and closing the door when the elf began to speak. "You lied to us, Church. You didn't tell us Fuchi was involved."

Chase sighed. "I don't know for a fact that they are."

"Bulldrek," snapped Falchion. "That's the Big Man's daughter. They gotta be involved."

Chase matched his gaze. "Have you heard anything about her?"

"No, but that don't mean—"

"No word at all? Nothing on the streets?"

"No, frag it, but you shoulda—"

"If Fuchi wanted her, the word would be out, wouldn't it? Somewhere, somehow, the word would be out and the Ancients would hear."

"Don't push it, Church."

"I'm not. I'm serious," said Chase. "I'll tell you what. You tell your people to keep an ear to the wires and the nanosec they hear *anything* about Fuchi and her, I pull her out."

Falchion looked at him and was about to answer, but Janey cut him off. "I'm surprised to hear the Ancients are worried about a corp."

Both Chase and the elf turned to look at her. She had her hands back in her pockets and seemed casual, but Chase sensed a tenseness.

"You don't know drek about us, chica," said Fal-

chion. "Don't try to guess what we're about or doing.
These are tricky times."

Janey looked about to retort, but Chase cut her off.
"Do we have a deal?" he asked the elf.

Falchion nodded. "Deal."

"Good," said Chase. He turned, but Janey turned
faster and moved through the door ahead of him.

"One other thing, Church," said Falchion to his back.

Chase stopped and turned slightly.

"You know the girl's a chiphead, right?"

Chase turned his head fully around. "Yeah, I know."

The elf grinned. "Good, 'cause we're gonna have to
charge you more for having to clean up her puke all the
fraggin' time."

Chase nodded. "If you need to, bring in a doc you
can trust. She needs to be clean in a few days."

The elf snorted. "You're dreaming, chummer. I don't
know drek about it, but I've seen others who had it the
way she does, and they don't ever get clean."

Something was blaring on the trideo in Cara's room,
but Chase had no idea what it was and suspected Cara
didn't either. He looked at her, wondering briefly if she'd
gotten caught in one of Seattle's all-too-common flash-
rains, but knew the elves would never have let her out.
It was sweat that had drenched her.

She was sitting too close to one of the room's speakers,
and Chase had to call out to her twice before she twitched
in recognition. He could see that her face was swollen
from crying.

"Cara," Chase said. "Are you all right?" It was the
stupid, obvious thing to say.

She didn't answer, but her gaze strayed to Janey and a
look of contempt slid across her expression. Her eyes
hardened and she turned away.

"We're going to start tracking your mother to set up a
meeting, Cara," Chase said. "You're going to have to
get yourself together for that."

He saw her tense, and her left arm twitched in that odd

way he'd noticed before. It had become more pronounced as they'd driven to Seattle and Cara was without the sim-chips left behind in Denver.

She shuddered slightly, then looked at him full in the face. The old fear was back in her eyes, but he saw something else, too: growing control. "I'll . . . I'll be ready."

"Good," he said. "It should be only a few more days."

She nodded.

"Need anything?" he asked.

Cara looked away without answering. He watched her for a few moments until the sun suddenly broke through the overcast sky sending a thin shaft of itself into the room. Cara shivered and moved slightly to bask in its feeble warmth.

22

A few days passed.

They were gathered in the spacious, nearly bare loft Chase had rented for use as their base of operations. Cara, still suffering painful withdrawal from her chip addiction, was asleep in one of the adjoining rooms. Dancing Flame, a teammate of Janey's whom Chase had never met before, had used magic to induce in her what the Amerindian shaman hoped would be a healing sleep. Cara did seem to be improving, but the psycho-physiological war going on inside her body was taking its toll on her health. Dancing had told Chase that he feared Cara's acceptance of the cyberware in her body had helped the chip addiction gain its foothold and was making it harder for her to shake it off. Chase accepted that and trusted the shaman. He'd shared a life with someone of that point of view for years before she was torn from him.

What he found harder to accept was the amount of cyberware Cara actually had. For someone who had shown such fear of enhancements as a child, Cara Villiers had grown into a woman who welcomed the modifications. He knew about and had seen the datajack, assuming it to be the simple neural interface port that more and more average people were having installed for convenience.

Liam Bough, another of Janey's teammates and a passing acquaintance of Chase himself, had looked Cara over when the elven gang had delivered her. Bough, so familiar with cyberware from personal experience, recognized the jack as a more sophisticated design able to handle higher rates of data flow with less system loss. For a chiphead, it was the difference between a sedan and a sports car.

Chase was less surprised to learn that she also had supplemental neural-trigger circuits that could be used to command a music system such as a keyboard or guitar. That made sense. The fact that Cara's left eye was artificial, but had no enhancements that made it more than normal, did not. Nor did the fact that Bough's cursory examination indicated that the long bone of her left forearm had been replaced. Bough suggested that perhaps she'd been in an accident. Chase was simply surprised. Cara had never said anything about it.

Once they'd all gathered, Dancing Flame erected a magical ward around the loft for protection. If anyone or anything tried to get through personally or via a spell, Dancing would know. The loft also had technological protection, white noise and subsonic systems to handle eavesdropping, and, against the windows and walls, tremblers to counter acoustic lasers.

A nod from Dancing, and Bough punched a code into the security command box at his side. The ward was up, and the electronics were active. They were isolated and protected, hopefully.

"So," said Chase as the green lights on his console came on, "what have we got? Janey?"

Janey Zane was curled up on one of the secondhand couches that had been in the loft when Chase rented it. That and other clues led him to believe that the space had been used more than once for purposes similar to his. As the job had become defined and the team's tasks assigned, Janey's energy level had risen to the point where she seemed more like a thirteen-year-old. A very professional thirteen-year-old.

"Well," she said, "I've been scanning the streets for any word on anything that might be directly connected, and like the Ancients said, it's dead. Nada."

"Interesting," said Chase.

Janey held up her hand. "*But* there's a lot of talk about Fuchi on the streets. It's just that none of it contains the key words Cara Villiers, Simon Church, or Alte Welt."

Across the room, Bough was nodding. Apparently he'd picked up a similar scan.

"What talk there is concerns a possible coup going on inside Fuchi," Janey said. Apparently, there's been a shakeup in their personnel and a general beefing up of personal security. It seems to be centered around the top, and trickling down almost all the way to lower middle management. The suits are expecting a shakeup, too."

"Does it look like a resolution between the Japanese elements and Villiers?" asked Chase.

Janey shrugged. "No way to tell. I did hear an interesting rumor that Fuchi's been staging runs against itself."

"Against itself?" said Dancing, obviously baffled.

"Yup. The beat is that Fuchi Corporate Services, their management consulting group, sent a run against the Systems Design group."

"Corporate Services was Nakatomi-run back when I was involved with Fuchi, and the Systems Design group is Samantha Villiers, Cara's mother," said Chase.

"Corp Services is still Nakatomi, though their consulting is mostly internal now," said Bough. "Villiers isn't actually in charge of Systems Design anymore. Doctor Ben Bleiler runs Systems since Villiers got pushed up to replace Darren Villiers as head of Northwest operations. But she keeps enough of a hand in that it could still be looked on as hers.''

"Any idea what the run was for?'' asked Chase.

"No,'' said Janey. "Street's quiet on that one.''

"My sources paint a slightly different picture,'' Bough put in. "I've been talking to some corp types who tell me the rumor mill about the infighting at Fuchi says it's between Samantha Villiers and Darren Villiers, whom she replaced.''

Dancing Flame leaned back in his chair and closed his eyes. "Now you've confused me completely. When we decide what to do, wake me up.''

Chase looked at Bough, who simply nodded and glanced back down at the datapad on his lap, and then at Janey who was grinning. "It's okay, he does this a lot,'' she said. "Dancing doesn't twitch on the corporate intrigue stuff, but he trusts us. When we get to the magical briefing part, we'll wake him up. It's kinda difficult to understand him if he's talking in his sleep.''

"You're going to have to stay with me on this,'' Bough said with a grin at Chase. "It gets pretty complicated.''

"Don't worry, I'm with you. Don't forget, I used to work for them.''

"Right,'' said Bough. "And since there are so many fraggin' Villiers in this mess, I'm going to refer to them by their first names.

"Darren is apparently going head to head internally with Samantha over her control of the Northwest operations. She was in charge only a short time before they were hit with a series of fairly serious personnel extractions that have given some of Fuchi's rivals access to vital proprietary information.''

Bough looked over at Janey quickly, who gave him a nod to go ahead. "We ourselves were one of those extraction teams. We pulled a Doctor Marie Palo from one of their robotics labs less than a week ago, right before you came to town.''

"Any idea where Doctor Palo ended up?" asked Chase.

"No," said Janey. "We could guess Ares Macrotechnology, but that would be based on who might want her, not any clues we picked up."

"Could Fuchi have done it themselves?"

Janey looked at him. "You mean, like the rumors say?"

"Exactly."

She looked back at Bough. "No idea. Maybe. Coulda been. Hard to tell. The hiring and pickup were very pro from our end. We had no idea who we were dealing with."

"Darren is apparently backed by at least the Nakatomis," said Bough. "Since Seattle is part of the Villiers' sphere of influence, Samantha's ex-husband Richard maneuvered her into Darren's position when he got moved up to Tokyo. Darren planted the idea in the ears of the Yamanas and the Nakatomis that he thought Samantha wasn't competent enough to manage the entire Northwest operation and he's been using these defections as proof that others in the company agree with him."

"What's Richard's position in all this?" Chase wanted to know.

"Very delicate," replied Bough. "He's always been on good terms with his ex-wife, but he's got to be very careful of the power balance within Fuchi. If the Yamanas and the Nakatomis get enough ammunition, they can block-vote their shares against him and cut him off at the knees."

Chase considered this for a few moments. "So, let's say that the Nakatomis are actually behind Richard's assassination, or are at least involved in the plot. If they've tipped off Fuchi internal security, specifically the non-aligned elements, that Cara is involved in a plot to kill her father things could get very complicated if they even spot her talking to her mother, Samantha."

"Yes," said Bough, "that's how I read it."

Chase leaned back and stared at the ceiling. "God, I love my job," he said, sighing.

There was a snort nearby. "Now you know how I feel," said Dancing Flame.

Chase glanced over at him, but the shaman still seemed to be asleep. Janey giggled.

"So," said Chase, "what we're going to do is get me in close to Samantha Villiers and play it by ear."

"Wouldn't it make more sense to have one of us do it?" asked Bough. "You might get IDed by Fuchi security."

"Maybe," agreed Chase, "but she'll listen to me sooner than she would someone she doesn't know. Time, I suspect, is of the essence."

"Right," said Bough.

"We've just got to figure out how we're going to do that. Janey?"

She smiled and reached over to key a speed code into the small voice-only telecom sitting on one of the box-tables. It dialed, another green light lit up on Bough's console, and there was a click over the telecom's speaker. Then silence, and another click, before a voice answered. Chase had never heard the voice before, but he knew whom they were calling.

"Janey," said the voice. "I expected to hear from you sooner."

"Sorry, Jack. We were jabbering," Janey said. "I'm here, obviously, and so's Liam and Dancing. And Simon Church." She looked up at Chase. "Church, this is FastJack."

Chase had heard of the decker, but had never worked with him. The name was held in almost as much awe as the Denver data haven, of which FastJack was said to be a co-founder. It was also said that, as part of the old U.S. government's Echo Mirage project, he was one of the first deckers, ever, to fight the computer virus that swept the world's databanks in 2029. Chase knew that rumor wasn't true, however, because he knew the names of everyone at Echo Mirage. FastJack couldn't have been one of that group. Their fates were all accounted for.

It was also said that no one had ever met FastJack in the flesh. Some said he had none.

"Just Jack will do," said the voice.

"I'm pleased to finally be speaking to you, Jack," said Chase. "I've heard a lot about you."

"And I you. Shiva asked me to tell you that Lachesis is doing better. The doctors think that with therapy she should be able to feed herself in a few weeks."

Janey and Bough both looked up at that and then at Chase. Chase simply stared at the phone. "That was uncalled for," he said.

"Perhaps," said Jack, "and perhaps not. I have learned something of who you are and what you were."

"All of which is irrelevant," snapped Chase. The past was not something he wanted dragged out here and now, if at all. There were parts of it that were too hard to explain. "She took her own risks, against my warnings. Shiva would have told you that, too, or is it Bash you listen to?"

There was a chuckle over the phone. "I don't 'listen' to either one of them."

"Glad to hear that. Now, have you come up with anything or do we need to hire a different decker who can handle it?"

Janey and Bough seemed tense. Chase was sure their loyalties were being stretched. They'd worked with FastJack on many occasions through the years, as had other groups in Seattle. They also knew Chase, though not nearly as well. And they had no idea what was really going on between the two.

"No, *tovarich*," said Jack, and Chase felt himself tense. "No need for that damning action. I have the information Janey requested. Liam, plug your datapad cable into the telecom jack."

Bough leaned forward and did as Jack requested. Chase was suddenly reminded of his own datadeck left behind in Denver. Immediately, information began flowing to Bough's datapad.

"I acquired as much as I could," said Jack. "You'll find Samantha Villiers' personal calendar for the next three weeks in there, Liam, complete with cross-referenced and verified ancillary travel data. There are also records of her security, the personnel, and their normal patterns. I also pulled what I could of the architectural and security diagrams of the Fuchi buildings downtown.

"There's one event on the calendar that I would recommend for a contact. She is attending a party the night after next at the Renraku Arcology in honor of one Hiroshi Uchida, who's been sent in from Chiba to stabilize the arcology's management following their recent problems. The event is actually being sponsored by United Corporation Council, who advise Mayor Schultz on corporate affairs, so nearly everyone who is anyone from the corporate sector will be there."

"Which will make it harder to get into than the Zurich-Orbital," said Chase.

"Normally, yes, but there are aspects of the arcology's systems that I've had access to for years now. The party is scheduled for the West Garden on the two-hundred fifty-eighth floor. I can get into and affect the subsystem that controls security access to that area."

"I'm impressed," said Chase.

"You, under an assumed name, of course, have already been added to a list of personnel with access to that area at the time of the party."

Chase nodded, but Janey seemed annoyed. "Gee, Jack, making up our minds for us?"

"No, Janey. I've simply prepared the most immediate option. It need not be taken."

"Yeah, it does," said Chase. "We're running out of time. The longer we wait, the more likely things are to spin out of our ability to intervene, and Samantha Villiers could very well be recalled to Japan for it. For good or bad, we've got no choice."

23

Chase walked the streets of Seattle. A light drizzle of cool rain fell, but neither he nor the city noticed it much. Both were far too engrossed in their own concerns.

Cara Villiers. Chase watched the traffic pass and shook his head. Days ago she'd been only a memory, vivid enough, but not one he'd ever expected to see made flesh again. The resurrection of ghosts had become all too common in his life of late, and it was not a particularly welcome phenomenon. He'd spent a lot of time, energy, and emotion trying to move forward. Seeing it all come sliding back was disorienting.

Down the street Chase saw a man and a little girl who was probably his daughter attempting to cross the heavy, swift-moving traffic. The man wanted to get across quickly, but the little girl was distracted, glancing back at the brightly lit soy grill they'd just left. He pulled her arm, she stumbled, and then their chance was lost as the temporary opening in the traffic vanished as rapidly as it had appeared. The father said something to the child, his expression harsh. She listened, smiled, and shrugged. He picked her up, and when the next opening appeared, dashed across.

Following them, Chase's gaze was caught by a sign that read "Spirit's Way." He walked toward it and watched the large, full-motion hologram in a shop window. A brook wove through a sparse forest. Animals moved in the underbrush. Shafts of sunlight slanted toward the ground, brightening the air in sharp pools.

Intrigued, Chase entered the shop, which reminded him somewhat of Farraday's in Manhattan. But where the Cat shaman's shelves were mixed almost evenly with items of interest to magicians of the hermetic or sha-

manic stylings, this one was almost completely shamanic.

At the far end of the store, an old Indian man was
sitting behind a handmade counter. Dressed in a loosely
woven pullover of tan and brown, he was reading a paperback novel probably as old as he was. He looked up
as Chase entered. "Can I help you?" he ask ed.

Chase shook his head. "No, thank you. I'm just looking."

The old man nodded. "Take your time. If you need
any help, just ask."

Chase gave him a small smile as his eyes roved over
the shelves. "Thanks, I will." Chase knew he probably
wouldn't need help. He was fairly familiar with the kind
of items the shop carried, or rather she had been, and
he'd learned from her. He winced. A minute ago he'd
been out in the rain bemoaning the raising of spirits, and
now he was inside helping them along.

"You all right?" the old man asked.

"Yeah," said Chase. "Just memories."

The Indian cocked his head. "That bad?"

"No, not so bad."

"Painful then?"

"Aren't they all?"

The old man seemed surprised. "Even the happy
ones?"

Chase nodded. "When they remind you of things
you've lost." He looked away, his gaze falling on a old
barrel. From it jutted a half-dozen rain sticks. He picked
one up and tilted it. The beads inside ran along its length,
filling the store with the quiet, calming sound of falling
rain.

"Perhaps you should be happy you have them at all,"
the Indian said, then grinned. "That's from the Big Book
O' Old Indian Sayings, page one-eighteen, in case you're
interested."

Chase tilted the stick again and smiled. "I know. I've
read it."

"I had a feeling you had."

Chase looked up, puzzled. "Really?"

The old man shrugged. "Most who come in here seem puzzled or surprised by at least one thing on the shelves. Not you; they reminded you of other things. Things other than what they were."

Chase nodded. "They sure did." He put the rain stick back in the barrel. "Thanks for letting me look." He turned and started to leave.

"You should buy something," the old man said.

Chase stopped and turned, smiling. "Oh?"

Cara was asleep when Chase got back to the loft. He'd wanted to talk to her, to see if there was anything more she knew and that he'd missed. Dancing Fire counseled against it.

"This is the first she's slept on her own since she got here. I'd be surprised if she's gotten much rest before this."

"What do you mean?" asked Chase. "She's done nothing *but* sleep. And it sure as hell is hard to wake her sometimes."

The shaman leaned back in his chair and folded his arms. "She's been asleep, sure, but she hasn't been *sleeping*. She's been dreaming—nightmares, bad ones. Very deep ones. You can only tell if you watch her aura. But she does not sleep."

Chase looked across the loft to the room where Cara was, hopefully, sleeping. "She's getting better then?"

The shaman nodded. "I think so, but I'm not a doctor or even a true healing shaman. I suppose you could say she's starting to reach some kind of balance within herself. What that balance is, and what it's between, I can't say."

"Thanks," said Chase. "I appreciate what you're doing."

The shaman shrugged. "It's my job, but you're welcome anyway." He paused for a moment. "I had a cousin, outta Sioux City, who got mixed up with BTLs. 'Dreamers,' he called them. Anyway, he had it bad, real bad. The chips drove him mad, and then they killed him.''

Chase stared at the shaman, expressionless.

''But your friend is different,'' Dancing said. ''At first glance I'd say she has it at least as bad as my cousin, but it doesn't sound like she had that much of a habit. Real chipheads spend *days* wired to their fraggin' decks. What she does have, though, is something that's keeping her from slipping away.''

''What do you mean?''

''My cousin had nothing to cling to,'' Dancing said. ''He'd completely lost his grasp on reality, had nothing inside to sustain him. She's got something, something hard and something sharp within that won't let her slip away. Whatever it is, she's got ahold of it and is using it to pull herself back out.''

The shaman turned his gaze to where Cara lay sleeping, dreaming. ''Chip-truth, though, chummer. I don't know if that's good or bad.''

24

Chase and Janey Zane were sitting in a battered Toyota Monarch sedan a few blocks from the Renraku Arcology. A kilometer above them, on the 258th floor, was the West Garden where that night the corporate elite were gathered to greet a new addition to their number. Chase would be there, too, but for entirely different reasons.

''This reeks of a setup,'' Janey said.

''Sure does,'' said Chase. ''I never like it when there's only one option available. That's why I'm not trying to bring Cara in with me. Who knows what might happen?''

''Remember, if you have problems, get to a window on the north facing.''

"I remember."

Static crackled in Chase's ear for just a moment. He adjusted the earphone he wore, a standard corp accessory for the man he would be tonight, though the electronics inside his were far from standard. Liam Bough's voice came over the ear piece, which had been set up to operate more as a radio than a phone. "Scout One, this is Scout Three. In position. Over."

"Roger, Scout Three. Over," Chase replied. FastJack had slipped Bough into the arcology a few hours earlier, having placed him tactically some floors below the party in the guise of a maintenance man. If the things went off according to plan, Chase would see him briefly, but would not be in real contact with him or any other member of the team while inside the arcology. Their radio system was sophisticated enough that Chase wasn't worried about Renraku security breaking it before he could get out, but the arcology's security systems were sure to pick up the presence of any unauthorized transmissions from within the building. If Liam was on top of things, he'd have transmitted that last message from as close to the outer wall as possible. There, the security people would have a hard time figuring out whether it came from inside or outside the arcology.

It was time to check on the rest of the team. Janey, he knew, was in position. "Scout One to Scout Three, report. Over," he said.

After a quick moment, Dancing Fire's voice came on the line. "Scout Three here. In position. No problems. Clear view. Over." Dancing and a small team of breaking and entering specialists had taken their places in an office building that gave onto the north facing of the arcology. If Chase got into trouble, Dancing was another option for escape.

"Roger, Scout Three. Over," said Chase. The audio pickup built into the top button on his chic, high-collared shirt allowed him to sub-vocalize with minimum chance of anyone nearby overhearing. To them it would sound like a mumble, if anything.

He turned toward Janey. "Looks like we're ready."
She nodded, able to hear everything over her own ear-phone. "Scout One to Scout Four, report. Over."

FastJack's voice filled his ear, digitally clear. "Scout Four. The main Renraku clusters are active, but nothing to be concerned about. There's some opposition present, but nothing serious. I'm in the lower-level security cluster and will watch for your arrival. By the way, I've added that augmentation rider you requested to your personnel record. Over."

"Roger, Scout Four. Will advise when we get started. Over."

Janey looked at him. "Augmentation rider?"

"I had Jack append the fake file he dropped into the Renraku personnel record to say that I've been in an accident and had some internal reconstructive surgery. I was concerned about security sensors picking up what I do have."

She nodded. "Makes sense. Liam wasn't sure if you had any or not, beyond the datajack. He's usually good at telling."

Chase smiled. "My stuff's unusually well-concealed." Movement on the street attracted his attention. A group of wage slaves, probably returning from dinner or a movie, were approaching the arcology. Chase adjusted his clothing. "We're rolling. Once I catch up to the group, let Jack know."

"I will," said Janey. "And be careful."

Chase was halfway out of the car. "Always."

The Renraku group was a mixed bunch of Asians and Caucasians. Chase cut across the street and matched their pace just slightly behind them. He wouldn't actually get close to them until they reached the arcology's entrance, not wanting to risk any of them being members of, or acquainted with, people in the department this ID connected him to. Renraku had thousands of people working in the arcology and the odds were low, but it was a risk he didn't want to take.

To his surprise, the group bypassed the arcology's main

entrance and began to walk toward one of the smaller
ones. He'd have preferred entering through the harder-
to-monitor main elevators that adjoined the massive public mall. He was close enough to the group, however,
that anyone watching their progress via security camera
would think him part of it. If he broke off now it would
look suspicious.

A few in the group glanced back and nodded at him,
but none spoke. Chase relaxed a little. They must all be
members of the same department and he, being unfamil-
iar, was obviously from a different department. They
wouldn't talk to him.

He was following the group up a short ramp toward an
employee entrance when Bough's voice came over the
earphone. ''Scout Three, dogs are loose.''

Bough had spotted members of the Red Samurai, the
elite of Renraku's security guards. Chase wasn't surprised. They were bound to be out in force for an event
like this. He was glad, though, that they'd been spotted.
He'd have been more worried if they hadn't.

The group filed through the entrance, one by one flashing their IDs toward the security sensor. The ID, about
the size of a business card, contained small micropro-
cessors that the security system could read. The security
computer cross-referenced and compared the information
on the cards with the info in its own databanks. Only on
a perfect match would a person be permitted to enter.

Chase held his own card up to the sensor as he passed.
He wasn't sure where they'd gotten it, but when Janey
gave it to him that morning, she'd assured him that Jack
had already encoded it with all the necessary information. It was one of the best he'd ever seen, and he wondered whether it was a forgery or a doctored original
acquired through some shadowy means.

A red light came on as the security system scanned the
card. The lone guard at the door glanced over wearily,
comparing the image that the system generated on his
monitor with the actual face before him. Chase was dis-
guised slightly, enough to throw off any casual observers

who might know him by his picture, but not enough to fool a sophisticated image-recognition system or anyone who actually knew him. Chase smiled and the guard frowned slightly. Good nature was apparently not the norm among Renraku employees.

Finally, the guard's second monitor flashed with data. After a quick glance at it, he motioned Chase through. Chase nodded again, and attached the card to his jacket's breast pocket, where it hung by the adhesive on its back.

Beyond was a short hallway and a bank of elevators. The group he'd been following was gathered waiting at one of them. Chase walked past them toward the executive elevators at the end of the bank. He felt the group watching him as he approached the elevator whose doors opened immediately in response to his card. He stepped in, then turned and gave them a smile as the doors shut silently. Rank, no matter how artificial, had its privileges.

The elevator, however, wasn't empty. A Japanese man in a Renraku service uniform stood there at attention, one hand near the elevator's control board. "Good evening, sir," the attendant said. "Your floor?"

"MIS."

"Would that be one-seventy-nine or two-forty-two, sir?" the attendant asked.

Chase looked at him like he was a fool. "Two-forty-two."

"Of course."

Chase felt the gentle acceleration of the elevator and knew it was traveling even faster than it seemed. In no time, the car began to slow, then came to a silky stop.

The doors opened. "Have a good evening, sir."

Chase ignored him and stepped out into the corridor, turning left, per Jack's earlier instructions. On either side of him were huge rooms filled with rows and rows of cubicles. Finally, he came to a set of double doors that took him into the domain of Management Information Systems.

He rounded another corridor and passed a small maintenance cart and a worker who'd pulled a wall panel to do some work on the air conditioning system. The maintenance worker ignored Chase as he passed and Chase ignored him, too. They were both right on schedule.

Chase spotted the door he wanted and stepped up to it. The door's sensor recognized the presence of his ID card, approved it, and unlocked itself. Chase pushed the door open and stepped quickly through, making sure it swung open as wide as it could. Behind him, the maintenance man, Liam Bough, reached in and slowed the door's closing.

Chase went up to one of the room's always-active computer terminals and quickly inserted a datachip into the primary data slot. As the system read and accessed the chip, he typed the access code FastJack had given him into the terminal. Then the terminal began to execute a series of instructions and commands fed to it by the datachip, given exactly as if someone were actually using the machine, complete with errors. It would run like that for two hours, finish up, log its "user" off using the same passcode, and eject the chip.

As the terminal ran, Chase turned and slipped out the door just as it was closing. Bough had slowed it down enough to give him time, but hadn't wanted to slow it unnaturally in case some aspect of the Renraku security system monitored how long doors remained open. They knew the system kept track, via ID cards and the door sensors, of which employees went through which doors and how long anyone stayed in a room. Certain sets of matched circumstances would alert the system to a potential security problem.

Tonight, the system watched as Chase's ID went through a door into the MIS Technical Oversight offices and then logged him onto the local system, where it would track his presence for hours.

Back outside, Chase stepped into the hall, pulled the ID off his jacket and handed it to Bough, who gave him in return another ID he'd just pulled from a sealed, shielded envelope. Chase would use that ID to continue up to the party via one of the local elevators, one used much more heavily for inter-floor movement and less monitored.

In two hours, Bough would use Chase's original card to open the door to the MIS office and retrieve the chip. The system would have logged him out of the computer by then, and then registered the door opening with that ID. FastJack had long ago noticed that the Renraku system had no way of discerning in which direction a person was moving through a door, only that someone had passed through. Tonight Chase's team would be using that to their advantage.

Chase headed off down the corridor toward the local elevators. He had two hours to locate and talk to Samantha Villiers before needing to return to this floor to reverse the procedure. As he approached the elevator, he glanced to his left as he passed the office of the man whose identity he'd borrowed. Chase could only barely make him out bathed in the glow of three computer screens. There was a problem, a massive one, with one of the building's local networks. A problem with software that *he'd* recommended, and it had to be repaired by morning. He'd planned to attend the party upstairs, but this sudden, unexpected system failure would keep him from it. FastJack had seen to it.

As Chase, he'd be there in spirit.

Chase entered the local elevator, then slipped his new ID card back into his pocket. Fortunately, custom dictated that one did not wear IDs to a corporate social function. Everyone was supposed to know who you were, and if they didn't, they didn't need to.

The elevator rose to the 258th floor, and when the door opened it revealed a large open space opposite the West Garden. Music and the hubbub of a festive crowd greeted him.

Chase was surprised. There actually did seem to be a party going on.

25

Chase stepped out of the elevator and into the perfect crossfire of two armed Renraku guards. He stopped, then realized they looked bored and had barely noticed him. Beyond them, though, was another guard looking suddenly annoyed. He wore a uniform of much finer cut with more red and less deep gray. A Red Samurai.

Chase did not keep moving, but instead stared at the nearest of the two guards. "Well?" he asked.

The guard glanced at his partner and then stepped forward. "Sir?"

Chase rolled his eyes toward the ceiling, then looked the guard in the eye. "You're not going to check my ID?"

The guard looked confused. "No, sir, this isn't an ID checkpoint. The downstairs entrance and the elevators are confirming entrance."

From where he was standing, Chase could see the Red Samurai, an officer by the rank markings, watching the scene. Chase raised an eyebrow. "You trust the systems?"

The guard immediately looked nervous, like he'd forgotten to do something, but couldn't remember what it was. "Yes, sir."

Chase nodded, noticing out the corner of his eye that the other guard had resumed standing at rest, or the Renraku equivalent, at some point in the exchange. Chase nodded to him.

"Good," he continued. "It's my job to make sure you have reason to."

"Sir?"

Chase sighed. "Trust the system."

"Thank you, sir."

Chase gave the guard a little smile and then moved past him. He nodded once to the Red Samurai, who looked a little perplexed, but returned the nod. A small set of stairs led down to a landing overlooking the party. From here Chase estimated the presence of perhaps a thousand guests, and he had less than two hours to find Samantha Villiers.

As he reached the landing he suddenly realized how informal and un-Japanese had been his exchange with the guards. Both were Caucasian, not the usual Japanese he'd come to expect for Renraku guards. That probably meant they were homegrown, local recruits into the corporation. Interesting. The Red Samurai, on the other hand, was Japanese. His nod to Chase had been formal enough, but still.

Chase hazarded a glance back, but could see only the two elevator guards. They were both standing at rest, eyes on the doors, waiting.

He stood at the edge of the landing, a few steps away from a pair of Japanese women he took to be of the same managerial rank as he was. He could not tell their department. Like him, they were watching the crowd. Every so often one would make a discreet gesture, pointing out someone to the other, and then whisper in her companion's ear.

The party was a sea of semiformal wear. Impeccably cut suits and beautifully cut evening dresses were everywhere. This wasn't exactly what was known in the corporate circles as a "peak" event, where the fashion rivalry was as fierce as the corporate. Nonetheless, Chase spotted a few individuals attempting to score points or to rise a notch socially, without overstepping their bounds.

His gaze roamed the crowd. Most were Renraku executives and their assistants. There were some from middle management: Chase's guise was as one of them. He suspected that was also the rank of the two women standing near him. Their attendance was a company incentive; they could be there, but not make their presence known.

Nice as that was, it would make it harder for Chase to converse with a senior vice president of one of the largest megacorporations in the world.

Of the corporate elite, Chase recognized precious few. It had been a while since he'd been associated, even peripherally, with that crowd. Some he did recognize: Sherman Huang, the eccentric head of Renraku America. Brian Gates of Microdeck. Bill Loudon of Lone Star Security, Seattle's "police force." Karen King of Ares Macrotechnology. They stood out, each at the center of some small tidal pool of interest.

Then he saw her. She was standing at the far side of the room, at the center of a group of about six men and women. She was laughing, with the same familiar wide smile. Her hair was different, though. Twelve years ago she'd worn it shoulder-length with a very slight reddish tint that shifted it from its natural black-brown. Now, it was stylishly short and natural. Chase could even pick out the attractive silver threads that had begun to highlight it. She laughed again, and somebody handed her a drink. She thanked him, and turned her gaze on another person in the group. She was working them. Chase smiled.

He made his way down into the party and moved through the crowd, catching no one's eyes. He was barely supposed to be there, after all. He slowed as he approached her group, taking stock of the situation. At first he thought it was going to be difficult to attract Samantha's attention without simply walking up to her. Then he realized to his relief how very, very simple it was going to be.

He moved past them, glancing up only once to see her nod and take a sip from her drink. She looked barely older than he remembered. The privilege of wealth.

The West Garden was set in an interior corner of one of the arcology's extended sections. Long balconies ran along the two sides, overlooking the city and accessible through pairs of ornate doors spaced out evenly every ten meters or so. Between each were shallow, landscaped

gardens artistically filled with small shrubs and larger
dwarf trees. They weren't exactly in the Japanese style,
but the influence was evident. Chase stood in the small
space between one of the gardens and the doors it bordered. He was directly in her line of sight.

He did not stare at her, but instead watched the crowd
while keeping her in view. He stood, watching and waiting.

She smiled, thanked someone for something, turned
her attention to a newcomer to her little circle, then
stopped. Her expression changed as she looked at him.
As always, she was difficult to read. He turned slightly
and nodded at her. She glanced away, then back again,
unsure. Chase smiled slightly, then very deliberately
turned and stepped out onto the balcony.

There were few people out there, so it was easy for
him to pick a section away from anyone else. He stood
among the ornate trees and waited.

She did not come.

Chase waited a few more moments, then became concerned. He walked to the edge of the balcony, then turned
back toward a different set of doors. From here he knew
he could be seen clearly by the shaman Dancing Fire.
Chase was starting to worry that he was going to have to
rely on the back-up after all.

He reached another set of doors and cautiously stepped
through. He was a good ten meters from the first door,
but Samantha Villiers and her group was still in view.
She was listening intently to someone, but Chase thought
she looked uneasy. A waiter came by carrying a tray of
hors d'oeuvres, and she set her half-empty glass on his
tray.

Still listening, she began to glance casually around the
room, shifting her gaze with slight turns of her head. She
was looking for someone.

Chase had begun to move back toward her direct line
of vision, when her head turned just slightly more and
she was looking straight at him. Again her expression

changed, but this time she seemed obviously surprised, a questioning look on her face.

Chase cursed quietly to himself, nodded again, looked deliberately out at the balcony, and then back at her. He thought she might have nodded in return, but wasn't sure. Again he stepped out through the doors.

This time, he chose a spot where he could still see enough of the brightly lit room to just barely keep an eye on her. She'd turned back to the group, and had resumed talking. Chase was so frustrated that he cursed again, more loudly, when suddenly she seemed to take a half step backward as though disengaging herself from the group.

Waiting until Samantha was almost to the balcony doors, he let her catch a view of his back as he moved to a more secluded spot nearer the end. He took a seat on a low bench, pulled out an electronic datapad and began to jot down nonsense.

After a moment, Samantha Villiers came and sat down next to him. She reached into her small, fashionable purse and pulled out a cigarette, touching its tip to the side of the case. Triggered by the chemical contact, the cigarette lit. She inhaled deeply, then let the smoke out slowly. He saw her eyes flick toward him.

"Hello, Sam," he said quietly.

She relaxed visibly and took another drag on the cigarette. "I wasn't sure if I was supposed to recognize you or not."

He suppressed a chuckle, keeping his eyes on the datapad. In one corner of its screen a small "OK" flashed, telling him that the circuits inside could detect no form of electronic eavesdropping. It would be up to Dancing Fire to make sure no one listened in magically.

"If you weren't supposed to recognize me, I'd have pulled my jacket up over my face the first time you looked at me."

She smiled, but tried to cover it up with another drag on the cigarette. "Did the Middle East get too dull for you?" she asked.

Chase was surprised. She knew where he'd last worked, even though he'd used yet another alias. Had Fuchi been tipped off and then she'd been briefed on him, or was it something else? "I missed the rain."

"I bet," she said.

"Look, I just wanted to say that I've heard about the shit flying around and I wanted to wish you luck."

"Thanks," she said, then after a moment, "So you don't work for Renraku."

"No."

"You went to all the trouble of sneaking yourself in here just to wish me luck?"

"It really wasn't so hard. I have my ways."

"That's true." She took another deep drag. "So do you want to tell me why all the James Bond drek when you could simply have made an appointment? Or dropped me a postcard?"

Chase reached up and rubbed the side of his nose. "Let's just say it was inconvenient to do it any other way."

She chuckled. "And this wasn't?"

He shrugged. "You should rejoin your friends before you're missed," he said, "but tell me, how is Cara? I've often wondered."

Her eyes narrowed and she put the cigarette out against the arm of the bench, turning toward him slightly. There was an edge to her voice. "I couldn't tell you. She's in Europe somewhere, dodging the fucking French police, from what they tell me. You probably have more chance of seeing her than I do." Samantha Villiers presented herself to the world behind one kind of façade or other at all times, but Chase thought that now, just for a moment, he heard real pain in her voice.

Chase let her words hang in the air for a few seconds, then said, "You're right."

She looked up at him slowly.

"Cara's here in Seattle. Now. She's in trouble and needs to talk to you, privately, away from your corporate army without them even knowing. Now."

Samantha Villiers stared at him. He thought she might be shaking just a little bit.

She looked down, then back up at him. He could see in her eyes the emotion she was trying to fight back.

"Whatever she wants," Samantha said. "I want to see her. I want to see my daughter."

26

"So?" asked Chase.

He was standing in an office of the Raynox Building next to the desk on which Dancing Fire was sitting Indian-style. Dancing was still watching the arcology and the party Chase had just come from. It was winding down.

Dancing shrugged. "I saw what I expected to see. Her aura was clean, nothing unnatural, maybe a little cyberware, but nothing serious."

"Her reactions?"

"Text book. She was a hard one to read, though. Kept up a front as long as she could, till you knocked it down."

"Tell me," said Chase.

"She came in nervous, a little confused. Then she relaxed, but there was still an edge, and some other interesting stuff lurking at the edges. When you dropped your bomb, she was all over the place—scared, angry, confused, worried. Lotsa worried."

Chase nodded. "But it seemed natural, nothing staged?"

Dancing turned toward Chase, was looking straight at him, but his eyes were unfocused. He was still seeing in astral space. Chase shuddered. "One of the reasons Janey lets me stick around is my ability to read auras," Dancing told him. "She was clean."

"So, then, apparently she doesn't know."

Dancing looked back toward the arcology and shrugged. "Would seem that way."

Chase nodded and patted the Indian shaman on the back. "Thanks. Stay till the party's over. Let Janey know if anything happens."

"Done."

As Chase turned to leave, the Indian's voice stopped him. "Ya know, it ain't my biz, but you do know she digs you, right?"

"We were always friendly. . . ."

The Indian stared at him.

Chase started away again. "You were right," he said. "It ain't your biz."

Returning to the loft, Chase passed quietly through the protection he'd arranged, some of it obvious and some of it so well-hidden that even he could barely spot it. If anyone was going to come gunning for Cara, they'd have to get through a small army.

He went upstairs into the silent apartment. There were two guards there, an Indian husband-and-wife team that Dancing had recommended. The perimeter guardians had alerted them to Chase's arrival, and they nodded as he entered.

"Anything?" he asked.

The woman shook her head. Her name was Leanna. "No, nothing. The girl is awake. She wanted to see you when you got back."

Chase nodded and gestured. "In her room?"

"Yes."

As Chase started across the loft toward Cara's room, the man, Jacob, called out to him quietly. "Janey Zane called. She said she'd begun the preparations, as you asked. Tomorrow night can be arranged."

"Good," said Chase. "Call her and tell her that's fine."

The Indian nodded, and returned to his corner of the loft, pulling out a cellular telecom.

At Cara's door Chase knocked softly.

Her voice was quiet and far away. "Yes?"

"It's me."

"It's open," she said.

When Chase stepped into the room, it was dark and smelled faintly of sweat. Cara Villiers was sitting on the far side in a small chair lit from above by the glow of the moon coming through the skylight. She looked very young, very tired. He walked over and sat on the edge of the bed.

"I saw your mother."

She shifted toward him slightly, and Chase could see the thin sheen of perspiration that still covered her, pasting the cloth of her shirt against her body. Her hair was disheveled, knotted, hanging like dirty string. Her lips were chapped, and her left arm showed a near-constant tremor. Her eyes, though, were clear, sharp, and focused. He almost flinched when she looked at him.

"Did she remember me?" Cara asked.

"Of course she did, Cara. She wants to see you. Right away. Our arrangements. Our conditions. No questions asked."

Cara stared at him for almost a minute, making Chase decidedly uncomfortable. "Really," she said flatly, and looked away.

"Tomorrow night. She'll meet with you tomorrow night."

"Did you ask about my father?"

"No. I didn't have enough time. Besides, I figured I'd leave that to you."

He saw her take a long, deep breath and then let it out. She closed her eyes wearily, then looked at him again, brushing strands of damp hair aside with her shaking left hand. She looked back at him.

"Yeah," she said. "Leave that to me."

27

The place they chose for the meeting was an "out of business" restaurant in Auburn that Liam Bough knew about. The Caretaker had long since stopped serving food, but the place still catered to an exclusive clientele. Its owner made his money conducting another kind of business, the kind that would be going on tonight.

Chase and Janey had rearranged the tables in the main area so that Cara and her mother could have a private talk out of earshot, but within view, of the others. Inside were Chase, Janey Zane, Dancing, and Cara, the Indian couple lurking in the background as extra guards. Bough was up on the roof coordinating the small army they'd moved here from the loft. At this point, Chase was assuming that if anything was going to happen, it was going to happen here. He was almost expecting it.

His earphone crackled. It was Bough. "Watcher One to Base. We've got a Jaguar XTC approaching, deep blue, tag reads FSG 101. Over."

"That's it," he said, and turned toward Dancing, who was sitting in one of the booths, looking almost asleep. "Juju time," Chase told him.

The shaman grinned. "Back in a second." The Indian leaned back in the booth and relaxed.

Chase keyed his microphone. "Watcher One, this is Base. Confirm vehicle. What else do you have? Over."

"Base, I have nothing. It's dead out here," Bough replied instantly. "I hate the fraggin' suburbs. ETA three minutes. Over."

"Roger Watcher One, keep us advised."

Chase took one last look at the meeting area and then walked to where Cara was sitting quietly next to Janey. Janey didn't seem able to talk to Cara the way Freid had.

Krista Freid. He shoved the thought of her from his mind. Before this was all over, someone would pay for what they'd done to Krista.

Cara looked better. She was wearing a pair of jeans, a T-shirt with the new Seahawks logo, and a lightweight jacket. With her hair pulled back, she looked more her age. She was tense, though, and distracted. Dancing had examined her aura earlier and surmised that her personal fight was almost over.

"Your mother'll be here in a few minutes," Chase told her.

Staring off into space, Cara didn't seem to hear. Janey did, however, and looked up. "She's been like this ever since we got here."

Chase squatted down in front of Cara. "Hey," he said, taking her hand, which she immediately yanked away. It was her left hand, and that got her attention. She looked at him and blinked a few times. In her eyes he read fear, but something else, too. The same something he'd first seen days ago. "You all right?" he asked.

Her brow furrowed, and she looked toward where she'd be meeting her mother. "I . . . I'm . . ."

"Scared?" said Chase. "I'll bet. Your mother probably is, too. She was last night. I think she misses you very much."

Cara spoke very softly. "No, not scared. Confused." She glanced back and forth between Chase and the meeting table. "I'm not sure—I don't remember what I'm supposed to say. . . ."

Dancing Fire spoke in Chase's ear. "I'm back. Checked mom out astrally—nothing. She's clean, just like last night. Nervous as hell, though. Pretty much what I'd expected."

Chase turned slightly so that he could see the shaman, and nodded. The Indian was staring at him and Cara. Chase returned his attention to Cara. "Tell her what you told me," he said. "Tell her what you have to, Cara. It's why we're here."

She closed her eyes and nodded. "I . . . I know."

Dancing's voice came again in Chase's ear. "She's twisted up, chummer. Bet her pulse is way over the speed limit." Chase ignored him.

"Cara," he said. "It'll all work out."

She didn't answer.

"Watcher One to Base, Jag in the lot," said Bough.

Chase backed away from Cara, leaving her once more lost in thought. Shit, he cursed inwardly, walking toward the door. Off in a far corner he could just barely make out the Indian Leanna. They nodded to each another.

At the doorway Chase waited.

"Here she comes," Bough said over the radio.

The doors opened, and Samantha Villiers walked in. Chase was surprised to see that she was dressed so similarly to Cara. Jeans, a stylish blouse in the green of her eyes, and a lightweight jacket that matched the whiteness of her boots. Dancing was right, she was nervous.

Chase stepped up and took her arm. She was looking past him, into the restaurant, but from the door, she could see nothing more than tables. Cara and the others were out of her view.

"She's here," Chase told her. "Do you think you might have been followed?"

Samantha shook her head, still looking beyond him. "No. I take off in my car a lot. They've given up following me."

Chase smiled slightly, and shook his head. "Not likely. Your car's probably got a tracer on it. I know it used to."

That made her look at him. "You're kidding?"

"No, I'm not. Security used to keep an eye on the whole family all the time. We wouldn't have been doing our job otherwise."

She managed a smile. "Never any secrets, huh?"

"None."

She took that and thought about it while scanning the restaurant again. "So am I going to get to see her?"

Chase nodded. "Yes, but I have to warn you about something."

She looked back at him and stiffened. "What is it?"

"Cara's been through some hard times. She's done lots of things you wouldn't like—"

"What's wrong?"

"She's got a chip problem."

Chase saw Samantha's gaze harden. "Yes, I heard something about that a year or so back."

"There may be some long-term effects. She's very confused right now. She's got some things to tell you, but I'm not sure she can. If not, I will."

Samantha put her hand on his arm. "Thank you," she said. "Thank you for bringing her to me."

"She asked me to. I'm just doing what I'm told."

Her gaze softened. "Yeah, that's you all right."

"If you can," he told her, "persuade her to go with you. She needs help—therapy, psychoconditioning, I don't know. We've used a little magic on her—"

She stiffened. "Jesus . . ."

"It's all right," he reassured her. "It seemed to help some, but she's still fighting whatever the chips did to her."

"Okay. Let me see her."

Chase motioned Samantha to stay where she was while he returned to the main area. Cara and Janey were off to one side, waiting. Janey was looking in his direction, but Cara was scanning the room, rubbing her arm and looking everywhere but at him.

Chase nodded to Janey, then back toward Samantha, the signal for her to step forward. As she came into view, Chase saw Cara's still-darting gaze light on her mother, then stop. She glanced away and then back again. Her expression was one of confusion, but a look of slowly growing determination was gradually replacing it.

Samantha was standing there, utterly still, looking at her daughter. She wasn't hiding her emotions now, maybe because a mother's fear and concern were too great even for her usual control. She stuffed her hands into her pants pockets, and Chase wondered if it was to hide their shaking. But she gave her daughter a smile.

Chase stepped between them to stand next to the seated

shaman. He motioned Samantha toward the main area. She started to walk that way, slowly, watching her daughter. Cara was taking long, deep breaths with her eyes closed. Janey had leaned in close and was talking to her quietly.

When Cara opened her eyes, Chase was surprised and heartened to see a calmness there. She turned away from Janey and moved toward her mother, leaving Janey in mid-sentence. Janey glanced at Chase, confused.

Samantha looked as though she wanted to reach out and take her daughter in an embrace, but was afraid to. Then she started to say something, but Cara seemed to cut her off.

Chase could see them, but not hear what they were saying. Cara's back was to him, while Samantha was clearly visible. He imagined that she'd just asked her daughter how she was.

Then Cara was talking, seeming to be explaining something, and Chase wished he could hear. Samantha looked alternately concerned, puzzled, and then slightly angry. She glanced quickly at Chase while the confusion was on her.

"Dancing," said Chase quietly. "What's going on?"

The shaman was staring out across at the two women, but his eyes held that same now-familiar lack of focus that Chase associated with astral vision. Dancing was examining their auras. "I . . . I'm not sure."

Then it was Samantha who looked to be trying to explain something, maybe defend something, to her daughter.

Cara cut her off. She was almost shouting now, so they could suddenly hear every word, yet her tone was still flat, expressionless. "—not that simple. People like him have a book of excuses." She'd grown tense, stiff, but Chase realized she was no longer looking at her mother's face. Her eyes were focused somewhere else, slightly lower.

"This is weird," said Dancing. "She seems to be emotionally all over the track, but her aura's stable, like a fraggin' *rock.* . . .''

Chase looked over at Janey, who was looking back at him. She keyed her microphone. "I don't like this. It's like she's fraggin' *reciting* something.''

Chase's gaze snapped back to Cara and her mother. "—situations demand action. Insults are not forgiven," Cara said.

"Cara," Samantha said, voice rising too, "I don't know what you're talking about.''

"That's fine." Cara nodded exaggeratedly. "That's fine.'' Her left arm was shaking, more even than the rest of her body.

"I don't understand," said Samantha, glancing at Chase, then back to her daughter.

"I've never seen anything like this." Dancing was shaking his head. He looked over at Janey, as did Chase, who turned his head just in time to see.

Cara's left arm had gone stiff at her side, her hand bent back at the wrist, poking out as though in some bizarre dance pose. She took a measured half step back from her mother. "That's all right," she said. "You don't have to. *He will.*''

Chase reacted instinctively, reflex being all his body had time for. He felt the warm surge rush through him as his artificially enhanced reflexes forced his body into action. Time slowed, the situation became crystal clear, painfully obvious. They were too far away to reach. Janey was the only one possibly faster than he, but she couldn't see what he could.

Milliseconds slid by. Watching Cara's arm, Chase heard the noise, the sound of ripping, tearing, as the long, thin, gleaming blade slid out of her arm and down along her pants leg, wiping itself of the fresh blood. Blood that flowed with it out of her wrist.

His arm moved, as did hers. Cara gestured slightly away from her body, then her arm began to trace a wide, shining arc through the air that would intersect with her mother's neck.

Wrapping his hand around the pistol, he pulled it clear, feeling some of the straps holding it in place tearing away. Instantly, the weapon activated and began to ready itself. He had no time for it to finish.

Cara's arm continued on, her mother only just beginning to notice the odd movement.

Chase lost sight of the blade against the paleness of Samantha's jacket and flesh. His weapon was up, clear, the targeting dot centered on another patch of paleness already tinged with red.

He fired, stiff-armed and single-handed. In the arm's-length space between Cara and her mother, he saw an explosion of blood.

Samantha flinched and stepped back, reaching for her neck. Cara began to turn, her body forced in that direction by the momentum of her swinging arm. A mist of blood trailed after the arm, following it down. The long thin blade, snapped off by the bullet, spun end over end, catching the light as it fell.

Cara hit the ground a few heartbeats before her mother. Chase's legs began to move and he reached her in a few steps, barely ahead of Janey, who had her own weapon out but unfired. Cara lay facedown, shaking uncontrollably, blood pouring from her shattered wrist and pooling under her. "DANCING!" Chase screamed.

His hand was on Cara's back as Janey began to roll her over, and he turned to look at Samantha. She was sitting where she'd landed, stunned, uncomprehending, her face and shoulders showered in blood. She slowly removed her hand from her neck and Chase saw only the faintest trickle of blood there. He wasn't sure whose it was.

Then the shaman was beside him, his hands already wrapped around Cara's shattered wrist. But his mere hands couldn't staunch this flow of blood. He began to chant, and Chase felt power rising around them as Cara's wrist began to glow, the light seeping out through the shaman's fingers with the blood.

Cara coughed, screamed, and thrashed. Janey held her down, saying her name over and over.

Cara's eyes snapped open. Chase started; she should've been in shock, unconscious. Her eyes were hard, cold, and dark. She smiled, but it was the wrong smile. She laughed, and Chase felt his blood run cold.

She said something Chase didn't recognize in a voice that was hers, but much deeper and harsher. She repeated it, then said it again, and Chase finally recognized the words. She was speaking German.

"I am the stone," she said. "You are two birds. Two *fragging* birds."

28

"I've read the reports, Simon, however sparse they may be," said Richard Villiers. "But I want you to tell me everything you wouldn't tell them." Villiers was facing the window, looking out onto the smog-enveloped skyline of Chiba, Japan. Beyond the buildings, through the gray clouds, could be seen the faint blue-gray of Tokyo Bay.

Chase was uncomfortable. The summons from Villiers had come shortly after Cara's admittance to Nightingale's, the sophisticated medical facility that Fuchi quietly fronted. Dancing's magic had stabilized her, but she'd lost a lot of blood. He'd also been forced to use his magic to tranquilize her when she continued to rave and thrash about. Chase had initially wanted to send Cara to some private facility, but Samantha Villiers insisted, once she'd recovered her wits, that her daughter be taken to the best medical facility she knew.

Cara was still in intensive care. The medical staff was doing its best to help her, and had taken advantage of Chase's and the corporation's connections to fly in a mage specializing in healing magic. The doctors and psycho-trauma specialists were concerned about the descriptions of Cara's behavior prior to the "shooting," as they called it. When Chase told them everything he knew of her chip problem, they nodded a lot.

Still covered in Cara's blood he sat in one of the private waiting rooms. He was still refusing to answer the questions of two of Fuchi's security people when the summons from Villiers had come. His ex-wife had apparently contacted him directly.

The clinic representative led Chase to a small room on the executive floor. In the middle of the room was a table and sitting on top of it was a commercial cyberdeck, a Fuchi Cyber-IVx.

Of course, thought Chase, Richard Villiers is in Japan. The only way we can actually meet is electronically. As he jacked into the deck, he wondered briefly how the images would compare to the sophisticated ones he'd seen in Denver during his meeting with Shiva. Arriving at Villiers' "office," he realized how stupid had been that thought. It was Fuchi who'd invented the technology.

Chase shifted in the chair again. It wasn't the chair that was uncomfortable. That was perfect.

"I know very little for certain," he said. "Other than the fact that I'm a fucking butthole." Villiers turned his head slightly to look back at him. "I really am sorry."

"You keep saying that."

Chase looked away and ran his fingers through his short hair. He dove into the story. "Cara came to me in Manhattan and told me that someone was going to try to assassinate you."

Villiers' eyebrows went up. "Assassinate?"

"In Frankfurt next month."

Villiers took a breath and looked away. "I see . . ."

"She knew because some of her friends had been recruited to carry out the hit. Members of a German political group called Alte Welt. Sound familiar? It means Old World."

Villiers shook his head. "No, never heard of them."

"Well, Alte Welt was getting corporate funding from Fuchi," said Chase. "Still doesn't ring any bells?"

"No, but if anything does begin to sound even remotely familiar, I'll let you know. Go on."

"Their contact at Fuchi was a woman named Katrina Demarque, who'd contacted—"

Villiers held up his hand. "There's a recognizable name. But not to me." In response to Chase's puzzled look, he said, "Miles Lanier has been listening. Let me bring him in so he can ask questions too."

A door opened across from Villiers at the far end of the office, letting in a tall, well-proportioned man. He was wearing a finely tailored suit, Spanish by the cut, and walked with the grace of a corporate aristocrat. Chase laughed inwardly; Lanier used the same aristocratic bearing for his electronic representation as he did in real life.

Lanier extended a hand in greeting to Chase, taking it in a strong, forceful grasp. "How are you, Simon?" he asked. "It's been a while."

Chase nodded. "Long time." Lanier had been head of one of the subdivisions of Fuchi's internal security when Chase had worked for the Villiers. He and Chase had often worked together to coordinate security for family trips or business meetings. Chase had always disliked the man. Now he was head of Fuchi's intelligence-gathering assets.

Villiers motioned Lanier into the plush seat next to Chase. "You've heard what's been said so far. Anything?"

"Well," said Lanier, clasping his hands in front of him, steepling two fingers and tapping them gently against his chin. It was a mannerism Chase despised. "The name Katrina Demarque is on file. It's an alternate identity used by a company woman of ours. I won't go into details about her, as there is no need at the moment." His eyes flicked to Chase while saying the last.

Villiers nodded. "Did she work mostly with any specific departments?"

Again Lanier nodded. "She often works with control officers who are more inclined toward the Japanese corporate view."

"And you, Miles?" asked Chase.

"Miles is with me, Jason," said Villiers. "Don't suggest otherwise."

Chase shrugged and avoided Lanier's glare. "One of the things Cara's friends told her was that they were receiving inside information about your trip from somebody close to you."

Villiers made a dismissive face. "That could be damn near anybody. My itinerary isn't that secret within the company."

"Unfortunately," said Lanier.

Villiers looked at Chase. "What happened next?"

Chase sighed and looked from one man to the other. "I take it you're recording this?" Lanier nodded.

"Good," Chase said, "because I don't want to have to go over it again."

Villiers was standing at the window, staring into the gray clouds by the time Chase had taken the story up through Cara's meeting with her mother, then the shooting. It had been difficult to talk about that part, but he'd done it and he'd have to learn to live with it. The doctors said they weren't sure whether they'd be able to save her hand.

"Well, Miles?" asked Villiers without turning.

"Sorry, Richard, I can't say at this point," Lanier said. "I've already got most of the assets I can commit doing verification. There's no way I can keep the Japanese from finding out, especially if Simon's story implicates the Nakatomis."

"Don't worry about it," said Villiers. "I'll handle them again. Hopefully, they'll be real sensitive about making me angry."

Villiers looked over his shoulder at Chase. A light helicopter passed outside, its warning lights brightening the smog for a moment. "What about you, Simon? What do you think happened with Cara?"

"Do you know what a 'loitering missile' is?" Chase asked. Lanier nodded, but Villiers' expression was blank. "It's a special kind of homing missile. Very expensive and requiring very special programming. Basically, it hangs around waiting for its target in the area where there's going to be a fight. Once it spots the target—usually by the fact that the target is using its radar—it homes in and hits."

Chase could see Villiers slowly putting the pieces together, but Lanier, who lived in a world where dirty tricks were the rules of the game, was one step ahead of him. "You think whoever it was set Cara up as a kind of homing missile, then made sure you hooked up with her, knowing that you would get her close to her mother?"

Chase nodded. "That's it. Except it ultimately makes no sense."

"Wait a minute," said Villiers suddenly. "Are you telling me that someone brainwashed Cara into trying to kill her mother?"

"Yes, I am," said Chase. "That's what I'm saying."

Villiers looked at Lanier. "It could be done, Richard," Lanier said in reply to his unspoken question. "Besides," Lanier continued, "the hospital's preliminary report indicates that she's showing all the textbook signs of what's known as EPS, Executed Program Syndrome. She's done what she was conditioned to do, and now her mind is collapsing."

Shaking his head, Villiers turned back toward the window.

"More reports have been coming in while Simon was talking, Richard," said Lanier. "I think you'll want to hear them."

Villiers didn't turn, but gestured for the man to go on.

Lanier looked over at Chase. "Unfortunately, they seem to confirm some aspects of his story."

"Unfortunately?" said Chase.

Lanier smiled thinly. "It would have been so much easier if you'd been lying and this was all your plan."

"Gee, thanks, Miles."

"Stop baiting him, Miles," said Villiers. "Just tell me."

"Well, for starters, the medical facility has compiled a report on your daughter's augmentations."

"Her cyberware," interjected Chase.

Lanier glared at him. "Certain parts are delta-grade, virtually unique. We're going to try and trace their construction, but I don't hold any hopes."

"Delta-grade," said Chase. "That's amazing. How the hell did she get delta-grade?"

"Exactly the question," said Lanier. "Her datajack and associated circuitry are high-grade, but standard, with one exception. Embedded in the jack's neural modulation circuitry, the part that takes the incoming electronic signal and adjusts it for the actual neural interface, we found a polyphase subcarrier decryption circuit."

"*Shit!*" Chase slammed his hand against the arm of his chair.

Villiers looked at him, then back at Lanier. "Which means?"

"As Simon has undoubtedly guessed, one or more of the BTL chips Cara was using contained, in addition to its normal psychoactive functions, a subcarrier signal that was either part of her conditioning or else served to reinforce it once she was out of their direct control."

"What?" asked Villiers angrily. "It was telling her 'Kill your mother' over and over?"

Lanier nodded. "Probably a little more subtly than that, but yes. But saying, 'Kill your mother' doesn't work in and of itself. The subject must also be conditioned to believe that there are valid reasons the mother should die. It's important that the subject's brain be able to accept the command in order to execute it without—"

"Whoever they were," interrupted Chase, turning toward Villiers, "they probably used Cara's estrangement from you and her mother as the foundation for their conditioning. They took whatever emotions were there and magnified them to the point where she could, and felt she had cause to, kill her mother.''

Villiers had paled and was again shaking his head in confusion, perhaps despair. ''But you said she seemed normal? Wouldn't you have noticed?''

Lanier answered for Chase. ''Not necessarily. Her conditioning was probably very deep, and only triggered when certain conditions were met.''

''Probably seeing her mother in person,'' Chase said.

Lanier nodded in agreement. ''The other significant piece of cyberware she had is the most important. It was a complete replacement of one of the long bones in her left arm, the ulna, if it matters. It has a synthetic calcium construction, laced with a harder plastic material for support. Inside the bone was a blade, made of the same material so that it wouldn't show up on X rays or any similar kind of material-density scan. The blade was triggered by a pseudo-muscle that snapped it free. There was no exit port built into her wrist, so it cut through her arm as it ejected. It severed the artery on the way out, as I suspect it was meant to, in an attempt to ensure her death.

''One use,'' finished Lanier, ''one shot. Very deadly.''

Villiers was sitting down behind his desk, one hand on his face, staring out across the room. He slammed the hand down hard on the desk. ''Those mother *fuckers*,'' he said.

Lanier glanced at Chase. ''Luckily there was a mage there who knew some healing.''

Villiers nodded.

''A piece of cyberware like that,'' said Chase, ''the delta-grade Miles mentioned, has to be custom-made. You can't just order it from the Wiremasters catalog. It was made for her, made to do that job.''

Villiers looked at him. ''But why? Why the frag would they want her to kill Samantha?''

''Actually, I think it was targeted at you. Indirectly.''

''At me?'' said Villiers. ''Then why didn't she try— why didn't they send her at me?''

"Because she'd have never gotten to see you," said Chase. "Her mother was much more accessible, and therefore much more vulnerable."

Lanier nodded. "I agree. They were taking their shot at you, through her. Use your daughter to kill your ex-wife, whom you might still have feelings for."

"Two birds with one stone," said Chase. "She kept repeating that. Not a direct analogy, but close enough."

"Why do you think this?" asked Villiers. Chase could see some real anger beginning to smolder in his eyes, not the usual bluster he tended to.

"At the meeting," Chase said, "she seemed to be berating your wife—ex-wife—for something. I didn't have the chance to ask her what it was, but I'll bet it wasn't about her activities, but about yours."

"Mine?" said Villiers.

Lanier nodded again. "Mrs. Villiers has given security a more complete briefing while we've been talking." He tapped his skull. "They've been feeding me the data. Shortly after the start of Cara's conversation with her mother, she apparently began to rant on about Fuchi's dealings with Hanburg-Stein and how that all ended up. It was a 'pre-programmed' speech, but it was apparently very explicit with regard to Hanburg-Stein and our dealings with Der Nachtmachen."

Chase bolted upright in his chair. Had he heard Lanier correctly? "Wait, you just said Der Nachtmachen. Cara's story connected Fuchi with Hanburg-Stein through Alte Welt. Der Nachtmachen doesn't exist anymore."

"I'm afraid you've been deceiving yourself, Simon," said Lanier. "Yes, your personal campaign against them destroyed their leadership, which they deserved for what they did. But the group rebuilt itself, toned down their terrorist activities. I guess they learned, but they are still very much in existence."

Chase stared at him. There was nothing he could say. No words.

"There isn't really any Alte Welt, Jason," Lanier continued. "It's one of their fronts. All of this, every bit of

it, has been carried out by the hand of Der Nachtmachen.''

29

"That's absurd," said Chase. "You don't know that."

Lanier sighed. "I'm afraid it all fits too well. The story
Cara told you is correct, more or less, except that Fuchi's
dealings were with Der Nachtmachen, not Alte Welt. By
our reports, Alte Welt exists solely for the purpose of
voter registration. The truth was distorted to ensure that
you'd get her to her mother."

Chase shook his head. "I don't buy it."

"I'm afraid it's true, Simon," said Lanier. "Der
Nachtmachen, under previous leadership, is known to favor exactly these the kind of tactics. As you know, they
aren't against killing innocents."

There was something deep within Chase that rose up
in him, demanding that Lanier be silenced. It would be
so easy for him to just reach across and . . . but no, that
wouldn't work here. Lanier was lucky.

"If it matters at all, Simon, what they did to your wife
weighed heavily on my decision to work with them,"
said Villiers.

Chase turned very slowly to look at him. He said nothing.

"I wouldn't approve it until I was satisfied that their
leadership had changed. I took a lot of convincing," Villiers told him.

"It's true," said Lanier. "In fact, it wasn't until we'd
dredged up a particularly amazing piece of information
that Richard was convinced."

"Oh?" said Chase. They were fools. Their information was wrong. Der Nachtmachen was ashes in the wind.

"Amazing, I suppose on one level, though not by

modern standards," said Lanier. "Der Nachtmachen was a cellular group. When you took them on in Berlin, you eliminated their upper echelon: Lieber, Veitman, Kaufmann, and then Steadman years later. I guess he was hard to track."

"I didn't kill Steadman."

That seemed to surprise Lanier. "Oh? We just assumed you had. Regardless, you quite neatly chopped off Der Nachtmachen's head, and that set off a bitter internal struggle that might have splintered the group completely, except that someone else stepped in."

Chase shifted in the chair. A dark thought was beginning to form at the back of his mind.

"This is the extraordinary part," Lanier continued. "The individual who stepped in is a great dragon. A Western dracoform by the name of—"

"Alamais," said Chase softly. Had this been what Shiva was trying to tell him obliquely that night in Denver? Damn the man.

Again Lanier was surprised. "You know this? But you just said—"

"I didn't. I just made a connection. I'd received some information, information I didn't think was related, that Steadman had been killed by the same person who'd ordered a hit on a woman named Shavan. She apparently used to run a group called The Revenants. Another Europoliclub, I would imagine. She was killed in Seattle a few years ago."

Lanier seemed suddenly distracted and Chase paused. Lanier motioned him to continue. "Please, go on. My people are telling me things while you talk. . . ."

"The reason she was killed was because she was about to cut a deal for corporate backing with Saeder-Krupp. Lofwyr, the great dragon that runs Saeder-Krupp, is Alamais' brother. Alamais had Shavan killed to stop that from happening. Apparently he and his brother are at odds over the particulars of the European Restoration."

Lanier looked over at him. "This is news to us. We'd assumed that you'd killed Steadman, or had him killed, as the completion of your vendetta. What little we have on Shavan indicates that she was killed in a place called Dante's Inferno in Seattle, though that was covered up to protect the reputation of the owner of the neutral meeting place where the death occurred.

"The Revenants were absorbed by Der Nachtmachen a year later, or rather, former members of The Revenants began to show up at Der Nachtmachen meetings. Those kind of groups don't do acquisitions the way corporations do."

Villiers cut in after sitting back and listening for a bit. "If what Simon was told is true, then Der Nachtmachen had Steadman killed. Why the hell would they do that?"

"I was never able to find Steadman in Berlin," said Chase. "He went underground. By then I'd . . . I'd had enough of the killing and didn't go after him." He paused a moment. "But maybe Der Nachtmachen kept operating, only in secret."

Lanier nodded. "That makes sense. That would also mean Alamais' story was a lie."

"A partial truth," said Chase. "Steadman's death was probably Alamais' bid to consolidate his hold on the policlub."

"Steadman was killed by a bullet," said Lanier. "The report we have from the Germans indicates some evidence of magic used on the body after death, but they seemed to think it was used to parade the body around, zombie-like."

Chase nodded. "They puppeted him long enough to soften the transfer of command."

"That's disgusting," said Villiers.

Lanier shrugged. "Resourceful."

"Wait," said Chase. "Was all this public knowledge? I would think a dragon taking over a policlub would rate at least a mention on the network news."

"No, it was all kept very quiet," said Lanier. "Der Nachtmachen's name had been dragged through the mud. Fronts, like Alte Welt, were set up to cover its activities. Splinters of the Der Nachtmachen organization still continued outside Europe, but those had changed into real policlubs using the radical Der Nachtmachen name.

"The core organization continued in secret, gradually rebuilding. According to what we've been told, Alamais was worried that admitting his leadership of the group might cause some concern among the membership. Instead, he issued orders through a front. Some members apparently still don't know he's in charge."

"A front?" asked Chase.

"A second-in-command, though to all appearances, he was the man in charge," Lanier told him. "He's the one we dealt with."

The dark thought at the back of Chase's mind loomed larger. "What's his name?" Chase asked.

"He referred to himself only as Alexander," said Lanier.

The dark thought bloomed as all sense of reality, of control, slipped away from him. The room actually seemed to waver for a moment.

"Could Alexander have been Adler?" asked Villiers, referring to the German who'd seduced Cara.

Lanier shrugged. "Possibly. It would be more likely that—"

"Do you have a picture of Alexander?" Chase cut in. He was staring out at the Chiba skyline, trying to sound calm, to stay calm. He was barely succeeding, and the other two noticed it.

"Yes," said Lanier, "we do. It'll take a moment, but . . . yes, my people are transmitting the image now. It'll show up on the wall over there." He was pointing to a bare spot on the wall. It was just beyond Chase's vision, but he peripherally saw the picture fade into view. He'd asked to see it, but now he didn't want to turn and look.

"There. That's him," said Villiers. "Never met the bastard, only saw his picture."

Chase turned slowly, rotating the chair instead of his body. There he was, larger than life. He was on the street, talking to someone, grinning broadly. His age showed.

Lanier and Villiers were staring at Chase. "You know him?" Lanier asked.

Chase stared at the face. "I know him." He turned the chair again, away from the face and toward Richard Villiers.

"Two birds with one stone. It didn't mean Cara and her mother," Chase told him. "It meant you and me."

"I don't follow," said Villiers.

"By using Cara to kill your ex-wife, he'd be getting back at you," said Chase. "And by having me unwittingly do everything I could to make that happen, he'd be getting back at me."

Villiers shook his head. "Getting back at you? What did you do to him?"

"Twenty years ago I killed him. I left him for dead in the Black Sea. I left a lot behind with him."

"Good God," said Lanier, somehow knowing and understanding.

"Who is he, Simon?" asked Villiers, now staring at the picture.

Chase closed his eyes and leaned back. He wished some dark oblivion would take him, but none came. "His name is Alexi Komroff. He's my brother."

30

Both Villiers and Lanier were staring at him, waiting for him to say something. Chase was quiet for some time. He was trying to remember his wife's face, her voice, her calm center, and take it for his own.

"I think you'd better tell us more, Simon," said Lanier.

Chase opened his eyes and sat up. He looked at Lanier. "I can't, not really." he said. "Prior obligations."

Villiers' eyes went hard. "God damn it, Simon. We're talking about my daughter—"

Chase cut him off. "There are some things I can't tell you, but I suspect you'll be able to figure most of it out anyway." He was looking at Lanier as he spoke. "What I *can* tell you is enough.

"My brother and I haven't been close since we were kids. He's a year older than I am. We were in the military together—I'll leave whose to your imagination—trying to prove which of us was the tougher son of a bitch."

"You had a falling-out, I take it?" asked Lanier.

"Yeah, you could say that," said Chase. "The circumstances are part of what I can't go into, but yeah, we had a falling out. Like I said, I thought he was dead, and I thought I'd killed him. But don't get me wrong, I lost no sleep over it. And that's all I know, until a day ago. Someone we both knew told me he was alive. That's the first I've heard in twenty years."

"That's it?" asked Villiers. "He'd do this for something that happened twenty years ago?"

Chase shook his head. "I wouldn't have thought so, but who knows? I guess I don't really know what the past did to him."

Lanier looked distracted. "My people have just pointed out something to me that I think bears some consideration."

"Oh?" said Villiers.

"It concerns Simon." Lanier looked over at Chase. "They tell me that we have only the most circumstantial, and I want to stress that, only the most unsubstantiated information that the man known as 'Alexander' has been active in Der Nachtmachen for a decade or so."

That long, Chase thought. "Really?" he said aloud.

Lanier was looking hard at him. "The plane crash, Simon."

Chase froze. He'd been avoiding that line of thought. Could Alexi have done that? Was it possible his brother had changed so much that he'd have killed her to hurt *him*?

"I know," he said very quietly.

Villiers had paled again. "That seals it," he said, placing his palms flat against the desk top. "Miles, get Peter Lindholm and Annie Dexter in here. Find out where the frag 'Alexander' is and work out a combat strike plan."

Villiers looked at Chase. "Nothing personal, Simon, but you had the right idea in Berlin. I'm just going to make damn sure nobody gets missed this time."

Chase nodded. "Whatever help I can give—"

"We can't do it," said Lanier, and both Chase and Villiers looked at him. He shrugged. "We can't."

"Don't give me that drek, Miles," Villiers told him. "I want you to figure it out."

"I have, and we can't do it. There are too many obstacles." His gaze was locked with Villiers'. "Should I go down the list?"

"Maybe you should," said Chase.

Lanier nodded. "All right. First off, this is more than a simple tac-ops job. We don't have a sufficient team in northern Germany, where Der Nachtmachen has its headquarters, if you will. You know the jurisdictional problems we have in Germany with regard to corporate operations. Arranging and staging a combat raid like this would be nearly impossible."

"Then don't tell them," said Villiers.

Lanier grimaced. "Oh, we could certainly do that, but then what? They'll figure out who it was, and we'll pay the price for the next ten years. Plus, Richard, you're forgetting it's not your territory. The Yamanas run Fuchi-Europe. Do you think they'd consent to this? You're only going to Frankfurt next month as a show of unity. They don't really want you there."

"I'll get them to agree."

"In exchange for what? Think of the politics, Richard. You, your nephew, your ex-wife? What about all that? Right now you're in a damn good position as far as the Japanese are concerned. You can exploit that and probably end this whole confrontation. Play combat cowboy and it could be all over.''

Villiers was staring at Lanier. Chase could see him thinking and analyzing everything his head of strategic intelligence was telling him, and not liking it. There didn't, however, seem to be any flaw in the logic.

"I can't let him get away with this, Miles."

Lanier nodded. "He won't. We'll track him and deal with him personally. It may take some time, but he won't get away with this."

"No," said Chase.

Lanier turned to look at him. "I suppose if you want to go after him—"

"Shut up, Miles," Chase said. "Depending on standard operations is never going to end the problem. That's what I did in Berlin. They're like a colony of bugs. You stomp on one and the rest run and hide somewhere else. The only way is to take out the nest all at once."

Lanier shook his head. "That won't solve it either. When you hit them last time, they simply splintered. They'll do it again."

Chase nodded. "Probably. But what happened last time? Sure they splintered, but most of the splinters ended up benign. Der Nachtmachen is a registered legal policlub here in North America. They're radical bastards, but they're legal bastards. It took me along while to get that through my head.

"The problem is the head, the core, the Der Nachtmachen that's behind this. From what you've told me, them we can hurt. Besides, hitting them hard and bloody sends a message. It probably won't get all of them, but those who get away will know they made it by only *that* much and that we're not playing games."

Lanier had been nodding in agreement with everything Chase said. "You're right," he put in. "But as I said, there's nothing we can do that won't cost all concerned more in the long run."

"Then we'll get someone else to do it," Chase told him.

"We?" asked Lanier.

Villiers sat up. "Who? The Germans? They can't think much of Der Nachtmachen."

Lanier made a face. "And I don't think much of the Germans. Compared to us, they're amateurs. Not to mention the national bureaucracy they'd have to deal with. Richard, you can issue an order and it gets done. The amount of time it would require to convince them that a combat strike was the only option . . ." Lanier sighed. "I hate to think about it."

"Besides, who's to say where the Der Nachtmachen influence ends," Chase said. "It would take only one wrong person in the German structure to hear about the plan and they'd be gone."

Villiers raised an eyebrow. "Good point, but I thought this was your plan."

Chase shook his head. "Get somebody to do it, but not the Germans."

Lanier seemed perplexed. "Not the Germans? Another corporation? Mercenaries?"

"Mercs," said Villiers. "We could do that. . . ."

Chase shook his head. "It would take too long to get them together. We need somebody who can move at a moment's notice."

Lanier was frustrated. "I take it you've got somebody in mind? Care to let us in on it?"

Chase shook his head and held up his hands. "Let me first see whether or not some bridges are burned. Miles, have your people compile a strike profile as if your forces were going to do it. Find out where they are, how they're protected, everything. Do it all through your own sources, don't use the Nexus in Denver. I wouldn't trust them with this."

Lanier looked annoyed and turned to Villiers. "I don't see how we can—"

Villiers held up his hand. "Work up the profile, Miles, and do it fast. Let's give Church here the benefit of the doubt." He stared at Chase. "His reasons for wanting this taken care of are as good as mine."

Chase nodded. "And I can think of at least one other group that may want Captain Alexi Komroff just as bad as we do."

31

Chase wasn't sure how tough it would be making the connections he needed. If he could have trusted Shiva and the Nexus, it would have been almost simple, but that was out. He had some personal contacts in the Middle East that might be able to point him in the right direction, but it wouldn't be easy.

Before that, though, he had something else to take care of. Something entirely personal.

The security guards at the door to the intensive care ward were eyeing him suspiciously as he approached, when suddenly another man stepped in front of them.

John Deaver didn't smile. Chase was surprised to see the mage here, but it made sense. Chase didn't reveal his surprise, however. His body was working at a level it hadn't achieved in years.

"John," said Chase. "Long time."

Deaver nodded. "You never did know how to handle her."

Chase leaned just a hair closer to him. "Don't start. Don't even think about starting."

Deaver returned the stare. "You can't go in. You're finished here. That's what you should be thinking about."

Chase glanced away for a second, and before his head swung back, his right hand shot out, knuckles extended, hitting Deaver in the solar plexus. The mage started to take an involuntary step back as his breath exploded from his chest. Chase pivoted slightly, his left foot coming up and glancing hard against Deaver's jaw line just forward of the ear. Deaver crumpled.

The two guards looked at Chase and then down at

Deaver. Chase raised his hands and gestured at Deaver's body with his head. "He's a butthole. You, on the other hand, are going to call your bosses and find out whether I'm allowed inside or not."

The one guard almost smiled. "That won't be necessary. We knew you were allowed in. Mrs. Villiers ordered it, and I sure as hell don't want to be the one to get her bent now."

Chase paused outside the isolation ward. From the hallway, he could see inside to the observation room and Samantha Villiers. She was standing, listening to someone, probably a representative of the medical facility. Her arms were crossed, and she nodded slightly as she listened. Beyond her, Chase saw a single medical bed. Lying on it was the small, still form of Cara Villiers.

He pushed against the door. It yielded to his pressure and opened with a hiss as the air seal was broken. The representative turned and scowled slightly at him. Chase was expressionless.

"Leave us alone," he said.

Samantha Villiers glanced up at the sound of his voice, then nodded at the representative. Without a glance, the man left.

Chase stepped up and placed one hand on Samantha's shoulder. "What have they told you?" he asked.

She took a sharp breath before answering. "They don't think the hand graft will take. You did too much damage."

He winced. He couldn't have done anything else. No options, only reflexes.

She turned slightly and touched his arm with her hand. "I'm sorry," she said. "I didn't mean it that way."

He shook his head. "No, you're right. I should never have let it happen."

She let her hand fall away, but turned to him full face. There were tears in her eyes, but also a calm strength that said much about who she was. "You did what you had to do. If it hadn't been you, it would have been someone else, and Cara and I might both be dead."

Chase shook his head again. "No, it had to be me. That was half the point."

She was confused, but he waved off the question. "Later," he said. "Ask Richard."

She nodded. "I will."

"I just wanted to see that everything was all right before I try to arrange some things." He looked through the inner window at Cara. "Some things that need taking care of."

Samantha nodded. "You do that. And then come back. I don't want you vanishing like last time."

Chase took a step back toward the door, but kept his eyes on her. "We'll see."

She nodded and smiled wistfully, then turned back to Cara. Chase couldn't read her expression, and he didn't have the luxury of pondering it. It was time to be on his way.

The telecom was supposed to be secure. He was taking Lanier's word for it, with Richard Villiers' behind it. Chase had spoken first with Janey, filled her in, then tapped in the number she'd given him. It was a private emergency number. Audio only.

FastJack answered on the first ring.

"Jack, this is Simon Church."

"How's the girl?"

"Well enough, all things considered."

"I was sorry to hear how it all turned out, " Jack said.

"Me, too," said Chase. "I need your help."

"Oh?"

"I need some information. I can't use the Nexus directly, I can't trust Shiva on this."

"That makes it difficult, to say the least."

"I'd like you to get the scan for me, Jack. Direct. Private."

"What do you want me to do?"

"I need someone's private telecom number. Somebody important whose number isn't listed publicly."

"That shouldn't be hard. Where is he?"

"In Moscow, Jack," Chase said. "He's in Moscow."

PART 4

GERMANY

Dragon, Great (*Draco sapiens*)   A sub-form common to each of the standard dracoform types (eastern, feathered, and western), great dragons are typically up to 50 percent larger than average lesser dragons. As a group they tend to be extremely intelligent, usually conversant in at least one human language and often many. They are also magicians of great power, tending toward shamanic-style practices, though the nature of their beliefs are undetermined.

Though alien in culture and psychology, dragons, particularly great dragons, show an unaccountable interest in human culture and motivations. As none of the twelve or so known great dragons will comment on this fascination, its nature and implications remains a mystery.

—Excerpted and abridged from *Soul of the Beast: Draconic Anthropological Studies,*
New World Press, Manhattan, 2051

32

The stealth transports were slipping neatly over the Baltic Sea, skirting Polish airspace and concealed from everything that looked their way. There were three of them, identical in design and in their absence of markings. They flew blind, relying on data from the three-dimensional electronic maps stored in their onboard computers and on detailed information fed them by a navigation satellite high overhead. The only sign of their presence was the slight electromagnetic leakage from those computer systems, the faint bloom of heat from the dampened engine exhausts, and their ghostly silhouettes in the night sky.

"Three minutes to Polish airspace," came a voice over the lead aircraft's intercom. Sitting in the converted cargo space of that craft, Chase shifted uncomfortably to adjust the load of his gear. Not for the first time did he question his decision to go in with the airborne contingent. Thinking about his long-ago training, he hoped it was true that such knowledge was never forgotten.

The group of aircraft would pass through Polish airspace for no more than a few minutes on their way to northern Germany. At the moment they were well within the zone watched by both German and Polish air-search radars, but those were not a concern. The mission's planners were more worried about accidentally crossing paths with an air patrol or a routine transport from the German port and military base at Bergen. Their flight path would take them across the northwest corner of Poland, about a hundred kilometers from that base.

Chase looked around at the other men in the craft, and marveled at how much had changed. Twenty years ago he'd been part of a team much like this one, but that team's reliance on technology had been minimal, a luxury their country couldn't afford, not even for their elite. Now, the sophistication and expense of each member's combat suits, let alone the aircraft that carried them, was staggering. It was far more than Chase had expected, but he'd lost the ability to be surprised a few days ago.

The one standing man, the platoon's senior sergeant, finished his last-minute briefing of the three squad leaders, then moved, combat rifle in hand, down the center of the aircraft toward Chase. The other men were seated against the sides of the aircraft, all of them garbed in mottled black and gray battle dress hung with matte-black equipment. Because they sat with the face shields of their combat helmets up, their faces were visible. They seemed relaxed, jovial, and continued the round of banter that had begun a few hours ago on the ground at the air base. Chase remembered only too well both the tradition and the anxiety it concealed.

The senior sergeant sat down next to Chase, forcing him to slide over on the slightly contoured bench. Gennadi Demchenko was still grinning at someone's last jesting remarks as he settled in his seat and handed Chase the assault rifle. Noticing another such weapon slung across the sergeant's back, Chase looked at him questioningly.

Demchenko shrugged. "Let's just say that the lieutenant has decided that the order to restrict you to carrying only a sidearm never filtered down through the proper channels. He expects to be very angry at someone, probably me, once we get back."

Chase smiled and hefted the weapon, examining it.

"This gun has a remarkable similarity to the prototype CAR-32 combat rifle Ares Macrotechnology was testing a few years back," he said.

The sergeant shrugged again, then smiled. "Our weapon designs are often imitated, and we suspect the AK-51 will be no exception."

The intercom crackled. "We are in Polish airspace. German airspace in six minutes. Mission standby in fifty minutes."

Chase glanced up at the words, then lifted the bullpup-style weapon, slipping his hand around the grip. It sprang to life immediately, sensing the presence of the smartgun weapon link in his palm. The rifle was ready and its status displayed in Chase's eye in a fraction of the time it took his heavy pistol to prepare.

Demchenko nodded. "I wasn't sure if your cyberware would be up to interfacing with the gun's systems. This has got the latest-generation hardware."

Chase released the weapon, slung its strap over his shoulder, then worked to find the most comfortable position for carrying it. He noticed that the gun remained active for a few seconds after he'd removed his hand, apparently just in case the connection loss was only temporary or unintended. Very clever design.

"Don't always go by what the files tell you," Chase said, turning the weapon upside-down. At his mental command, the ejection mechanism engaged and the clip popped up a few centimeters. He removed it and examined the color-coded striping across the top. He chuckled. "Well, I'm impressed. Caseless, light armor-piercing round, explosive tip. What's the red and black stripe?"

"Depleted uranium."

Chase raised an eyebrow.

"Just the very tip, for penetrating vehicular armor," the sergeant told him. "Just in case."

"Aren't you worried about blow-through?"

"The round fragments well," Demchenko said. "Besides, this isn't a hostage situation."

Chase noticed that the weapon's visual status display

indicated that the rifle had an under-barrel grenade launcher fed from a magazine of eight minigrenades. The ammo counter, however, read zero. "No grenades?" Chase asked.

The senior sergeant grinned. "I give you an automatic rifle instead of your pistol, and now you want grenades?"

Chase shrugged, distracted for a moment by a round of laughter from the other platoon members. The sergeant turned briefly, then looked back at Chase, shaking his head. "Too many of them don't understand," he said quietly. "What we're doing may not be unprecedented, but it's explosive politically if we're discovered."

Chase braced the combat rifle against his thigh and powered it down for safety. "How many of these missions do you pull a year?"

"I really shouldn't say, but it's probably no more than what would have been normal when you were active." The sergeant looked down and began to work an invisible bit of dirt off his boot. "But not at all like the one you were involved in."

"How much do the others know about that?"

"Nothing," said the sergeant. "Only the officers, and me, because the lieutenant thought that it might be a good idea since I'd be looking out for you."

"How do you feel about that?"

The sergeant eyed him oddly. "About covering you or about what you did?"

"Both."

Demchenko shrugged. "When I was in tactical school, we actually looked at your mission profile and execution files once. It created quite a controversy when the administration found out, but . . ." He leaned back against the aircraft wall. "It was all very unfortunate. Many wrong decisions were made by everyone involved. But the loss of a guided missile cruiser is not something that can be tolerated, regardless of whether it's called a 'theft' or 'defection.'"

"No," said Chase, "I suppose not." He sighed. "I'm

amazed to this day that I never thought to question those orders. To go in and just kill them . . ."

"He was your commanding officer and your brother. You had no reason to doubt the veracity of what he told you. Why would you?"

Chase looked at him. "Because I'm a human being."

"You were a soldier. Soldiers receive inhuman orders all the time. It's why there are soldiers. We do the things human beings will not."

Chase looked away and then leaned back as well. He looked at the tarpaulin-covered crates, possibly mechanisms, that were built into the aircraft near the rear cargo ramp. They were also immediately adjacent to two normal-sized emergency exits. Nobody would tell him what those crates were. Chase tilted his head back.

"I'm not a soldier anymore," he said.

"Then why are you here?"

Chase closed his eyes. "It's something I have to do," he said. "I have to see it to the end. I'm playing the game, and these are the rules."

"Sometimes," the sergeant said to him, "we must be soldiers even if we don't wish to. Those are the rules, and until the game changes, that's the way it will stay."

33

The transport was in the midst of a gliding, banking turn as Chase dropped from it, the second to last out the rear of the aircraft. Last out was Senior Sergeant Demchenko, as befit his position as assistant platoon leader. The platoon's leader, Senior Lieutenant Grachev, had been first out into the clouds, his men following. The cloud cover was heavy, but high, and Chase was only lost in the black soup for a few moments before he fell into the open.

The sophisticated circuits in his battle gear were monitoring the drop the entire way. They'd flashed a warning on the visor of his headgear just as the automatic deployment system slid him down the rail and out the back of the aircraft. Now, in free fall, it told him exactly how far below him in the darkness was the hard, unyielding ground. He wasn't sure if he was pleased to have that information.

The air was misty, but with enough visibility to just make out the foggy glow of Magdeburg kilometers to the south. A message crackled over his headset radio.

"Rocks inbound." It was the voice of the company commander, Major Abdirov, alerting Fourth Platoon on the ground that the airborne elements were incoming. Because of the real danger of the Germans intercepting their radio transmissions, they'd decided to make all communications, radio and personal, in English. None of the soldiers carried anything that marked their country of origin. Chase suddenly thought of the combat rifles. They *were* Ares CAR-32s; the unit wouldn't be carrying actual Kalashnikova weapons for that very reason. Where had they obtained the weapons?

He twisted in flight to get a look at the retreating stealth transports, but the cloud cover now obscured them completely. He'd have to take a good look at one of them later when the V/STOL craft picked them up after the mission. He hadn't been able to see much of the transport when they'd loaded up; only the rear profile was visible as they'd transferred from the trucks to the aircraft. It looked familiar, but Chase had dismissed that impression as a debt of design. Now he wanted a better look.

The altimeter display began flashing. It and every other gauge on the helmet's heads-up display was red to maintain his night vision. The flashing was an early warning that it was almost time to deploy his chute.

He rotated again and faced the ground. Without moonlight, all that lay below him was almost impenetrably black. He raised the light amplification in his own eyes as high as he could, trusting them over the helmet's system. There was only a slight increase in clarity; without moonlight there was little light to amplify.

Even his heat-sensitive thermographic systems were of little help. The ground and the base ground cover were all the same temperature, and so offered no differentiation between them to his sight. His vision systems, coupled with what light amplification he had, were sophisticated enough to separate the larger trees from the ground, however. Fortunately, the sun had shone earlier in the day and both trees and ground were retaining, and radiating, uneven amounts of heat.

Then he saw them clearly. Small infrared signals, probably no bigger than his palm, but large enough to be seen from above. The company's Fourth Platoon had been infiltrated into the area the day before by conventional means. They'd crossed the border with fake passports, and had moved into the area earlier to isolate it. A small bridge had been demolished, and flares and barricades set up to block the road. The only other road in was to have been blocked by a delivery truck that had lost control on the slick road and rolled onto its side. The truck was to be abandoned there, with no license plates, leaving the local authorities with a slow and sorry mess to deal with once it was found.

Isolating the area was only a precaution, for traffic in this part of the countryside was highly unlikely at the time of the night for which the raid was scheduled. Still, the mission's planners had wisely chosen to play it very safe. There was always the danger of local authorities getting involved once the shooting broke out, and any actions that could delay their arrival at the site were necessary.

Chase knew little of the actual plan, because its creators had decided to keep him uninformed. He'd almost been barred from the mission, despite the fact that he'd been the one to give them the information—quietly, via Fuchi—that permitted it. It was only in the last few hours that word had come down from higher up the military chain that he be allowed to take part. They'd even tem-

porarily restored his old rank to get around the rule that
civilians were forbidden to participate in special military
operations.

Chase wondered about that, too. Was it an offering,
part of a bid to bring him back into the fold? Or had it
simply been decided that "accidents" were easier to arrange in combat. He just didn't know.

Falling, he focused on the infrared signals. Some
member of Fourth Platoon had placed them in the middle
of the small fields that surrounded their target. A single
infrared light, invisible except to thermographic systems,
indicated the landing and eventual pickup point for First
Platoon. Two lights for the second platoon, and so on.

The transport and the deployment systems had func-
tioned perfectly, putting him and the rest of the platoon
almost directly over their landing zone. Chase could
barely make out the others falling below him, even with
his thermographic vision: one component of their combat
suits dampened and absorbed their body heat. It made
them harder for Chase to see, but it also made it harder
for an enemy using similar vision systems to spot them.

Shapes blossomed between Chase and the ground as
the parachutes began to open. He watched the display on
his own visor, and when the solid red box appeared, he
pulled the cord to open his.

The abrupt change in velocity as the chute deployed
was what he'd expected, and remembered. It was fully
open within seconds, and his descent to the ground
slowed to a much more survivable rate. He glanced up
to confirm its deployment as best he could in the darkness. Everything looked fine. Seeing the control cables
and handles where they should be, he reached up to grab
them.

His chute was actually a paraglider, steerable within
reason to allow for a more controlled landing. Chase
needed to make only a slight adjustment to his course as
he came in on the single light.

At the last moment, he shifted to the right as the
ground detail became clearer and he saw the rough shape

of what could have been a collapsed chute directly below him. Fearful of landing on top of another of the platoon members, he twisted and landed off-balance, hitting hard. Bulky as the combat suit was, Chase was thankful for the protection of its body armor as he hit, having had little time to prepare. He felt the breath rush out of him, and then the slight drag of the chute as it began to collapse and pull him along the ground. He dug in as best he could, and with no real wind to fill the chute, it collapsed completely.

Chase scrambled to his feet as ground commands began echoing in his ears from the helmet radio. All three platoons were down, with only a few minor injuries. The four men who'd been injured were being redeployed to secure the landing zones for their pickup. The rest of the platoons were being quickly restructured to make up for their absence. Chase was amazed at this display of high-level training that permitted the troops to adapt so quickly. His own former platoon members, good as they'd been, would never have been able to handle a rotation of members in the field.

"Apache Three, this is Apache Two. Do you read?" It was Sergeant Demchenko's voice coming over Chase's radio. Chase was Apache Three, the third "commanding" officer in A platoon. The other platoons were coded "Bandit" and "Cobra," and within each of those, the squads were referred to as "Alpha," "Bravo," and "Delta."

Chase acknowledged the sergeant's call. "Roger Apache Two, I read."

"Apache Three, activate your tac unit, please."

Chase cursed, reached down, and activated one of the systems at his belt. He could, if he wished, call up a tactical display of the area as best as they knew it, which would also show the positions of all the members of the company. Each man emitted a low-powered scrambled and coded tactical signal that could be read by the others in the company. Its use was limited by the environment, obstructions, and interference, but the tactical benefits

DOUG 92

were enormous. It also allowed squad, platoon, and even
company commanders to keep separate track of each of
their unit's members.

"Roger, Apache Two. Unit on."

"Thank you, Apache Three. Nice of you to join us."

"Roger that, Apache Two."

The platoon commander's voice cut in. Because Chase
was technically attached to Sergeant Demchenko, he was
on the command channel, the one reserved for communications between platoon and squad commanders.
"Units advance to waypoint one," Grachev said.

While calling up the tactical map, Chase listened to
the individual squad leaders acknowledge. There was
enough obvious movement around him that he could have
followed any of the other platoon members, but he
wanted to see bearing and distance for himself. As the
image assembled itself on the inside of his visor, he heard
someone approach from the rear. Chase tilted his head
as Demchenko clasped his shoulder with one hand.

The sergeant pointed off to the left. "This way," he
said. Chase couldn't see the other man's expression behind his face gear, but he could sense a big grin.

"I know," Chase told him. "I was just checking the
progress of the other squads."

Demchenko grabbed at one of the straps on Chase's
gear harness. "Don't worry, they're where they're supposed to be. Let's do the same, eh?"

Chase laughed, and the two men took off at a quick
jog for the first waypoint.

34

An unknown voice spoke in Chase's ear. "Confirm
two guards; one in front, one in back. Both armed. Light

automatic weapons. No evidence of body armor, no evidence of personal magic.''

Chase glanced to his left. Each of the platoons had a single magician, a hermetic mage, and the one in Apache was crouched a few meters away. As the recon report came over the radio, the mage nodded. Chase knew the man's name was Kunayev, but nothing else beyond the fact that when he moved his head it was always at a strange tilt. He was garbed and armed identically to the other squad members to prevent enemy snipers from selectively picking off the magician. He was also bearing the magical tactical support load, in addition to the mage from Cobra platoon. The Bandit mage was running recon along with the rest of Bandit.

Chase was surprised that they had only three magicians along, considering that Der Nachtmachen was known to have magically active members. More to the point, though, was the fact that the policlub apparently had the backing of the great dragon Alamais. That, in and of itself, was reason enough to bring along extensive support. When Chase had pointed that out during mission planning, they'd told him that magical support would be present, but that they had other means for dealing with a dragon.

He shifted the vision magnification gear on his helmet into place, then glanced at the estate nearly a kilometer away. It wasn't large by the standards of other chalets in the area, but it was imposing. Fuchi intelligence estimated that it possessed about thirty rooms, but intel had been unable to dig up any further floor plan data before the raid commenced. Chase could see many windows lit up, especially on the second floor, and noted the presence of a number of ground vehicles at the rear of the building—the side facing them. He could also see a single guard, dressed in jeans and a button-down shirt, pacing back and forth. A cigarette dangled from his mouth and a submachine gun from a shoulder sling.

The unknown voice spoke again in his ear. Chase knew that the reports were being routed to all circuits to save time and pass-along errors. "Limited magical recon of the site completed. Report no evidence of paranatural security patrol. Main building is fully protected by a high-powered ward that prevents penetration."

The Apache mage was crouched next to platoon commander Grachev. Chase could barely make them out. "I'm a little surprised," the mage said. "I'd have expected something."

The senior lieutenant nodded. "Perhaps they think they don't need any?"

The mage shrugged.

Grachev tilted his head as he received his own orders. A moment later, Chase heard him over the radio. "Apache One. Everyone stand by." Demchenko shuffled over next to Chase, not bothering to push aside the brush between them. Chase nodded at him, and received a short salute in return.

Grachev's voice returned. "Bandit will secure the immediate area, Apache and Cobra will lead the assault. Apache heads straight in while Cobra backs them up. As per the plan, gentlemen. Any questions?"

If there were any, Chase couldn't hear them.

"Apache, move out!" Grachev said.

Chase and Demchenko would be among the last in, but just before Cobra, whose members would move in and secure the positions the previous unit had just vacated. Two squads each of Apache and Cobra were positioned around the front of the chalet, and would be advancing from that direction. The one remaining squad from each platoon, with Chase and the senior Apache sergeant, would be entering from the rear. Bandit, in addition to securing the area, would be covering their immediate approach.

They advanced steadily but cautiously through a thin stretch of woods to the southwest of the building. Their progress was so silent that Chase was almost certain the Apache mage traveling with the group was using his magic to achieve the silent movement. The Cobra mage was with the squads at the front of the building.

When they reached the edge of the trees, some twenty meters from the building, they stopped, waiting for the final signal.

Then Chase saw the guard at the rear of the house pull a small microphone or radio from his belt, apparently to report in. The moment he was done and the radio safely back at his belt, he was hit by a single, silenced high-velocity round. It came right on target, and his head exploded. The suddenness of it startled Chase as he watched the man's head snap back and his body crumple immediately after it.

The squad moved in, advancing in two ranks toward the rear of the building.

Then explosions began to blow out the windows, as Bandit fired concussion and shock grenades through them, the flashes lighting up the ground around the building. Chase imagined that the Bandit mage was also making some kind of mystical assault on the magical ward that protected the building, to keep anyone monitoring those defenses busy.

The two squads rushed on, reaching the edge of the building. He heard gunfire from the front and a scream from somewhere in that direction as the lead men reached the rear door. They deployed around it while two squad members examined the lock and the door frame for booby traps. They found nothing, except that the door was locked. A small, shaped-charge explosive took care of that.

Two other squad members opened fire, their thermo-graphic gun sights cutting through the smoke from the door explosion. From his position, Chase could not see into the building, but the hand signs from the two gunners indicated that they'd hit two enemies who'd been waiting in ambush beyond the door. Then the squad began to enter.

They moved through the foyer and began working their way into the house. Chase heard more gunfire from ahead of them. Demchenko's voice came over the radio. "Most of them seem to be up front. We're going to—"

The rest of his words were lost in the sounds of the surrounding walls rupturing, burst by waves of cyan energy that rippled and then arced around them. Chase was knocked backward by the blast, landing sprawled on top of a now-broken table. A large framed painting fell from the cracked wall and shattered all over him. Magic, thought Chase, and of a scale and type he'd never seen before.

Pulling himself up, he looked ahead to see the rest of the squad rushing forward, Demchenko in the lead. Beyond them, he could see a ruined hallway and room doors, and at least one figure in black and gray battle dress being dragged to safety. There was gunfire, heavy automatic fire, in that direction as well. But no more magic. A mystic booby trap? he thought.

Barely heard above the gunfire, something broke behind him, and Chase spun, dropping to one knee and bringing his gun to bear. Two men were there, panic on their faces. One carried a submachine gun, the other some kind of double-barreled shotgun. The one with the shotgun made the mistake of raising it slightly, and Chase fired. The burst tore into him, knocking the man back flailing into the room from which the pair had just come. The other froze.

There were more flashes of cyan and red behind Chase, but he didn't turn. The second man winced and took a half step backward, dropping his gun. Chase sprinted over and slammed him against the wall.

"Where's Alexander?"

The man glanced furtively between Chase and the direction of the gunfire. His eyes were wild.

"Tell me!"

The man looked back at Chase and it seemed in that moment that the reality of what was happening sank in. "Upstairs," he said.

Chase released him, turning as he did and reaching for the man's submachine gun. Chase slammed his elbow backward, catching the man just above the solar plexus.

There was a sharp crack, and the man collapsed. Chase tossed the weapon on top of a nearby cabinet.

He entered the room from which the men had come, stepping carefully over the bloody form sprawled just inside the doorway. It seemed to be an auxiliary kitchen area that was partially used for storage. Across from him, a flimsy door stood open. Approaching it, Chase just barely made out a narrow stairway beyond.

Pushing the door open with the barrel of his combat rifle, he scanned the stairs. They were old, but showed signs of recent repair. More gunfire, followed by two quick explosions. More grenades, Chase thought.

He used the noise as cover and vaulted up the stairs. Quickly reaching the top, he flattened himself against the wall just inside the door. He tried the handle, found that the door was not locked. He twisted the handle, giving it just enough pressure to swing the door open as he dropped to one knee.

The corridor beyond was dim, but lit sporadically by the flare of gunfire from farther beyond. Chase could also clearly hear the automatic fire: the distinctive tones of the combat rifle, and closer, the sounds of more conventional assault rifles. He stepped into the hallway, and glanced in both directions. Clear.

He moved quickly in the direction of the gunfire, passing a blown-out doorway. The room, shattered by the concussion grenades at the start of the raid, contained three bodies, one a woman's. He didn't stop.

Coming to an intersection, he could see flashes and bursts of gunfire just around the corner. Then came another flash of brilliant red, with barely any noise accompanying it, followed by a shudder of the whole building. The fight was there, just ahead. And so, he expected, would be Alexi.

Chase squatted down, turning into the other corridor, leading with his combat rifle. At the end of the short hall, maybe a half-dozen meters from him, was the enemy. Magical energy flowed around them, shielding their position from the sustained gunfire below them. They were in position on a balcony overlooking what Chase assumed was the main entrance, though he couldn't see it.

There were four of them, three heavily armed, and Alexi. The three were firing at those below, while Alexi had apparently stepped back to catch his breath. Chase was amazed to see the last energy shards of some spell dissipating around him. He looked tired but defiant.

His brother. Alive.

Chase stood up slowly, keeping his weapon trained on them. Doubled over, Alexi was still trying to catch his breath. Sweat dripped from him, and he wiped it away with the already-soaked arm of his jacket.

Alexi was older than Chase by two years, but looked younger, even worn and battered as he was now. There was an energy about him that he had rarely ever expressed, but that Chase had always seen burning in his eyes. Now it raged through him, driving him.

The men with his brother suddenly dashed forward, beyond their magical protection. Had the squads fallen back? Chase had heard nothing over the radio. . . .

Alexi straightened, pushing damp hair back from his forehead with one hand. He ended up staring directly at Chase, and froze. Chase centered his targeting site on the center of his brother's chest, where even a loose grouping of rounds would be effective. Alexi stared at him, an unknown opponent in black and gray. How fast was his magic? Chase wondered. Faster than his own cybernetic trigger? Faster than—

Alexi moved, his hand coming up to point at Chase, blue-white energy trailing from it. Chase fired. He was faster.

The sustained burst tore into Alexi, knocking him backward into the wall. Chase fired again. His brother's body began to fall, but the hammering rounds held him up, balanced against the wall as it too was torn up by stray rounds.

The weapon emptied, and Alexi Komroff fell forward

to crash facedown against the ground. His legs twitched for a moment and then his form was utterly still.

Chase stared at him as more gunfire echoed up from below. It had been so quick . . . Another explosion from somewhere else and a voice behind.

"Almost anticlimactic, wasn't it?"

Chase turned slowly, acutely aware that the clip in his combat rifle was empty and he had not reloaded. A man stood there, garbed in a dark suit cut so beautifully that it seemed too perfect to be real. His hair was almost gold and flashed oddly with red highlights. His eyes too were gold, almost like molten ore. A sense of power surrounded him and filled the hallway.

"He never even knew it was you," the man said in a deep, resonant voice that rooted Chase to the spot. "Kind of disappointing. I was hoping, at the very least, for some kind of last-minute realization, just before one or both of you killed each other."

Chase let his left arm drop, holding the combat rifle. He still had his heavy pistol.

"I'm being rude, though, aren't I?" the man continued. "You of course are Mikhail Komroff, brother to that half-mad corpse around the corner." He smiled, beguilingly. "And I am Alamais."

Chase started. Alamais, the great dragon. But he didn't—

"No, I don't, do I?" Alamais said. "Simple trick of shape-changing and mass displacement. Besides it's much easier getting around buildings made for humans if you look like one. Displeasing form, but it has its uses."

Chase heard some movement on the stairs far behind him, and so did Alamais. "Ah, company," he said with a frown. "I had so wanted to talk to you alone."

Another solider in black and gray stepped up alongside Chase. It was Demchenko, and the weapon he had leveled at the great dragon wasn't his combat rifle, but a large, boxy-shaped pistol. Chase didn't recognize the design.

Alamais barely glanced at him. "If we can't talk now,

then I'm going to leave you with a bit of information so that I can be sure we'll talk again later. And that bit of news is that your brother didn't know.''

Chase stared at Alamais and suddenly felt weightless. He wasn't aware of anything but the dragon, and his words.

"Oh, he despised you, to be sure," said the dragon, "but that intriguing human emotion called 'loyalty' stopped him from hunting you down. In this case it was the familial connection. So I took those steps for him.

"Through it all he never knew that 'Simon Church' was his brother. I wanted to see what he would do, and you as well, when your respective identities were revealed.'' Alamais smiled. "I wanted to see how alike you were, how much, as brothers, you shared the same values.'' The man-shaped dragon sighed. "I have my answer, but still more questions.''

Chase started to speak, but he heard Demchenko suck in his breath. "No more questions,'' the senior sergeant said. His weapon fired, at least Chase thought it did. He felt a sensation, an odd tingling, and noticed some lights on the weapon change. Chase also noticed a thick power cable running from the grip of the weapon to the pack on Demchenko's back.

Chase turned to look at Alamais, who'd glanced down to where he presumed the weapon was hitting him, or at least where it was aimed. There seemed to be no effect.

"Again, how disappointing,'' the dragon said, frowning. "What is it supposed to do?''

The air felt warmer. Chase sensed Demchenko's grin. "Aim.''

There was light everywhere.

It entered through the ceiling in blinding shafts. Pulses brighter than the sun struck the dragon, enveloping him in a corona of energy. A roar began, the mix of a dragon's pain and the rush of superheated air. The shock wave tossed Chase and Demchenko to the ground, and they felt the building buckle.

Light flashed, and Chase felt a searing pain in his legs

as an enormous shape suddenly passed over him. Gold
and red scales appeared around him as the dragon re-
verted to its true form. The floor broke, and Chase began
to fall.

He was enveloped in darkness, then tossed aside by
the passing of a giant clawed foot. The dragon was roar-
ing, deafening him, the light still everywhere. Chase
rolled over onto his back as best as he could, ignoring
the terrible pain in his legs.

The dragon was rearing above him through the shattered roof, wings extended and fighting to clear the debris. A sphere of green-white energy surrounded him.
Light flashed down from the clouds, long streaks of
blinding energy pulsing against the shield the dragon had
erected.

The hidden weapons in the transports were battle-grade
lasers, and the weapon Demchenko had used was some
sort of targeting device, Chase realized.

Light flashed again, and Chase couldn't look any longer. He rolled and spotted Demchenko's limp form a half-
meter away in the rubble. Chase dragged himself over to
the senior sergeant, then stopped in horror. Half of the
man's body had been nearly burned away, and the side
that remained was blackened.

The light came again, and Chase covered himself,
fearful of the searing heat. It never came.

Chase looked up as Alamais' shield blocked the laser
beams again. There were red flashes high above in the
clouds in response to something the dragon was doing.
It was a stand-off. The shield protected the dragon, but
the clouds blocked him from being able to see the aircraft
and to directly affect them with his magic. Alamais,
though, was shaking the remains of the building loose.
Chase had no doubt that once free and able to fly, the
aircraft would be no match for him.

The lasers fired again from a different part of the
clouds, and again Chase ducked. Brilliant light surged
around him, but again he felt no heat.

He was within the shield. He was inside Alamais' protection.

Chase's gaze fell on Demchenko's combat rifle lying a meter away. Dragging himself, Chase reached it and felt it respond to his grip. It was working. Checking its status he found that the clip was full, as was the small magazine that held eight minigrenades.

Chase rolled onto his back, and pointed the weapon at the dragon rearing above him. The last part of the roof fell away from the dragon's wing.

Light flared again, and Chase fired, shifting the weapon from burst to full-automatic fire. The stream of bullets caught the dragon in the exposed underside, and the recoil pulled the weapon, tracking it toward the creature's head. Chase cybernetically adjusted the timing of the minigrenades so that they'd detonate almost immediately after launch, rather than on impact.

The gunfire did little damage, but the dragon glanced down. Chase fired again, and a minigrenade launched from the under-barrel of the weapon. It exploded just shy of the dragon's head, rocking it back. Chase felt the blast, winced, and fired again. The dragon had twisted, and the second grenade glanced off its wing before detonating, tearing into the wing's membrane.

The dragon howled, and energy grew around its head, centered in its eyes. Chase felt those eyes turning toward him, and fired. The grenade exploded high above him, and beyond the blast Chase saw the green-white shield flicker, and dissipate.

The dragon reared back its head and howled in fury.

Energy lanced down from the clouds.

This time Chase felt the heat.

35

It took a careful, knowing eye to notice the change in the color of the black plasticrete runway rushing below the aircraft, now moments from contact. Jason Chase did not watch for them.

He knew they were there.

That was enough.